I0785542

The Music Makes the Man

Nicole Fratrich

Cover image, design, and typesetting by Tyler Friend.

Typeset in Baskerville, Daniel Black, and Helvetica.

ISBN: 979-8-9866111-0-5 (Print)
ISBN: 979-8-9866111-1-2 (eBook)

The Music
Makes the Man

Chapter 1

Steel City Dreams

Luke Cavarelli had never felt so alive in his life. But he wondered, could this feeling grow even stronger? Or, could it be snatched away in a second? The bright lights shone down on him where he was standing on the stage. The heat was taking its toll on him; he could feel the sweat rolling down his face, but he didn't care. The fire rising inside of him was pure joy.

While the strumming of the guitars and the pounding of the drums behind him grew louder, he felt the music flowing through his veins. When the bass guitar solo ended, he came back in on the downbeat. His vocals soared through the club, and he kept going until he sustained the last note and concluded with a gentle cutoff.

The usual bar patrons shouted and applauded, but they did that regardless of whether they actually liked the song; half of them were drunk out of their minds anyway.

Luke stepped away from the microphone and helped the rest of the band pack up the equipment.

"Did you get the money yet, Luke?" Ryan Delhart, Luke's best friend, was the lead guitarist and backup singer in the five-member band known as The Steel City Boys.

"No—wait. Here comes Mr. Silva now." Luke jumped offstage.

"A fine job tonight, as always." The gray and elderly club owner handed Luke a wad of cash. The man was kind and fatherly, but his short build made him look like a child compared to Luke's naturally tall and broad figure.

"But when are yinz gonna go big?" Mr. Silva reached up to lay a hand on Luke's shoulder.

"Sir?"

"Kid, you need a record deal. The world needs to hear

whatcha got. I love having yinz perform, but you can't be here forever. You'd be wasting your talent!"

"Um, no offense, Mr. Silva," Luke was taken aback by this comment, "but there's no way that we could ever make it to the big stage. There's no way we could ever compete with the big guys. I mean, our lyrics are weak sometimes and I can get a little pitchy…" Luke trailed off as he glanced up to find Joe carrying a drum across the stage and down the side steps.

"Oh, have some faith, kid. This city ain't what it used to be for young people. You got the talent, so give it whatcha got and yinz'll make it outta here one day."

Luke grinned weakly and gave Mr. Silva a nod of acknowledgement.

When he went back onstage, Ryan shot him a curious glance. "What did he have to say?"

"I'll tell you later." Luke pushed it out of his mind.

"All packed and ready to go." Ryan lit himself a cigarette before he picked up his guitar case and set it near the stage steps.

"Really, dude? Those things will kill you eventually."

Ryan scoffed and took the cigarette out of his mouth, emitting a huge puff of smoke. "You took that Surgeon General warning too seriously. Dude, that warning came out nineteen years ago when we were kids. Look, we're all doing a-okay."

"Fine, but don't come crying to me when it ruins your vocals." Luke flung his arms up in the air.

"Relax, man. What's your problem anyway?"

"I said I'd tell you later!" He huffed, stomped down the stage steps, and sat down at a nearby table.

Luke watched as Ryan gave the other band members

their share of the $280.

"Great job tonight, man," Ryan told Tyler, the other guitarist who played both electric and bass.

"Thanks!" Tyler pushed his black hair out of his face and took the money. The tallest of them all, he loved being up with the current trends, and he couldn't stop talking about the upcoming *Return of the Jedi.*

"Your solos were spot on! Our improvs were killer tonight, but I might have slipped out of tune."

"Ah, you worry too much!" Ryan said.

"Speaking of worrying," Adam wandered over for his share and whispered, "is Luke okay?" He was the keyboardist, but he also played any other instrument the band needed. And, even though it was the '80s, Adam had the shortest hair out of the whole band.

"I think he's fine. I'll talk to him," Ryan said.

"Has anyone seen my other drumstick?" Joe called.

"How do you lose only one?" Tyler asked.

Joe shrugged and took his money from Ryan. "It's like losing a sock in the dryer."

"You don't do your own laundry," Tyler said. "Your mother does it!"

The boys laughed. There was no doubt that The Steel City Boys had chemistry. Between Luke (the serious one), Ryan (the calm one), Tyler (the trendy one), Adam (the compassionate one), and Joe (the quirky one), there was never a dull moment.

"Luke, you good?" Adam shouted down to Luke at the center table.

"I'll be fine," Luke said.

Tyler jumped down from the stage and patted Luke on

the shoulder. "I'm going to grab a drink. Do you want anything, Luke?"

"Nah, it's getting late."

Joe and Adam made their way to the table after buying drinks, and Joe sat backwards on the chair across from Luke.

When Ryan joined them, he heard Tyler rambling on.

"If compact discs become more popular than cassettes, then everyone will need to buy new stereos."

"Oh no," Ryan joked, "I'm not getting into this discussion with you again! CDs will never take off. Luke, are you ready to hit the road?"

After saying goodbye, Luke and Ryan headed outside. Luke shook his head slightly as Ryan, with his nicotine craving satisfied, flicked the cigarette to the ground. Ryan hopped in the red Pontiac Firebird and turned the key in the ignition.

Luke sat in the passenger seat with his head in his hand, leaning on the armrest console. The air from the open window rustled his light hair. His cobalt eyes sparkled like tranquil ocean waves ebbing under a golden sunset. And though he wasn't smiling at the moment, the usual gentle smile on his clean-shaven face was like the last ray of sunlight shining down below on the ocean's surface. He stared at his reflection in the side-view mirror as if it would somehow vanish if he dared to look away.

They rode in silence until Ryan, not being able to stand it any longer, cranked up the radio. In an instant, an opera song came blasting through the speakers at full volume.

"What is *this?*" Luke said.

"Uh, I don't know. I didn't put this station on." He tried to hide his crime.

"Really, opera? That's not exactly our style, Ryan, in

case you haven't noticed."

"You know what? I'd spend a night or two with that opera chick."

"Oh, shut up!" Luke punched his best friend's arm.

"But listen to her voice; she's amazing, man. I've seen her on TV, and she's incredible. I'd die to spend a night with that body."

Luke couldn't help but tease. "Yeah, but you wouldn't get around to it because you'd be dead!"

Ryan rambled on while the car rolled through the heart of Pittsburgh. The steel mills were no longer booming, but scaffolding towered above, as what would soon be Oxford Center, Mellon Tower, and PPG Plaza were being erected.

"Renaissance II," Ryan narrated as they passed, transfixed on PPG Plaza. The bottom half of the tower was plated in mirror, and the workers would soon be moving upward. At night, the city lights reflected off the mirrors.

"Beautiful," Luke said.

"Yeah, but it's a shame both of our old mans lost their jobs at the mills. A few towers aren't going to make up for it."

"We named ourselves after a proud and successful city."

"Ah, it'll have its day again," Ryan said.

They entered a tiny parking lot just outside of their apartment building and squeezed into an empty space. When they entered the lobby, they were bombarded by sunflowers. The landlady loved her large and faded sunflower wallpaper, but Ryan had other thoughts.

"I know she loves her sunflowers, but I feel like they suck out my soul every time I see them." With the edge of his guitar case, Ryan patted an upturned corner of wallpaper.

"This old place may be worn out, but it is comfy," Luke

said. They took their time up the windy, green-carpeted staircase. They passed rows of mauve doors with golden letters. Each hallway was lit by lamps surrounded by frosted sconces decorated with pastel flowers.

On the third floor, they stopped, and Ryan fished the keys from his pocket.

"You know, I bet Tyler could redecorate this building in a heartbeat," Ryan said as he thrust the key into the lock.

Luke nodded. "With him, each floor would have a different interior design."

Ryan chuckled. "And I hear no one cares about color-matching these days."

The living room was in the center of the apartment with a chocolate-colored couch and a recliner; currently, a denim jacket was draped over the couch, while a box of crackers lingered on the coffee table near the television. A leaning tower of mail sat on the corner of the kitchen counter, and a few crusted plates waited in the sink. Luke wasn't a fan of disorganization, but Ryan felt otherwise.

Ryan set his guitar case at the foot of the end table, plopped himself on the couch, and turned on the TV and VCR. Luke walked over to the fridge and grabbed a bottle of water, always dehydrated after a performance. "We have to talk." He swiped the remote and turned the machine off.

"Dude, it's American Bandstand night! I taped it!"

"Yeah, well, Dick Clark will just have to wait."

Luke put himself in the recliner, but did not allow it to recline. This was serious. "Ryan, what're we doing with our lives?"

"What do you mean? We're musicians. We're in a band."

"A band that isn't going anywhere, Ryan. We can't stay in this jag-off band forever. Our day jobs aren't going to pay the rent for the rest of our lives. I mean, we're lucky if anyone outside the city even knows our name."

Ryan slouched down even further into the couch. His slicked-back ebony hair and stubbly chin made him think he looked cool and chic. With his sharp green eyes, which were always so full of light and unwavering optimism, he scanned over his best friend's anxious expression.

"Then we'll find ourselves a record deal," he answered simply like it was no serious matter.

"You know it's not that easy. Even if we do, there's no way we can compete with the big guys."

"Come on, we sent out some demos. Just be patient. I'm sure someone will respond soon."

Luke knew very well that Ryan wasn't worried about the band's future. Ryan accepted long ago that securing a record deal takes a long time, so he wasn't in a rush. The Steel City Boys had a following, even if it was only local. Still, Ryan believed anything was possible.

Luke sighed heavily, stood up, and started to pace. "We have to keep reaching out to people. We need to put ourselves out there more. We need to do something else, Ryan. We already play at Silva's club twice a week, but maybe we should try booking more than once a month at the Renegades' club. I was talking to Adam's brother the other day, and he said that there are a couple of places that some of the Steelers go to regularly, so if we bring our 'Steel City' brand there, then maybe…"

"Luke, it's only 1983," Ryan said to soothe Luke's rambling. "I know your ten-year plan is for the band to sign with a record label, but it's early and plenty of people know who we are." He reached for the remote and began fast-forwarding through the show. "There are thousands of record labels out there."

Luke pondered this for a moment. "I guess you're right." He slowly sat down.

"You know it, dude. We'll just have to give it all we got. What made you think of this anyway?"

"Mr. Silva said we should find a record deal."

"So that's what he told you. We'll be fine, don't fret about it." Ryan finally found something of interest and hit the play button, while Luke got up again and prepared to head to his room. "Luke, wait." Ryan called him back.

Luke leaned over the top of the couch, his attention brought to the TV. "Who are they?"

"They're Brits," Ryan said, mesmerized. "Called Wham!"

Once Luke turned his eyes to the screen, he was glued to the energized performance of a song called "Young Guns (Go For It)." He couldn't stop watching George Michael and Andrew Ridgeley jump almost carelessly to the proud beat, leather jackets flapping as they danced. Accompanied with dazzling, perfectly white smiles, they spun their way across every inch of dance floor. Even though the dance was choreographed, Luke had a strong feeling that the friendship was very real.

"This is us," Ryan pointed at the TV.

"We're not exactly bubblegum pop," Luke said. "We're rock that sometimes blends with pop.

"True, but we'll be famous young guns!"

"Keep dreaming."

Ryan sighed. "We have their energy and passion. Their chemistry isn't much different from ours. We're young and free. Unstoppable. I don't know about you, but I'm not settling down any time soon."

By then, the song ended and Dick Clark was interviewing the band.

"They're 19?" Luke was amazed. "We don't stand a chance!"

Ryan tilted his head back to glare at his friend. "Really? Dude, this is proof that we can make it. We're only three years older than them."

Unconvinced, Luke rolled his eyes and retreated to his tightly-packed bedroom. Most of the crap was stuffed into various nooks to make room for his vinyl and cassette collections. Luke loved nearly all mainstream genres of music, but rock was his first and foremost obsession. Although his tastes varied, his entire bookshelf was crammed to the top with the likes of Tom Petty, Billy Squier, .38 Special, Foreigner, Rick Springfield, and Stray Cats, as well as staples like Billy Joel and the Rolling Stones. He brought out his Walkman and popped in his most cherished cassette: the *Heartbreakers Only Live Once* album by The Leather Heartbreaks. He started humming and singing under his breath with the song:

I'm a heartbreaker.

Girl, i'll bring you down.

I'm a heartbreaker,

don't care 'bout no one but me.

Looking up, he stared at the large poster on the wall of his favorite band. The Leather Heartbreaks were a pop/rock band much like The Steel City Boys, but they were where they wanted to be, leaving their mark on the music industry. Why did it have to be so hard? He stared at the lead singer whom he admired the most. Tony "The Buff" Bellano. Bellano gave off a bad boy vibe with the excessive amount of leather he was wearing, along with his slanted smile, but the music he produced was catchy, vibrant, and thrilling. Luke had no desire to change his personality, but he wanted to fly out into the music world.

The three members in The Leather Heartbreakers were close friends. Although Bellano was the lead singer, and highly respected, Ace Holloway was often the face of the band: a guitarist extraordinaire, not unlike legends Keith Richards and Jimmy Page, Ace had raw talent and skill, despite his rough childhood.

Scanning the poster, he focused on Frankie Pierce, the bass guitarist, in the left-hand corner. He kept the band in line with his easy-going style and lured in the girls with his perfectly crimped hair.

Luke loved him too, but his eyes returned to Bellano. Luke had looked up to Bellano since his junior year of high school. Bellano was cool and confident, and Luke admired those qualities. He loved how Bellano's style and image matched. As a singer himself, Luke appreciated Bellano's vocal range and quirks, and he wasn't half bad at emulating Bellano's sound. He knew every lyric to every song and owned every album. He instantly knew the answer to any trivia question that could be asked.

Many superficial Leather Heartbreak fans spread fake stories of how the band arrived at its name. It had nothing to do with the band members being dumped by girls. On the contrary, Luke would often find himself explaining to other "so-called" fans that the band's origins started with the three members growing up on the harsh streets of New York. Far from rich, sometimes all they could rely on was the little warmth from their leather jackets. As a band, their sound and image was durable like leather. They were not boys to be messed with, and all the girls who swooned for them needed to be careful and treat them right. They were determined to rise to the top, but any girl who didn't share that goal was a victim of a "leather heartbreak."

Sometimes Luke couldn't understand why he was a big fan. The music could always boost his spirits, sure, but the bad boy stuff just wasn't him. He didn't go around breaking girls' hearts or go out partying every night. Yet Bellano's deep and raspy voice came through each time, telling him that everything was going to be okay, no matter the situation. Over the years, he decided that it was the band's grit, determination, and authentic sound that kept him falling in love over and over again with the music.

The first time he saw him on stage was exhilarating. Bellano took control of that stage like he was singing to the entire world. His voice echoed triumphantly and the band in the background only enhanced the feel-good sensation. The music pumped through Luke, and he wondered if the crowd surrounding him could feel it as well. He knew right then and there what he wanted to do with his life. He often wondered how Bellano would perceive a singer like him, especially because he wasn't cut from the same cloth. Bellano grew up in a rough neighborhood. His father was stuck doing the mob's bidding, and his mother had to make her living as a prostitute. Tony Bellano had to be rough and tough to leave his mark in the world. Luke, however, had no such background.

In fact, Luke almost met Bellano a few years earlier when The Leather Heartbreaks toured in Pittsburgh. Luke had entered and won a songwriting contest that The Leather Heartbreaks' manager devised to gain more publicity for the band. Luke gave it a shot; he knew that his song captured Bellano's style of rock, complete with lyrics fit for a true heartbreaker. Winning the contest gave Luke backstage passes to meet Bellano.

Ryan had to work the night of the concert, so Tyler joined Luke. Honestly, Luke wished that Ryan would have been there. By the time the band took a break halfway through their set, Tyler was swaying with alcohol in his system, and Luke didn't know if he would be brave enough to talk to Bellano on his own. When the security and stage managers let Luke backstage, he was shaking, and Tyler had slumped himself in a chair, half-passed out. Luke waited and waited for Bellano to come over and greet him. The stage managers kept apologizing for Bellano's lateness, but the longer Luke stood there, he realized that Bellano was likely to stand him up. As hopeful and excited as he was to meet his idol, he also knew that Bellano would rather meet pretty fangirls.

Luke understood how chaotic the rock star life could be, but he himself felt like a new victim of a leather heartbreak. How could Bellano just forget him like this, especially when the contest had been promoted on major radio stations for months? To top it off, Bellano never did record the song Luke wrote, like was promised in the contest details. At the end of the night, all Luke had received was a small plaque, a few pre-autographed pieces of memorabilia, and disappointment. He was so angry that he couldn't listen to, talk about, or even think about, Tony "The Buff" Bellano.

Over time, Luke justified Bellano's no-show with a million reasons that left everyone but Bellano to blame. Luke was still obsessed with Bellano, and he didn't see why that should change. In those days following the concert, he also realized that he didn't want to let the fame or the management consume him when he became big and famous.

"I'll sing like you one day," he told his poster. Then, even though he was exhausted, he picked up his own guitar and strung a couple of chords softly as he contemplated the situation. He picked up pen and paper and began to write. He scribbled notes and lyrics until he finally fell asleep.

Chapter 2

Ladies' Man

When Luke woke up the next morning, it took him a second to realize that he had fallen asleep while writing. He put on his Sunday best before heading out into the kitchen, where he found Ryan buttering a piece of toast on the formica countertop.

"I wrote a song last night," Ryan announced with his mouth full.

"Uh, so did I," Luke said.

"Cool."

"Wait, you wrote a song? You were too submerged in *American Bandstand*. Besides, that's my department."

"I can multitask!"

"Alright. If you want, I can look at it later." He turned around and slid two pieces of bread in the toaster.

The newspaper was sitting neatly on the countertop—the one thing Ryan didn't crinkle or disorganize every morning. At first glance, Luke didn't notice anything out of the ordinary. But when he looked at it again, the front headline caught his attention. Jake Hexton was getting married.

Jake Hexton was the son of successful international entrepreneur Richard Hexton. The Hextons were one of the richest families in all of Pittsburgh, so it was going to be the wedding of the year.

"Hexton's getting hitched. Why can't we get a gig like that?" Luke once again found himself depressed. "His father can probably help us get the band moving. He has the money and the resources."

"Maybe we need more advertising."

"Maybe." Still, Luke was very doubtful. All he wanted was to sing and make people happy. He never wanted anything so much, except perhaps a wife one day.

He went to church, like he did every Sunday. He knew that no one would expect a wannabe-rockstar to be a holy-roller. The truth was, Luke grew up a cradle Catholic and had a firm foundation in his faith. The two people who kept him confident and true to himself were Jesus and Bellano, a completely ironic duo.

Luke came straight home to work on the new songs. While Ryan was putting in his shift at Giant Eagle, Luke had the apartment to himself. He played around with different lyrics until he thought he was satisfied.

"Well, that just sucks," he admitted after singing what he wrote.

He stared at his piece of paper until the phone rang, making him jump.

"Hello?" Luke cradled the phone receiver between his ear and shoulder as he continued to hold the lyrics in his hand.

"Luke? Hey, son, how are you?"

"Oh, hi, Dad. I'm okay, just working on a new song while Ryan's at work."

"Any news on a record contract?"

Luke sighed. His father asked him this question nearly every week, and the pressure made Luke hate answering the phone every Sunday.

"Not yet," Luke said, "but we're going to record new demos soon."

Mr. Cavarelli's gravelly voice struck a nerve. "Have you given any thought about a different career path? Luke, it's not too late to change your mind."

Luke paused for a moment and closed his eyes. His parents had never been thrilled about his decision to pursue music. "Dad, I don't know what else I would do. We've been through this a hundred times."

"Son, I'm just looking out for your future and wellbeing."

Luke started to grow angry. "I know, music isn't manly. It's not medicine, law, or construction. You're always trying to change me!"

"Luke—"

But Luke hung up the phone. He hated doing that to his father, but he was in no mood to justify himself to his father again. His dad just didn't understand.

To calm himself down, he turned his attention back to the song. After singing what he wrote, he said to himself: "That's worse than the last version." He threw down his pen.

"Take a break, then." Ryan slammed the door shut. "Let's go out tonight." He was grinning from ear to ear, but then the smile faded. "What's wrong?"

"I'm not sure. I took what you wrote last night and used it as a basis. I want this song to reflect how we truly feel about music, show who we are. I just need some time to work with it."

"You changed my song?"

"Yeah. Do you mind?"

"N—no," he hesitated. "It's cool."

Luke shrugged. "Okay, let's go." He returned the guitar case to its home in his room and hunted down a pair of shoes.

"You're not taking that with you," Ryan pointed, indicating the sheet of lyrics in Luke's hand. "Luke, bars are for beer and women, not songwriting. How're you going to pick up women?"

"Oh, I have my ways," Luke answered, repeating Tony Bellano's catchphrase.

Ryan grinned. "Okay, Bellano, let's just go downtown. Any requests?" he said as he flicked off the lights and locked the door.

"Nah, you can pick the club."

An acrid combination of cigarette smoke and beer attacked them when they set foot in the new club. The neon lights cast down barely enough color to see by. Instead of having a live band, predetermined music siphoned through the speakers, loud and electric.

Ryan twisted his way to the bar with Luke close behind. They sat up front directly at the counter, and Ryan ordered his Rolling Rock beer.

"For you?" the bartender asked.

"Just ginger ale, please," Luke said.

"Really, dude?" Ryan slapped Luke on the arm after the bartender turned away. "I know you drink."

Luke took the song lyrics out of his pocket. "But you're not driving home."

"Do you ever break the rules?"

He didn't respond. Instead, he sipped his carbonated beverage and stared intently at the lyrics written on the page. It wasn't that Luke didn't fancy a stiff drink now and then, but he was too focused on the song. Once he got into the writing groove, he was very reluctant to snap out of it until he was ready.

Meanwhile, Ryan busied himself with girl-watching. He spun around on the barstool and faced the tables, arms propped on the edge of the bar. "Hey, babe."

A thin, blonde-haired girl walked past. She glanced up

at him and scoffed, but then hopped up on the stool next to
Luke.

"How can you concentrate in here?"

He scratched out the line he was working on. "I can't,"
he admitted. He pushed the paper aside.

Their eyes met. Hers were gentle and she had an ac-
cepting smile, as if he could tell her anything and she'd agree.

"Could they find any better music?" she complained
before bringing her glass to her lips.

"I know. What would you want?"

"I could really go for some Rush or maybe Def Lep-
pard. This stuff is terrible. You?"

"I could go for Loverboy right now."

"Seriously?" Her eyes sparkled as she scrunched up her
face in disgust.

"Not a fan?"

"Not especially."

"How about The Leather Heartbreaks?"

Her eyes lit up. "Tony Bellano is such a knockout! I've
never heard someone sing like him."

Luke nodded. "His tone is raspy and silky; he's got a
perfect blend."

"Totally! Frankie has always been cute, but Ace Holloway, though…" The girl shook her head. "He was always on
fire."

"Do you remember where you were when he died?"

"Don't we all?"

He looked down at her drink. "No alcohol?"

She shook her head. "Not for me. I just come here because my friends make me. I'm the driver."

"Me too!" He shifted in his seat. "I'm Luke."

"I'm Barbara."

"So what do you do?"

"Oh," she blushed, "I'm studying to be a French teacher. I go to France next month. What about you?"

"I'm the lead singer of The Steel City Boys," Luke said. "Have you heard of us? I mean, we've been trying to boost our local following."

She thought for a moment. "Yeah, actually. I was at the city's music festival last year. You guys were pretty good. I liked that song you sang about the river."

"Oh, you mean 'Monongahela'? Out of all the songs I've written, it's one of my favorites so far."

Someone across the bar yelled out to her.

"Those are my friends. It was nice to meet you."

"You too," he said as she started to leave. "Au revoir."

She turned around and grinned.

After her departure, Luke whirled around to face whatever it was Ryan was doing. And, not surprisingly, he was flirting with a curvy girl who had huge, flowing brown hair. Her smile was a bit menacing and her jade-green eyes shot off a devilish stare.

"You know, you're like a music rush... Do you know what that is?"

Luke hung his head and glared at the counter top. Not the music rush again. Ryan used this rehearsed routine whenever he tried to get women. He was a sappy Casanova. His pick-up lines were so stupid, but funny. It made him an adorable puppy that no woman could resist—except for Barbara, apparently. Luke put up with it because, at the same time, Ryan Delhart was a polite, affectionate guy. That was also his saving grace with women. It never lasted long, though.

He was a series of one-night stands. He couldn't keep a girl-friend long if he tried because he was never ready to settle down.

"A music rush," Ryan continued, "is the feeling *musicians* get when they're in the zone playing a song. It's what makes us feel alive."

The bartender came to refill drinks as Ryan droned on.

"But now a music *high* is completely different," Luke mouthed the words as Ryan said them. "That's the part in the song that makes the *listener* feel alive..."

The girl batted her mascaraed eyes and listened with the utmost interest. She had no clue that Ryan invented these terms. She rested her head in her hand as he draped his arm around her.

"What do you think you're doing?" A man wearing a navy suit jacket popped up out of nowhere and dragged Ryan off the barstool. "Get away from my fiancée!"

Within seconds, Ryan met the ground.

"Sara, are you okay?" her husband-to-be asked as he smoothed his silver tie and pushed back his already-neat dark hair.

"Fine," she answered smoothly. "I'm glad you saved me, Jake. This guy was starting to creep me out."

The light bulb above Luke's head lit up. "Jake Hexton?" Luke stood.

"Yeah. Who are you?"

"Luke Cavarelli from The Steel City Boys." He extend-ed a hand.

Jake shook it cautiously. "Heard of you, but never heard you sing."

"Ask him about the wedding," Ryan said to Luke

through clenched teeth.

"He's with you?" Jake was annoyed.

Luke hesitated. "He's our lead guitarist."

Ryan jumped up. "Look, man, I didn't know she was your girl. If I knew, I never would've talked to her. How can I make it up to you?"

Standing there with his arms folded, Jake said, "Don't worry about it."

"We'll play for your wedding," Ryan offered instantly.

"Ryan!" Luke reprimanded. "You can't just ask him that."

"No!" Jake said. Then he had a second thought. "Well, we do still need a band. I'll tell you what," he began pacing, "let me hear you first."

"Okay. Tomorrow night, Silva's," Luke said.

"Cool." Jake took Sara's hand and led her out of the club.

Ryan looked at Luke. "See, we could get a gig like that."

"He didn't say yes yet."

They turned back to the bar, and Ryan searched for cash in his wallet. After paying their tab, they headed for the door.

"Why didn't you ask that girl out earlier?" Ryan got ready to shove the key in the ignition.

"Huh-uh. I'm driving." Luke held out his hand for the key, and the guys switched places, Ryan using the hood to steady himself as he walked around to the passenger seat. "That's what you're thinking about?"

"Are you sure you're—"

"I'm straight, Ryan!" Luke exclaimed. "She was nice, but not the one."

"Well, Luke, if you don't start a relationship with a girl, you're never going to know if she's the one."

"You're one to talk! I'm telling you, I'll know her when I find her."

* * *

The next night, The Steel City Boys prepared to impress the son of one of Pittsburgh's richest men. After hearing through the grapevine of friends that Jake was a mega Queen fan, they decided to do their version of Queen's "Crazy Little Thing Called Love" just for Jake. The band was a mix of emotions.

Luke kept pacing back and forth on Silva's stage. Per Luke's request, the band arrived an hour earlier than usual to rehearse.

"Am I putting enough emphasis on *thing*?" Luke asked after singing the chorus.

"Don't accent it too much," Adam suggested. "Don't keep it too short."

Ryan and Tyler disagreed.

"Look," Ryan said, "Jake Hexton's not going to be able to tell the difference. We just have to sound good overall."

Luke rolled his eyes. "You'd tell me everything's fine if the sky were purple."

"If you're that worried," Tyler piped up, "then make lots of eye-contact with Jake."

"Pfft!" Joe burst out laughing. "Tyler, he's not trying to marry Jake Hexton! It's not like girl-catching."

Waving his hands up in the air, Luke shouted, "I'll just practice it again. Joe, count us in."

When it came time to perform, Luke took a deep breath. He felt his voice tremble, but he closed his eyes and imagined that Jake wasn't in the crowd. He owned the stage like usual and allowed the accompaniment to lift him up, using all of the emotion he could. He didn't write this song, but he performed it like it was personal. He disappeared into each note, into each crescendo, into each instrumental riff. When he sang, he was absorbed. He was the song.

The drums echoed off the walls and Ryan's last guitar chord rang out. The applause were generous as always. Not long after the conclusion of the band's set, Jake Hexton strode over wearing a neutral expression.

"Oh boy," Luke told Ryan, "he doesn't look happy."

Jake just stood there staring at them. "That wasn't great." He beamed. "That was awesome, and we'd be so totally stoked to have you play at our wedding."

The boys started writing new songs to mix into their set with the covers they usually played. Confident, they wanted to make an impression to show that they were serious and well-rounded in their music repertoire. Even though the family would have some say in the music, it was mostly up to the band. Hopefully, the rich Hextons wouldn't think of Luke Cavarelli and Ryan Delhart as reckless boys who played their guitars too loud and out of tune.

Chapter 3

The Servant Girl

Rigby Mansion stood high and proud in the center of sixty acres of lush green land. The mansion was a behemoth with beige siding and bay windows. There were three main floors to it and half as many bathrooms as there were bedrooms. There were other facilities on the property like a pool and golf course. The estate was located a half-hour from the city; some parts were exposed while others were more secluded.

All Samantha Denvy could see was the trash from the previous night, not the grandeur of the mansion. If she were to take a photograph of it, she'd call it "Trashed Treasure." Crushed up beer cans littered the floor, and some of the furniture was askew. Every room had something out of place, including a knocked over lamp in the hall. The night still haunted her as she went about her day. Jake and Sara's engagement party had indeed been a real party. The mansion was as jam-packed as a high school gymnasium on pep rally day. People ran from room to room, floor to floor. The music couldn't have been any louder or the speakers would've burst. She couldn't comprehend how Mr. and Mrs. Hexton were fine with the revelry.

Her name was called endlessly throughout the night. Between food setup and cleanup and any other needs the guests complained about, she had no time to breathe. She and Gina were supposed to be working, but she was the only one dashing around like a maniac; Gina was lost in the party scene.

Nearly every muscle she owned ached, and she kept imagining her name being called. She was stuck in the basement mindlessly folding the laundry which, in her opinion, should have been someone else's chore. She only took the job at the Hexton mansion because she needed the money to put herself through college and become a professional photographer. The only jobs that were still around didn't satisfy her in the least because they paid too little. At the mansion, she could do her work without being in the public. She liked keeping to herself.

Finally, she finished folding and then took her time walking up to the third floor. Why should she bother hurrying up just so another bothersome task could be flung in her face? Let Gina do something. Samantha's work ethic had always been superior in the eyes of Mr. and Mrs. Hexton. Really, she was entitled to take it easy every once in a while.

The Hextons had a whole crew of employees to take care of their mansion; however, there were only two maids on the housekeeping staff, and Gina never went out of her way to do much, but Mrs. Hexton believed in second chances. Emily, Samantha's best friend, was also the Hextons' cook. Meanwhile, the landscape and maintenance crews worked non-stop to keep the rest of the property up and running.

After two flights of stairs, Samantha made it to the long hallway. She continued on the hardwood floor until she came to the string of bedrooms where the empty drawers were anxiously waiting on the arrival of their occupants.

"Taking all day to do one job again," a voice sneered from behind her.

Mr. Hexton's sister loathed Samantha. She was the only one who didn't view Samantha warmly. Charlotte had moved in with her brother years ago in order to mooch off of his wealth. Because she had taken care of her parents in their old age, Richard Hexton always granted Charlotte's requests as if he were indebted to her.

Samantha had devised many ridiculous theories over the five years as to why Charlotte hated her. The only logical theory, however, was that Charlotte believed photography wasn't a valuable or prosperous career; it was an endeavor for lazy people. Therefore, Samantha's dream was a moot point for Charlotte.

Charlotte Hexton was a plump lady with her hair pinned up to her head, which went well with her beady eyes and crooked nose. She was always so meticulous. She stalked around the mansion just searching for trouble. She maintained a posture that made her straighter than the point of the Empire State Building, and she never refrained from speaking her mind.

"I'm not taking all day," Samantha said.

"Don't give me attitude, girl!"

Instead of answering and making matters worse, Samantha turned around and intended to keep moving, but she accidentally ran into the wall, and the hamper dropped, tumbling fresh clothes to the floor.

"Ha! Look what you did now. Can't do a blessed thing right."

Samantha knelt to the ground and pitched the jumbled-up clothes back in the hamper. She stood up and hurried into the nearest bedroom with Charlotte cackling and insulting her the entire time.

"It's not like I don't do anything," she muttered to herself once she was safe from the Hexton witch. She refolded the clothes and thrust them into their respective places in the dresser drawers.

She was in the master bedroom. The walls were painted a luscious green and the large queen-size bed was pushed up against the left wall. The big oak dresser rested adjacent to the bed. The window on the other side of the room emitted a slight spring breeze, compelling the white curtains to sway with ease.

"I work so hard here and this is what I get? If she knew how much I did these last two days… If I could only quit…"

"Who's quitting?" Gina pranced into the room.

"Why are you in here?" Samantha snapped, still annoyed at Gina's disappearing act from the night before.

Gina was the ultimate Valley Girl, except that she was from Latrobe. "I came to get the dirty laundry."

"Don't bother. I washed it all. Wasn't this your week for laundry, anyway?"

"Well, you're, like, so much better at it than me." She slid over to the mirror and stared at her slightly-squashed, round face. "And I had to redo my makeup."

"Yeah, just like when you couldn't work last night because you were too busy partying."

"Omigod, do you have a problem with me?" Gina's high-pitched voice rose even higher.

"No." Samantha left the room and continued her job in the other bedroom. When she was all finished, she peeked out the door and exhaled loudly when she found that neither Charlotte nor Gina were lurking the halls.

At the end of the day, Mrs. Joanne Hexton, the true lady of the house, was waiting patiently for her.

"All done, my dear?"

"Yes, ma'am."

"Can I talk to you for a minute?"

"Of course."

Mrs. Hexton motioned her into the den. Like Charlotte, Mrs. Hexton was middle-aged with fine lines and gray-streaked hair. Her face was mellow and seemingly carefree. She could put on the rich lady attitude, but she really was empathetic. After all, she had the patience to endure Gina.

The den was enormous and surreal, holding many pieces of furniture. There were sectionals, recliners, and tables galore. The grand fireplace in the center of the back wall had a mantle with precise, decorative moldings.

"Sit, please."

Samantha complied, perching upon a couch. Mrs. Hexton sank elegantly into a chair and folded her hands in her lap.

"Samantha, I want to apologize for the way Charlotte has been acting towards you lately. You know how much I appreciate you, and I realize how much work you do for us."

"Thank you." Samantha nodded.

"That's why I'd like to offer you a raise—and help you showcase your photography in a gallery setting."

Samantha was in shock. "Mrs. Hexton, that really isn't necessary. I mean, how can you get that past Charlotte? She—"

"No, no, I insist! Look, Charlotte isn't my favorite person in the world, and Lord knows I've tried to change her beliefs about things like photography. She's never worked a day in her life—unlike you and me. She's had everything handed to her. You remind me of myself when I was your age. Richard and I were always hard workers. Everything in this house came from our work and devotion. Samantha, I have the money and the resources; I can help you. I want to. You're my best employee. Please don't leave."

Samantha shook her head. "How did you know that I

was thinking about quitting?"

"My dear girl, it's all over your face; I can tell that you're miserable. A girl as young and intelligent as you shouldn't have to go through this."

"What, work?"

"Arbitrary grief! Besides, you should be doing the work you want to do, not what you have to in order to make ends meet. So, what do you say?"

"Um, sure. Yes. I'd be more than grateful."

"Good, it's settled!" Mrs. Hexton said. "Believe me, I need you for the wedding. There is so much to be done and your legs are among the youngest!" Samantha stood up.

Mrs. Hexton walked her to the door. "I'll have your pay-check fixed at once. Have a good evening, dear."

"Thank you." Samantha prepared to leave, but then she turned around. "Mrs. Hexton?"

"Hmmm?"

"I can't thank you enough. You've no idea how much this means to me. You don't have to go through the trouble—"

"Samantha, I'm overjoyed to help you. Really, it won't make a dent in my pocket!" The old woman winked and watched Samantha head down to the driveway and into the employee parking lot.

Samantha traipsed through her apartment door, exhausted, but still giddy. She threw her purse on the couch and hung her keys on the nail protruding from the wall by the door.

It wasn't a small apartment. Its high-end quality wasn't necessary for the two people living there, and the rent was expensive. The front door led straight into the living area with a couch in the center across from the TV.

"Oh, good, you're home!" Her roommate, Natalie, came out of the hallway that led to the bedrooms. She stood in the area behind the couch, which included the dining room table and the sliding doors that led to a balcony.

In contrast to Samantha, Natalie was heftier with natural auburn curls and dark eyes. "It feels like your shift at that place gets longer and longer."

"Well, it'll be a lot longer once the wedding comes closer."

"Oh, yeah. How's that coming?"

"The planning's underway, and I took Mrs. Hexton's offer to help the vendors and waitresses for overtime pay."

"That means you won't even get to enjoy the wedding."

"Probably."

Samantha had met Natalie in one of her college classes. Both girls were looking for a new place to live while they finished school. They quickly discovered that they had the same fashion sense and the same taste in art. Natalie was a business major, and she always said that she wanted to be a higher-up someplace. It was either that or acting. Natalie's family helped the girls pay the deposit and first few payments. Following an argument, Natalie's parents stopped sending support, leaving the girls to financially fend for themselves.

"Hey, the A/C's not working again." Natalie pointed.

Samantha turned her head. "Again? I don't think you should be blasting it all day long. Natalie, you know we're on an extremely tight budget! If we have to pay to have it fixed, we'll never have enough to go on that Gateway Clipper cruise with the other girls.

When the girls had moved in, Samantha quickly realized that Natalie enjoyed the finer things in life, from expensive lamps to shag carpets. Samantha loved the luxury, but she also knew that she shouldn't (and couldn't) be too careless with her money.

"Chill, girl, I called, and it'll only cost $100 dollars to fix the A/C."

"Oh, only?" She scoffed. "That's still $50 from each of us! We can barely pay the rent now!"

Natalie's grin faded instantly, turning into a shameful frown. "Landlord called today."

"Now what?"

"Rent's late. They might kick us out."

"How can they kick us out over one late payment?"

"We've missed four months, actually," Natalie mumbled under her breath.

"We've what?! How is that possible? I set out my portion of the money and you were supposed to write out the check and make the deposit. You didn't put the money in your account?" Samantha yelled.

"I must've misplaced it."

"Misplace—NO! Money doesn't just disappear!" Samantha shouted.

"Uh, I have to go," Natalie grabbed the car keys and bolted out the door.

"Where do you think you're going?" she called after her, but it was no use.

Despite the late hour, Samantha knew that she had to sort out the bills and determine if she could scramble up four months' worth of rent. She was about to write a check when she realized that it was time to begin a new checkbook. "What drawer did I put that in?"

There was a large, not to mention pricy, filing cabinet next to the dining table where she had been working. After rummaging through drawers and thumbing through files, she found what she was searching for, but there was some foreign object in there with it that had caught her eye.

It looked like a wallet wedged in the corner of the drawer. Curious, she picked it up and examined its smooth, leather exterior. But her excitement disappeared quickly when she flipped it open and discovered fake IDs proudly gleaming at her. Natalie's bright and toothy grin seemed to mock her. There were two in total, each of them bearing different names and ages, obviously over 21.

"So that's where my money's been going!" she shouted as she threw the wallet on the table. She could feel her face grow hot, and she really had the desire to scream. Samantha wasn't completely oblivious to Natalie's penchant for partying, but she never realized it was this bad. *I guess I was too naïve for thinking that she was really taking all of those night classes.* She had trusted Natalie enough to assume that her money wasn't going to fake IDs and booze. But, sometimes Natalie did withhold information from her. There were times when Samantha would ask about what was in the mail, and Natalie would shake it off. Natalie was typically the first one home and sorted through the mail. *Did she hide late payment notes? Eviction notices?*

Beyond frustrated, she checked all of her monetary resources and concluded that she couldn't find enough money for the rent, so she called the landlord.

"You signed the contract," he said. "I'm sorry Samantha, but I can't make any more exceptions."

"It's not like I knew that she wasn't paying the bills."

"You guys live together; that's your problem. I'm just trying to do my job. Besides, I talked to Natalie myself and she blamed it on you."

"Seriously? What did she tell you?"

"She said that you weren't working because you had to go home and help your family after your mother's death—I'm so sorry for your loss. She said that you'd pay your share when you got back."

"What?! She totally lied to you."

"No way."

"Yes way! Call my mother and ask her! How'd you fall for such a bogus lie?"

"But you did go away for a long time," he said.

Samantha scoffed. "It's called spring break. I went home to see my parents, who are both very much alive."

"Oh," he said softly. "You know, I wasn't exactly sober when she told me."

Are you ever? Samantha thought.

"That was around the time my girlfriend dumped me," he continued, "so I wasn't really thinking straight. Listen, don't worry, I got you covered."

"No, I'll pay my share, but not hers," Samantha negotiated. "It just may take me a little longer."

"Cool. Maybe I'll throw in fifty bucks or something. Just get out of there so you don't have to deal with her."

Samantha rolled her eyes. How he ever became a landlord was beyond her. "Thanks." She slammed the phone down and buried her face in her hands. This can't be happening.

She couldn't believe that Natalie had played her. She has seemed so sweet and innocent. Natalie had wanted the best of the best, even if it was expensive. Samantha had come from a conservative family, but lately she found herself in a rut. Her parents always controlled the spending in her house because both of her parents had experienced poverty growing up. Her limited allowance money forced her to learn the "penny-pinching" game early on in her childhood. Now that she lived on her own money, she chose to live a more luxurious life; so campus-living was out of the question. It was difficult to live luxuriously at home, so when she moved to the apartment, she indulged in this lavish spending. As she grew older now, she also realized that, for a little bit anyway, she'd have to control her spending. Well, until she had so much money that it wouldn't matter how much she spent. But, being poor just wasn't an option. She wasn't really worried when she moved in with Natalie, but eventually she got wise. If she was going to finish putting herself through college, then she couldn't afford to waste any money—she could only dream of being rich, famous, and free.

Chapter 4

Dudes in a Firebird

It was well past midnight and there was no sign of Natalie. Samantha spent the night packing. After she had finished, she decided to wait up for Natalie so that they could endure one final confrontation.

Yes, she knew it was terribly late, and that she was going to regret this decision in the morning, but this needed to be done. She kept catching herself nodding off, and she cursed Natalie even more.

At last, the lock on the door turned and in stumbled a tremendously-intoxicated Natalie, along with some strange man trailing behind her. Natalie was cheery until she found Samantha sitting fully alert and serious on the couch.

"Oh, uh, this is my roommate," Natalie explained to the tall and dark-haired man standing behind her. It was clear that he was much older than she. "I didn't think she'd still be here."

"I wouldn't still be here? I live here." Samantha got to her feet, arms crossed. "Natalie, it's two o'clock in the morning on a Monday. Look at you: you're drunk out of your mind and bringing strange men home. Do you know she's not even 21?"

The stranger's eyes danced around the room now that he knew the truth about the woman he was hoping to score with later.

"You can't prove that!" Natalie slurred.

"I can't?" Samantha held up one of the fake IDs, and Natalie gasped. "Yeah, that's right. I know where all of my money's been going. Instead of using it to pay the bills, you're out getting drunk and bringing home strangers. I know I'm a sound sleeper, but I don't know how on earth you rushed men out before morning!"

Natalie's mouth opened and closed. All she could do was stammer.

"Whoa, I gotta book," the man said, hurrying to the door. "My wife can't find out about this."

"You better leave, jerk!" Samantha called.

Natalie glanced up. "Samantha, I—"

"Just shut up! I don't want to hear your apologies. I thought you were better than this. I'm exhausted. This is the last night I'm sleeping in that bed. After that, I'm gone. I can't believe you betrayed me like this. Haven't I been a good friend to you?"

"You can't mean that. Where will you go?"

"Like you even care." Samantha stormed off.

She planned to leave her things in her apartment until after work, so that she wouldn't be late. Then, she would pick up everything and check into a nearby motel. The only problem with that plan was that she couldn't afford too many nights, and she wasn't about to flee back home. Her paycheck was decent, but she still had other expenses to pay.

She got everything legally squared away with the landlord. She eventually scraped up enough money to recompense her four-month debt. It took a great deal of budgeting, and Samantha almost went crazy by having to buy cheaper shampoo, use less hairspray, and cut back on snack food. She dwindled down her "necessities" until she paid back the debt. At least this time she actually knew where her money was being deposited.

Maybe it would've been simpler to throw Natalie out of the apartment, but the apartment was too expensive anyway. It'd be better to just find a cheaper place for the time being. Why was it that people like Charlotte and Jake Hexton had everything handed to them? Even Sara was about to fall into the money thanks to a ring on her finger. Was working hard and going to college even worth it?

The plan worked out fine for the first week or so. Nobody bothered her, and nobody knew that her backup stash of cash was beginning to run thin. But, all of that changed when her alarm clock didn't ring. Or did it?

She still didn't understand how she missed it. Normally, she was up on the first ring. One minute it was 5:15 and the next it was 6:30. On a regular morning, she woke up at 5:30, and work started at 7:00.

After throwing on some clothes and stuffing a granola bar in her mouth, she rushed out of the door and into the parking lot. She tried to start the car. *Whir. Whir. Whir.*

"Oh, come on!" She swung the car door open and headed to the front where she lifted the hood. An opaque emission of iron-gray smoke diffused into the warm air. "No, no, no! I don't have money to fix this!"

She let out a disgusted grunt and rushed to the nearest bus stop. She needed all of the cash that she had in her wallet, which really wasn't much at all. By the time the bus screeched to a halt in front of her, it was already pushing 7:30. Traffic in the heart of Pittsburgh wasn't any better than traffic on the parkway. Her conflicts didn't cease there. The bus stop closest to Rigby Mansion was two miles away from the mansion itself, so she had to walk—no, sprint—to get there.

I'm going to lose that promotion! Come on legs, move faster!

She was about a half-mile in when she tripped over what apparently was a camouflaged rock on the side of the road. Her ankle twisted, forcing her to the dirt.

It was a beautiful spring day. The sky was a pale indigo with a few puffy, marshmallow-like clouds hanging around. Samantha cursed the weather. Why should it be such a beautiful day when she felt so miserable?

As she stood up, her ankle throbbing, a shiny, ruby-colored Pontiac Firebird rolled up alongside her.

"Need a lift?" a voice called out.

"Depends. Where are you headed?" Samantha knew that there were several other houses up the road besides the Hextons' massive property.

"Wherever you need to go, babe," a second voice said.

"Shut up, Ryan, honestly! Hextons' place. You know, Rigby Mansion."

"That's where I have to go."

"Hop in."

"Thank you so much," she hobbled over to the car and slid into the middle of the backseat. "Um, I don't mean to be rude, because I'm really grateful for this, but can you please hurry? I'm already late as it is."

"No problem." Luke allowed his foot to put a bit more pressure on the gas. He stole a peek at her through the rearview mirror. She had pretty, glowing eyes. He was curious. "What do you do at the Hextons'?"

"Oh, I'm a maid there."

"Really? You've got to be kidding. A girl as hot as you should be a—I don't know—a model or something," Ryan said.

"Dude!" Luke shot back.

"Hey, you insisted on driving. It's really my car," Ryan shot back jokingly.

The boys couldn't see it, but in the backseat, Samantha

was blushing like crazy. These boys seemed pretty fun.

"I'm sorry, I didn't catch your names."

"Luke Cavarelli."

"Ryan Delhart."

"Nice to meet you," she said. "I'm Samantha. Hey, I don't mean to sound nosy, but what's your business with the Hextons?"

"We're The Steel City Boys," Luke said, like she should have known who they were.

"The who?"

"We're a band, babe," Ryan clarified.

Samantha gasped. "You're playing for the wedding, aren't you?"

"You bet. We're meeting with the family this morning."

"Well then, I can't wait to hear you play. I'm helping with the wedding to make a little extra cash."

"Aww," Luke said. "I hope you still get the chance to enjoy it."

"I hope so too."

It was a little after 8:15 when they pulled into the driveway and passed the sign that spelled out "Rigby Mansion" in gold lettering.

"Why is it called that?" Ryan asked. "Their last name is Hexton."

"It's Mr. Hexton's mother's maiden name. He wanted the property to be named in her memory. He had a really close bond with her."

Meanwhile, Joanne Hexton was frantically pacing the porch. Her eyes lit up instantly when the car approached.

Samantha jumped out of the car despite her ankle and shouted, "Mrs. Hexton, I'm here!"

She didn't hear Ryan say, "Whoa, hold on babe. The car hasn't even stopped yet!"

The old woman was overjoyed and met Samantha in the driveway. "Samantha, I was worried. You're never late. Is everything alright?"

Samantha quickly narrated what had happened that morning.

"You better get some ice on that ankle. As soon as you're able to work, get to it. You and I will talk later."

Samantha nodded and made her way inside while the two gentlemen who helped her followed Mrs. Hexton to the front porch.

* * *

"Are you the band?" Mrs. Hexton asked.

"Yes, ma'am, The Steel City Boys." Luke said. "Well, two of us anyway."

The boys introduced themselves and shook hands with Joanne.

"Jake and Sara are inside waiting for you. I'm sorry that Richard couldn't make it," she rolled her eyes, "but my husband's business means more to him than planning tiny details of a wedding."

She led them into the parlor. Jake and Sara were sitting on the main couch. Mrs. Hexton and Luke each took a chair, and Ryan insisted that he'd rather stand in the archway.

"Ok, here's a list of songs I want played." Sara handed Luke a sheet of paper.

Neither Sara nor Jake showed any signs of remembering Ryan's flirtations. Instead, Sara clung onto Jake as if he were a comfy pillow.

The boys scanned over the wish list, which was by no means short and sweet.

"Do you know this one? How about this one?" Luke pointed to songs on the list.

"Huh-uh. How're we supposed to play songs we don't know?" Ryan said.

"What do you mean you don't know them?" Sara got testy. "Don't you listen to good music? What kind of garbage do you people play?"

"Opera," Ryan mumbled under his breath so only Luke could hear.

"Well," Luke said, trying to make peace, "We can learn them and do the best we can."

"Sara, please, it's not the end of the world," Jake said. "Maybe they can play your songs and their songs. You guys do write your own songs too, right?"

"Yeah. Actually, we wrote a couple just for this. Plus, we have all of the other songs that we usually perform for gigs," Luke said.

"Let me see," Sara demanded.

Luke gave her several papers with lyrics scribbled on them and hummed a few bars.

She read them carefully. "No way!" she said. "I can't have this junk played at my wedding."

"They can't be that bad." Jake took them. "Dude, these are killer!"

Sara scoffed.

Luke smiled faintly. "You really like them?"

"Solid. I love them. As a matter of fact, this one should be sung for our first dance."

"Ugh. Which one? Eww, no!" Sara got up and stomped out of the room. Then she turned around and said, "And don't forget to ask about the entrance song."

"Oh, yeah. Can you guys play 'The Bridal March' on guitar?"

"Sure," Luke said.

"Awesome! You'll have to excuse her. She can be kind of dramatic, but I love her anyway. Play what you usually do. She'll come around."

With that, the short meeting concluded and Luke and Ryan were able to leave earlier than they had expected. When they got back to the car, Luke just happened to glance in the back seat. To his surprise, he discovered a leather purse lying there. He retrieved it and hurried to the Hextons' front door. He knocked gently and waited for a reply.

"Hi," Samantha held onto the doorknob.

Luke hadn't expected her to answer the door. "Hi," he said softly. "This belongs to you?" He held out the purse. She was even more beautiful than he first thought.

"Yes!" she exclaimed. "I'm so stupid! How could I have forgotten it?" She put a hand to her forehead.

"It's okay… You were just in a hurry."

"Thank you." She took the purse out of his hand.

Still breathless at the sight of her, Luke couldn't help but notice how this blond beauty happened to appear out of nowhere. Surely, he thought, her light and smooth complexion, along with her pale azure eyes like a crisp winter morning, would make her stand out in a crowd. She seemed to have an angelic radiance that could follow her on her darkest days.

"See you around." He turned to leave.

"Bye! Thanks again."

Luke waved and slid into the passenger seat, as Ryan took control of his car again.

After a few minutes of driving, Ryan said, "She's smoking hot, dude."

"Who?"

"Jake's girl."

"You're crazy. She's engaged! Didn't you learn the first time? Seriously, I don't know what goes through your head. She's nothing but attitude and trouble. I don't know about you, but I definitely don't want a girl like that."

"Man, what's your issue *now*? Is it that girl?"

"No, I'm fine!" Luke kept his eyes focused on the road, though Ryan was driving. For some reason he couldn't explain, an angelic maid was swirling in his mind.

Chapter 5

If Money Grew on Trees

"You met The Steel City Boys?"

"Yes! Emily, is it really that big of a deal?"

Emily was the hard-working cook at the Hexton's and perhaps Samantha's only true friend at work. A girl around Samantha's age, Emily Weston had long, wavy red hair and freckles on her high cheekbones.

"Totally! Haven't you ever heard of them?"

"No."

"What's wrong with you? Don't you ever go down to Silva's club on the weekends?"

"College."

"On the weekends?" Emily's acorn-tinted irises shot Samantha a look of sheer disbelief.

"Work."

"As if! Have you forgotten we both work here?"

"I have to work on my photography."

"Try again."

Samantha sighed and kept dusting, while Emily shook her head in disbelief.

Mrs. Hexton constantly stressed the importance of cleaning a house. She made sure that hers was dusted down from top to bottom, every knickknack, every shelf. In her defense, which the maids knew by heart, company could drop by at any given moment, so the mansion just had to be spotless. The list of Hexton family and friends was rather lengthy. Estranged, yet wealthy, cousin Claudia may show up out of nowhere, or high-end Mrs. Walters may need to stop by to dispel her grief over her husband's careless gambling habits. No matter the situation, the house had to be pristine (or at least give that impression). If she found a speck of dust that hadn't been wiped away, she wouldn't get angry about it, but would only jokingly hint to one of the maids about it.

Samantha dusted off the dressers in the master bedroom, and Emily was taking a break, waiting for the meat to cook in the oven.

"I wish I wouldn't have wasted two years gallivanting all over the country trying to get my photography to take off. I spent all the money my parents gave me. What good did that do? Everyone told me I was too inexperienced. Look at me now, trying to make ends meet while I get an education."

"Why don't you move back in with your parents? It'll save you like a load of money."

"No." Samantha shook her head. "I'm not about to lose my pride. I can't just show up poor and homeless. Besides, they live outside of the city. It would take forever to get to work everyday."

"Where are you going to go?"

Samantha shrugged.

"You can stay with me if you need to."

Samantha stopped for a moment in thought and sighed. "You know, I could've rented a cheaper place instead of moving in with Natalie. Actually, I was going to. But that was before I sold that piece as my own."

"What?" Emily asked.

"I needed a place to live after I spent my parents' money. I had to do this group project with a girl I didn't really like. She didn't take back any of her photos after the project was finished, and someone approached me about buying a few of the photos. I, um, sold them and said they were mine. No one ever knew the difference, and I had enough money for my safety deposit."

"Was this after the breakup with Nick?"

Nodding, Samantha stared at the ground. Then, she shook her head. "I couldn't pass up the apartment."

"Well, if she didn't want the photos back…" Emily trailed off.

Several minutes later, Mrs. Hexton trotted into her room. "I take it your ankle is feeling better?"

"Much, thank you," Samantha said.

"Wonderful! Look, I explained your situation to Mr. Hexton. He and I have decided that you may stay here for a while until you are prepared to get your own place."

"Wait, I don't need to stay here, Mrs. Hexton. I'm perfectly fine with living in a motel for now."

"For now? My dear, you told me that you're running out of money. You and I both know that you can't live in a motel forever. Please, we can give you a home until you're ready to go back out on your own. We won't charge much for rent, and you'll already be here for work. Will you please consider living in a guest room?"

Samantha stopped dusting and thought about it for a moment. It was the best offer she had. Mrs. Hexton was unfortunately right: she couldn't live in a motel all her life. And she still had to pay to have her car fixed in order to get to school.

"Okay." She smiled weakly. "I'll take you up on your offer."

"Wonderful!" Mrs. Hexton said and clapped her hands together. "And before my old mind forgets, would you also do the photography for the wedding? We'll pay you, of course."

"Uh, sure. I'd love to."

"Plus, I was thinking that maybe we could use some of your original work as displays in the reception hall."

Samantha gasped. "That'd be perfect! Mrs. Hexton, how can I ever repay you?"

"Just keep working, dear. Like I said before, you're one of my best employees." Mrs. Hexton winked at Emily. "You're one of the best too."

"Thanks, Mrs. H." Emily blushed.

Suddenly, there was a crash in the hall downstairs, and the women stared at each other.

"Gina's dusting the vases," Emily pointed out.

Mrs. Hexton sighed. "Not anymore, she's not."

After Mrs. Hexton left, Emily put a hand on her hips. "Did you just choose an old lady over me?"

"Yeah, but she's rich." Samantha grinned.

Emily laughed. "Can't argue with that. Go for it. But you do have to cook your own food!"

Within the next few days, Samantha moved into Rigby Mansion. It felt odd at first because most people don't live at the place where they work. But, after she set herself up in the large guest room, she began to feel at home.

As the wedding grew closer and closer, a sort of bubbly anticipation built up inside of her. The problem was, she couldn't figure out why. She had to work and that wasn't her definition of fun. Maybe it was because she hadn't been to too many weddings. Perhaps it was something entirely different. It was something that she didn't want to admit, something deep down that longed to be unveiled and proclaimed to the world. Could it be that she was looking forward to a locally-acclaimed band called The Steel City Boys?

Chapter 6

Passed Out on the Parkway

"Hey, man, wake up!"

Ryan groaned.

"Ryan, wake up, dude."

"Let me sleep!"

"Come on, dude, the wedding's today."

"It is?" Ryan shot up in his bed looking dazed.

"Yes, don't tell me you forgot."

"No, I didn't forget. This is the day we might finally make it big." Ryan chuckled and jumped out of bed. "But why'd you get me up so early? We don't play until this evening."

"This afternoon."

"Same difference."

"No, there is one, Ryan. You see, afternoon comes before evening."

Ryan threw a pillow at his best friend.

"Okay, okay! I got you up because we have prep work to do. We have to gather up the equipment and do a final run through of the songs."

"Get real, that's not going to take all day."

"Fine. I'm excited, that's all."

"To see your girlfriend again?"

"What? No, I'm in this thing for the music, you know that. Wait a second. I'm not hooking up with that girl."

"Want to bet?"

"No—I—do—not." Luke walked out of the room.

"You scared?"

"No, I just don't want to risk any money."

"So, there's a chance?"

"Would you eat and change clothes?"

"You are not my mother." Ryan made his way past

Luke into the kitchen.

They double-checked their arrangement of "Bridal March" for acoustic guitar and edited the setlist for the reception.

Time seemed to drag on for an eternity. Finally, it was time to leave. Dressed in neat, pastel-colored suits, they grabbed their guitar cases and took off for the door. But, before they could make their escape, the phone rang, beckoning them back into the living room.

"I got it." Ryan ran to answer it.

Luke watched as Ryan's smile faded. The wedding was at 3:00, and the band was to be setup by 1:30. It was already pushing noon.

"Is he okay?" Ryan asked. "Well, do what you can. Let us know if anything else happens."

He hung up and trudged over to where Luke was standing.

"The others might not make it."

"What? Why?"

"They were on the parkway, but Adam passed out."

"Oh no. He wasn't driving, was he?"

"No," Ryan shook his head, "but they're at the hospital now. It's so hot out there that the doctors think he got dehydrated. They're running a few tests just to be sure."

"What are we going to do?" Luke said. "I mean, we can't blame Adam for getting sick, but we won't even have Joe now on drums. We could do it without Adam's keyboard."

Luke and Ryan were capable of performing alone, but they didn't want to blow this chance to impress Mr. Hexton. Without their normal instrumentation, the songs wouldn't sound the same.

"The dream is lost, Ryan. We may as well forget it. Hexton won't help us if we sound like—He might not help us anyway—"

"Luke!"

Luke glared at him.

"Go. Get in the Firebird."

The lead singer cocked his head in confusion. Ryan wasn't usually one to get snippy.

"Now, Cavarelli! I am not giving up that easily. Whether they like it or not, they're getting the best dynamic duo they'll ever hear, drummer or no drummer."

Luke complied and went ahead of Ryan, looking over his shoulder as he walked.

Chapter 7

The Lead Singer

It had been a terribly long morning for Samantha. Even though the wedding was not until the afternoon, she had to wake up extra early because of the preparations that needed to be made.

There were going to be a little over 250 guests in attendance. The chairs were already arranged, but there were still a few tables that Samantha needed to set up. Most of the decorating was finished, but there was a laundry list of little things that couldn't have been done until today. The wedding was going to be catered, so Emily divided her time between helping in the kitchen and helping Samantha.

Samantha tried to make the best of it. She was excited to do the photography, but the only problem was that she also had to help prepare the reception hall.

Mrs. Hexton had told Samantha a thousand times that she would've preferred a traditional church wedding for her son, her only child, but Sara wanted no such thing. Mrs. Hexton lost the battle, so the wedding was to take place right at home.

Thanks to Mr. Richard Hexton's prosperous company, the Hextons were able to do a lot with their property. The mansion took center stage, but they also constructed other buildings on the land. Some of these structures were reserved for company use, others for either private or commercial.

Besides owning a golf course, they had the R.H. Hexton Reception Hall, which was used to host fancy galas, dinners, and other events. They rented it out for public use and donated the money generated to charity. For the wedding, the hall was ideal, spacious, and just perfect in the eyes of Sara.

The Hexton estate, even though mostly private and dis-

creet, was considered a paradise all in itself because of its surroundings. While most of the area had been cleared for the
Hexton additions, there was still a natural beauty to it. Circling the majority of the mansion on either side was a large
cluster of woods. Down the hill from the house was a serene
and transparent pond, free from weeds and moss, thanks to
the maintenance people that the Hextons employed. The reception hall sat adjacent to it, exuding a relaxing feel.

Samantha had to change outfits two times that day. To
photograph the wedding, she dressed in all black so that she
could remain unobtrusive. Her slacks would help her crouch
down with ease. She had also pulled her hair back, since she
would have much running around to do later. Along with
that, she clasped a short pearl necklace around her neck and
let matching earrings dangle a few inches from her ears.

It was a picture-perfect day; sky was nearly cloudless.
The temperature rose, and humidity clung to the air.

Samantha, Emily, and Gina made their way down to
the hall. As they got closer, Samantha admired the building
with its flat and level entrance, off-white siding, and russet
shingles. There was a small driveway and parking lot, but,
because of the number of guests, cars would eventually be
scattered in the grass. The Hextons even hired valets for this
special event!

"This place is always so gorgeous," Emily said, reading
Samantha's mind.

"Totally fabulous," Gina whispered.

Right inside the doors was a small room that resembled
a parlor. The green-blue carpet acted almost like an ocean
welcoming the guests. There were a couple of sofas, tables,
and decorative lamps assembled before the archway that led

into the main hall.

The main hall was a wide room that normally had round tables that provided seating for eight to ten guests comfortably. Tables were added or removed depending on the number of people expected to attend the scheduled event. However, the tables were pushed out of the way, and only chairs were lined up from the front all the way to the back wall. The massive room would have no trouble holding all of the guests.

The floor was hardwood, unlike the parlor area. The front of the room had a removable, polished wooden platform. This low platform was usually used for less formal gatherings, but today it was reserved for the band; the stage was for the couple to be joined in holy matrimony. After the ceremony, the band would be allowed to move onstage.

The stage wasn't very large, given the size of the rest of the building. The crimson curtains that were tied back followed the wedding's color scheme of red and purple.

The mature red was for Jake and the royal purple for Sara. The backs of the chairs were tied with bows. The guests related to Jake were to sit on the red side while the guests related to Sara were to sit on the purple side.

The Hexton employees, except Samantha, put themselves in the back. They watched the hall fill up quickly. There was an aisle that had a purple carpet rolled out for the bridal party processional.

While Samantha got out her brand new Nikon FA camera, a gift from the Hextons for the wedding, her mind wandered to dreamy thoughts of the band. Should she make a big deal out of this? Was she ready to move on after what happened in her last relationship? Maybe it would be better to just ignore them.

To her surprise, she found only two of the band members walking along the far side of the room, swinging guitar cases.

Apparently, it had been to Mr. Richard Hexton's surprise as well. Although older like his wife, he was a bit grayer with a broad build and a warm, dimpled smile. He had the precise stature of a businessman, but he wasn't cocky. He was reserved and professional.

Samantha tried to listen to the conversation.

"You're the band? There's only two of you!"

"Our keyboardist got sick, and the other guys are with him. We're not sure if or when they'll show up," Luke said.

"Can you play without them?"

"Yes." Luke sounded confident.

When she chanced a glance at the boys, she discovered something that she hadn't before. They were both quite handsome-looking young men, but their smiles were also comforting. They gave off a sense of pride, but not so much they were unappealing or seemed like bad boys. There was a seriousness about them, the sense that they were passionate about what they did, and they didn't need to flaunt it. They were humble. Maybe they were what she was looking for after all.

She shook her head softly in an attempt to chase away the thought from her mind. She felt her face flush, so she looked away in hopes that no one had seen her.

Suddenly, she realized that she had forgotten to light the candles. Around the room, there were wall mounts that held single votive candles. Mrs. Hexton, wanting to enhance the mood, had purchased candles that matched the wedding theme.

"I forgot to light the candles," she said to herself. Quickly, she left her camera and hurried out into the parlor where the lighter was located. She began to light the wicks and, coincidentally, there was one candle very close to where Mr. Hexton and the boys were conversing.

"I've been immersed in music ever since I can remember," she heard Luke say, "but the two of us formed the band about five years ago."

"We're looking forward to hearing you. Jake spoke very highly of your music."

"I think you'll be quite satisfied," Luke said.

Meanwhile, Samantha came to the candle she had been dreading. After taking a breath, she clicked the lighter. Nothing. Again: nothing.

She sighed. "Must be empty." Her finger kept slipping off the trigger. She tried checking the gauge on it, and it seemed pretty full. One more try: nothing. She threw her head back and grunted, glancing at the crystal chandelier above. Her whole body broke out in a sweat as she banged the lighter against her glistening palm, hoping that would help. She knew she was drawing attention to herself. The guys that she may or may not have had a crush on were staring. Although she couldn't deny that both gentlemen caught her eye, she found herself glancing at Luke the most.

"Need some help with that?" Luke asked while roaming over.

"No thanks. I got it."

"You sure, babe?" Ryan made his move. "Oh, it's you!" He recognized her instantly.

"Samantha, right?" Luke pointed as a soft grin spread

across his lips.

"You remembered." She pressed the button again. This time, a bright orange flame radiated out of the lighter's tiny tip. *Figures it'd work now. They'll think I'm a complete idiot!*

"See, you got it. I guess I'm good luck," Luke said.

"Good luck?" Ryan scoffed. "You?"

"Well, it most definitely isn't you."

"What do you mean? You've been all doom and gloom lately."

Luke's smile faded. "Later, Ryan." He slapped Ryan on the back. "Let's go set up."

Ryan shot him a dirty look and headed to the platform. Mr. Hexton had exited the scene. Luke turned to leave.

"What was he talking about?"

He spun around. "Ryan? Oh, it's nothing. I've just been worrying a lot about where our band's going to end up in the future. He's too reckless to care, some days. Look, I'm not normally depressed." He said this last bit with a huge smile.

She laughed. It was a sunshine-filled, light-hearted laugh. He liked it. It felt good to make somebody happy, even if he wasn't 100 percent.

"Well, good luck."

"Thanks. I'll need it."

"Are you nervous?"

"A little, but that's only because there are so many rich people here to impress. Other than that, it comes pretty naturally to me." He paused to change the subject. "You'll be on that dance floor, right?"

"As soon as I can. I've actually never heard you guys before."

"Never?" He was surprised.

"Nope."

"Then I hope you enjoy!"

They said a quick goodbye and went their separate ways. She made final preparations to her camera and waited for the wedding to start. She kept her eyes on the boys up front, especially Luke. There was just something about him, something she couldn't describe. He seemed like a sweet guy with a big heart. If he were to sweep her up, he would never let her go. She continued to watch them as they set up their microphones and guitars. She stayed mesmerized by all of it until Luke approached his mic.

"Please rise."

Chapter 8

Rich Man's Wedding

The Bridal March sounded unique, but not so much that it was in bad taste. Ryan's strumming made the song gentle and absolutely beautiful. He played the main melody, while Luke played simple chords in the background. They were so comfortable, knowing each other's movements and feeling every note. Their sound grew fuller as the notes swelled and faded softly and sweetly. By the end, Mrs. Hexton was sobbing as Mr. Hexton guided her to her chair.

The bridal party carried on the color scheme, and Jake Hexton stood on the stage with a nervous, yet joyful expression.

Samantha began snapping photos right away, moving from one side of the room to the other.

Sara was escorted down the aisle by her father, who already had tears forming in his eyes. She wore a strapless, ball-gown-style dress, which was complemented by a glittery silver belt that surrounded her waist. Her stiff, curled hair stayed pushed back so that her glowing face could be admired.

The ceremony seemed to last forever, at least for Samantha. She was proud of the pictures she was taking, but her thoughts kept wandering. It still bugged her that Sara was simply marrying into money and, in 10 more minutes time, Sara's dreams would be reality. Why do people always have everything handed to them? No matter what side of the room she was on, she found her eyes darting over to Luke and Ryan, who were sitting in the end row closest to the stage. They definitely didn't look snobby like the rest of the guests. They reminded her a little bit of herself. Finally, the vows were said and the words, "I now pronounce you man and wife," were fervently announced.

The guests filed out of the room and congratulated the newlyweds. They had the choice to either stay in the parlor or roam outside while sipping drinks. Meanwhile, Samantha lined the bridal party up for photos.

"Okay, can I get Sara's family to gather around Sara and Jake? We'll put Mom and Dad next to her and Brother and Sister on the other side of Jake. Alright, everyone look this way please, big smiles… Just a few more… Wait, Jake, you have to smile. It's your wedding day, come on! Great. Now, I want Mr. and Mrs. Hexton next…"

She scrambled to gather up her equipment so that she could help set up for the reception. She found a safe place to keep her camera and lenses, keeping in mind that she would have to take many pictures later. Satisfied, she hurried to help bring out tables and rearrange the chairs. They decorated the tables with alternating red and purple tablecloths and placed more candles around the center pieces.

These elaborate center pieces took Samantha and Gina days to prepare. They were glass vases filled with colorful glass roses. Each vase had lights in the bottom of it, so the entire display glowed, bathing the room in various neon colors. Apparently, real flowers weren't chic enough for Sara.

Samantha hurried to decorate. The quicker she moved, the sooner she could enjoy the wedding and The Steel City Boys.

* * *

Meanwhile, the boys were preparing to play for the reception. The rest of the band still hadn't made an appearance. Regardless, there was a gig to do.

"I hope they show soon. It's going to be awkward without a backbeat," Luke said.

"I know. So, we're just doing an upbeat instrumental for their arrival into the room, right?"

"Yeah, and then we do 'Forever Mine' for their first dance."

"And we're not doing 'Carry On Wayward Son' until later? Luke? Luke!"

"W—what?" Clearly, his mind was elsewhere.

"The Kansas song, Luke."

"Yeah, it's in the middle along with 'Sir Duke.' I don't want to do too many covers."

"Dude, your mind's not on the music. Hey, will you quit staring at that girl? I'll admit, she's hot, but remember: the music comes first."

Luke sighed. "Definitely. I know, it's just—she piques my interest. That's all." He couldn't forget Samantha's sunshine-filled, light-hearted laugh. He liked it. It felt good to make somebody happy.

"She's right for you, man. She's your type."

"How do you know?"

"I'm a ladies' man. I know about ladies."

Luke rolled his eyes.

"I'm just saying. Either way, focus on the music tonight. We have a lot of rich people to impress."

"Sounds like my usual pep talk to you."

Ryan smirked. "Funny how roles can change."

The guests were just filtering back into the room when two men walked in carrying several framed pictures. Samantha recognized the pictures instantly. She rushed over and told them where to hang her photography. She had made sure to do her very best work for the occasion.

Finally, it was time for the party to commence, and Ryan took over announcing. "Please join me in welcoming Mister and Missus Jake Hexton!" He hung on to each word as he shouted them.

The packed room of guests cheered and hollered in delight when the couple, clasping hands, danced their way into the hall.

The platform that was used during the ceremony had been taken away and the tables were pushed back away from the stage, leaving a spacious dancing area. The couple meandered over and waited for the music to start.

But nothing happened.

Luke and Ryan looked at one another. Should they start without the rest of the band? The "Bridal March" was arranged for two guitars, but the rest of their set relied on background instruments so the songs wouldn't sound empty. They thought Tyler and Joe would have been there. They didn't have much of a choice, and the people were starting to gawk.

Sara angrily charged onstage. "What're you waiting for?" She tried to lower her voice so the guests couldn't hear.

"The rest of the band," Ryan said weakly, as if she were going to rip his head off.

"We don't have time for that. Either play or beat it. You are not ruining my wedding!"

Although some of the guests were rich and snobby, no one booed. Instead, the guests sat silently, staring at them.

Luke's heart fluttered, and he felt his stomach drop.

"We can play, but it's not going to sound right. Do you want it to sound good, or do you just want it to be done and

over with? You can't have both. Meaningful or meaningless."
He couldn't believe he was telling off Sara Hexton. Yes, it
was his voice speaking the words, but he didn't feel like himself at all.

Sara's face grew redder, and Ryan pulled Luke aside.

"I think we should play," he whispered.

Luke shook his head. "'Forever Mine' isn't going to
sound right without the guys."

"And you and I both know that we've practiced the song
in the living room dozens of times by ourselves."

Luke sighed, knowing Ryan was right. But this wedding
reception could be a pivotal moment in their careers, and the
last thing Luke wanted to do was screw it up. He scanned the
crowd again, half-hoping the band would pile through the
doorway. Some people were whispering, others still staring.
What about Samantha? This was also his moment to impress
her. He had a job to do.

Luke nodded to Ryan. "Play the intro an extra time to
give me a minute to prepare."

Waiting for Ryan to start the song, Luke held onto the
microphone stand, his eyes closed. This was his song. This
was his moment.

Slowly, Ryan's strumming began and flourished into a
sweet and soulful melody. Luke didn't have Joe's jazzy back-
beat on drums, but he dominated the song from the very first
lyric.

It feels like I've been waiting a lifetime,
    To find someone I can call mine,
    Someone to glue me together—

You will be mine forever.

The exhilaration I feel when I'm with you,
Wipes all sinfulness from view.
When I gaze into your eyes full of love
and tenderness,
I am compelled to always keep my vow of
faithfulness.

As our love continues to flourish,
My worries and despair gradually vanish,
To a small follicle of my imagination.
My heart explodes with utter exaltation.

And as the music crescendoes:

You are mine,
I have been shown the sign,
Nothing can tear us apart,
We are no more just lonely hearts.

Oh, when i see your face,
I'm reminded of that first embrace,
Each of us now intertwined—
You are forever mine.

The song concluded simply, and Luke felt the last few notes pour out of him. It was like releasing some foreign magic that had the power to heal the world. It felt so good. And even though the song was composed in more of a traditional poem format rather than a normal song, the crowd didn't seem to care. Their thunderous applause echoed, bouncing off of the walls. It didn't begin to taper off until after Jake and Sara headed over to the Bridal Party's table.

"Do you think they liked it?" Ryan said with a sarcastic, but joyful tone.

"I think they were applauding for them."

"I wouldn't be so sure."

During dinner, the rest of the band arrived. Joe and Tyler rushed through the room, fighting to get to the stage with equipment. Adam staggered behind, looking sickly but eager.

Luke and Ryan glanced at each other and grinned.

Then Luke said to Adam, "Are you sure you're okay to play?"

Adam shrugged. "I'll be okay," he said wearily. "I can sit to play a keyboard." He tried to smile. "I'll stop when I need to."

Meanwhile, Tyler plugged his guitar into the amp. "And The Steel City Boys are here to rock the top off this joint!"

* * *

Samantha finally finished serving tables. Since she volunteered to help out for overtime pay, she worked alongside the caterers—Mrs. Hexton's direct order. She had just enough time to change into a floral-patterned dress, which she had replaced with more comfortable clothing in order to mess with food. She grabbed a plate of leftovers and ate them in the corner of the kitchen before venturing out into the party with her camera. All the while, "Forever Mine" was stuck in her head. Why did the song sound so familiar? It was as if she had heard the song before, but that couldn't be since she had never heard Luke sing. She left her plate by the sink and didn't at all pity whoever's shift required clearing tables and washing dishes. In fact, she hoped that it was Gina's job.

When dinner was mostly over, Ryan invited everyone to the dance floor. The Steel City Boys did what they did best and entertained the wealthy partygoers.

Ryan Delhart rarely got any solo vocal parts; he always got the backup parts because Luke was the better singer. That night, however, he had the privilege of sharing lead vocals with Luke on the band's cover of "Carry On Wayward Son." In their version, Luke sang the chorus and Ryan took over the verses. This way, Ryan could come back in on the instrumental interlude with "the rockin' guitar parts," as they called them.

Mostly, the song went well. Luke had to hold his breath, though, when Ryan went to start the first verse. It was the first time that the audience had ever heard Ryan's voice. He was two lines in when he was momentarily distracted and almost missed the downbeat of the third.

Some girl on the dance floor let out a huge 'woo' clearly directed at him. Luckily, he saved himself and finished out confidently.

The night continued on strong. Luke was ecstatic to see so many people packed on the dance floor. The round of applause after the end of each song seemed even greater than the last, but that could've been his imagination. What wasn't imaginary, though, was Samantha Denvy out there on the floor enjoying the—his—music with her camera in her hand.

He thought that maybe the night would never draw to a close. He loved singing his heart out, but waking up early was beginning to catch up with him. Nevertheless, he felt a twinge of disappointment when the final song had been belted out. The reception hall was almost empty. The newlyweds had departed and a few straggling guests lagged behind, prolonging their exit.

"I'm impressed, boys." Mr. Hexton approached the band. "I didn't think you were going to make it in the beginning, but I have to say that you didn't disappoint. I want to apologize for doubting you. Really, I think you guys have something going on here, and it's amazing. First, I have your check. Thank you for taking time out of your busy Saturday night for us. I know you could've played at a different venue. Now, I don't know anything about music. I'm a businessman, not a Grammy Award winner, but I have a good friend in the music industry. It's a shame that he couldn't make it tonight. I think he'll love you guys. Here's his contact information. You should send him some recordings." He handed Luke the check along with a folded-up piece of paper.

Luke and Ryan stood there, not knowing what to even say. It was too unbelievable. Neither of them actually thought it would happen. It was just wishful thinking, maybe even partly a joke.

"Look, it may sound too good to be true," Mr. Hexton had read the boys' minds, "but I feel like I need to help you out. Maybe you were hoping this would be your big break. I don't care. I'm more than willing to get you guys on track. I don't have personal contacts and high-profile friends for nothing. I believe in helping young people make their dreams come true. But please, don't waste your talent. Don't give up, and don't make me regret my decision!"

Mr. Hexton thanked them once more and, likewise, the boys couldn't stop expressing their utmost gratitude.

Luke and Ryan shared a sideways glance after Mr. Hexton left, and they checked their surroundings before gleefully hugging each other.

Then, Luke glanced down and read the piece of paper. "Wait a second." He hesitated, absorbing the words. "Sforzando Records?!"

"You mean The Leather Heartbreaks?" Adam cocked an eyebrow. "As in, Hexton's contact works at the same label that signed Tony Bellano?"

"I can't believe this!" Luke laughed.

"You and me both, brother!" Ryan exclaimed.

Slowly, the rest of the band shouted in jubilee.

"This can't be happening!" Tyler said.

"This could be our big break!" Joe tossed a drumstick in the air and watched it twirl back down before he caught it.

On the way out, they passed Samantha, who was talking to a man holding a framed photograph in his hand. He had just handed her a check. She seemed so happy, and Luke saw his chance.

"Hey," he said casually, walking towards her.

"Hey! I can't believe that guy just bought one of my photos for $1,500!"

"Whoa," Ryan commented.

"Wait, I didn't know these were yours!" Luke exclaimed. "I saw that you were taking pictures earlier?"

"Yeah, photography's my passion. Well, I'm trying at least."

Luke and Ryan took a minute to observe her other work that hadn't yet been removed from the wall. They complimented her and then turned to make their escape. Ryan kept moving, but Luke stopped dead still.

His eyes remained transfixed on one of the photos. It captured a lighted boardwalk with the end of it protected by a tiny roof. It looked out into the vast, calm sea. The dull, puffy clouds covered the pale blue sky. For some reason, he felt like he had been there before, yet he knew he never had been. It felt so comforting. It was like he could go to this place in his mind and forget the rest of the world. He looked at Samantha and everything made perfect sense; he wanted to go to this paradise with her.

If he didn't ask her out, he would never forgive himself. He felt fuzzy with nerves. A warm sensation shot through his body, and he suddenly felt breathless. This was it. This was her.

"Samantha?"

"Yeah?" She had her back facing him and was taking down a glowing photo of the Pittsburgh skyline at night.

He exhaled. "Would you want to, I don't know, maybe go out on a date with me sometime?"

Now her stunning beauty was staring at him, and her

cheeks were glowing bright pink.

"I—I don't know. My schedule—"

"I'm flexible. I can work around it."

"Okay," she said. "I'd like that."

"Great!" Luke lit up instantly. Then he realized his mistake: "Um, I guess I lied about being flexible. We may have to do it on a Sunday; Fridays and Saturdays are usually booked with gigs."

"That's fine," she said, still grinning.

He waited for her to finish up and escorted her outside. It was much cooler out; the sun had hidden itself beyond the horizon.

They made their way out in silence until they came to where Ryan had parked the car.

"I'll call you," he said after they exchanged phone numbers.

"Can't wait!" She waved goodbye and headed towards the Hexton mansion.

Luke watched her walk away, half-stunned that he actually just asked her out, and even more surprised that she'd said yes. Slowly, he got in the car.

"Well?" Ryan was anxious.

"Could you wait until I shut the car door? Got her number. I'll call her in a few days. "

Ryan scanned the radio for a station without commercials. "Good for you, man. Look at you getting hot girls!"

"Ryan, please."

"Just saying."

"Just drive."

"You're no fun."

"And you're too much."

"Who cares? We're going to be famous!"

"Yeah." Luke chuckled to himself. "Things are looking up."

Chapter 9

Open Minds, Tender Hearts

Everyone seemed to know about the date. Samantha couldn't remember telling anyone about Luke calling her to see if she'd like to go out that following Sunday, but the secret had seeped out like water breaking through a worn-out dam.

"That's awesome!" Emily said.

"And he's in a band," Gina said, whipping back her beach-blonde hair.

"Don't forget, he's smoking hot," Emily rambled on.

"Omigod, like, total stud," Gina continued, dramatically.

"Guys, really, it's nothing," Samantha said, blowing them off.

Charlotte Hexton walked by the girls, who were in the kitchen. "Yes, it is, whatever you're talking about. It's nothing. Now get back to work, or I'll tell Joanne that she has lazy bums working for her!"

"She's such a witch," Gina whispered.

"She's been a lot worse lately," Emily said.

"I just thought it was menopause," Samantha said.

They all giggled softly.

"I better get going. Luke's picking me up at 6:00." She wiped her hands on a nearby towel.

The other two let out high murmurs of excitement as she headed upstairs.

It was a large guest bedroom. By no means should it have housed a maid. It reminded Samantha of a hotel room, but with richer decor and a lot more furniture. The bed had been pushed up against the right wall, and the bathroom was in the corner. The closest was on the other side of the bed on the far wall. The room had a beige and green theme because Mrs. Hexton wasn't huge on vibrant colors. Unfortunately, there was no television, but the medium-sized window captured a picture-perfect view of the Hexton property.

Whenever she would come back from her evening classes, she would watch the golden sun sink lower and lower into the horizon, stretching its last beautiful rays of light behind the trees. Camera always ready, she would capture whatever was occurring outside her window. Her joy had nearly doubled when, one evening, a family of deer strolled out of the woods and grazed in the backyard.

Now, what to wear? She stared into the abyss that was her closet. How dressed up should she get? Surely, Luke wouldn't roll up in jeans and a T-shirt. Or would he?

After much debate and contemplation, she chose a denim miniskirt and a black crop top. She put on her best jewelry and generously applied hairspray before observing her overall appearance in the mirror. Once she deemed herself satisfactory for a first date, she grabbed her purse and hurried downstairs.

Shutting the door behind her, she walked out into the warm air and roamed the yard. While she waited for him, she felt her stomach twist. Was it getting hotter out here, or was it in her head? *Alright, Samantha, calm down. Why are you such a nervous wreck? He can't be worse than any other guy you've dated, especially… Never mind. You'll be fine. Just be yourself.*

She thought she was prepared and composed until Luke pulled up in the Firebird. Suddenly, the mix of emotions rushed back over her.

Luke stepped out of the car and made his way up the driveway to meet her. Dressed in off-white pants and a blue shirt, Luke immediately impressed Samantha with his style—not too fancy or too casual. He met her halfway and opened the passenger-side door for her.

A gentleman, she thought to herself. *That's promising.*

They only made small talk on the way there.

He decided to take her to a chic place called The Edge of Town. Not only did it serve as a restaurant, but it had its own dance floor where a different band or DJ would perform every weekend. Because it was Memorial Day weekend, it was fairly crowded for a Sunday night. The club's bar was located on the left side of the building, and there were many tables scattered about.

Her heels clicked on the wooden floor, which made her feel too well-dressed for the occasion. She let him lead her back into a corner booth. Once they ordered their food, the conversation began with, "What part of Pittsburgh did you grow up in?"

"Well, I come from a pretty small family." Luke kept the conversation going. "I hope I'm not a spoiled only child."

"That's kind of funny because mine is huge!" She took a sip of soda. "I love my brother and sister, but we were one rowdy household! To top it off, we always had to watch our money, so I've suffered through a lot of hand-me-downs."

They each laughed as the waitress served their food and then left them to eat and talk the night away.

"So, how did you end up at the Hextons' anyway?"

She sighed heavily and told him the condensed story of her photography failures and how now she was confined to school and the Hextons'. "I don't know. I just feel like I'm never going to get anywhere. Does it seem too selfish to say that I'm tired of worrying about money constantly?"

Luke shook his head. "Not at all. I get it. I just wish the band would score a record deal already. I feel like I'm at the bottom and I'll never rise to the top." He pushed his plate aside. "I'm sorry for all you've been through. I mean, it seems that we both feel the same about our current situations. I'm sure things will look up for you. I think you have a better chance of getting a job in the photography business than I do of becoming a pop star."

"You sound amazing though. I think you guys have what it takes." She smiled.

"Thanks, I appreciate the confidence," he said. "My parents always pushed me to settle down with a high-paying job, so I don't always get support from my home base."

"Hey, I get it," Samantha said. "It took a lot of convincing, but my parents finally approved my career route. Can we talk about something maybe less depressing?"

"Be my guest."

"Okay. Um, how did you and Ryan meet?"

"Really, we've always been together. We lived next door to each other, so we grew up together. Now look at us; we're still joined at the hip!"

"No offense, but why does he think he's a ladies' man?"

"What do you mean?" Luke laughed. "He is a chick magnet. Somehow. He charms them and then that's it. I can't explain it. I've never had that much good luck. Then again, I've always distanced myself from romantic relationships." He felt like he could be so open with her.

"Why?" She looked at him skeptically.

He shrugged. "I just tune it out and focus on my music. Ryan jokes that I'm married to music. I guess it's because he's been with so many girls. I've realized that I don't want that kind of life. I don't want to be a one-night-stand kind of guy. I like to think of myself as quiet and reserved."

"Yeah, a 'quiet' singer."

"But you know what I mean."

"I do, I do." Her eyes scanned around the room as she searched for something to say. What hadn't they talked about? She caught a glimpse of the crucifix around his neck. "So, you're religious?"

"Catholic. Born and raised. I'm at church every week with bells on. I know, it's not what most guys my age are into these days. It doesn't make me seem cool."

"No! It's fine. Honestly, it makes them less cool and you even better. I'm more of a Christmas and Easter churchgoer."

The night zoomed by as the singer and the photographer chatted away. Samantha's flair for detail led her to keep track of how they were alike; he liked the Pirates, and she preferred the Steelers, while they met in the middle on the topic of cheesecake. Luke would rather live in an apartment, while Samantha dreamed of a mansion like the Hextons'—provided she didn't have to clean it. They both acknowledged their nerdy sides by saying that they loved *Jeopardy*. Still, neither of them had successfully solved the Rubik's Cube.

Eventually, they ran out of things to talk about.

Sitting in silence, they watched those having a blast on the dance floor.

Samantha smiled to herself. It wasn't going bad at all. She liked him. A lot. Maybe too much. Would he ask her to dance?

One of the popular DJs played that night. He made the announcement that it was the final song, and, in mere minutes, a slow and lyrical melody flowed through the speakers. Luke exhaled. "May I?" He held out his hand.

She stared at it for a moment, shoulders tensed. This

could truly be the start of a new relationship. Was she ready? Then, she realized that Luke seemed different from other guys. She didn't know how to describe him; she just knew he was special. She nodded and stood up.

The crowd thinned as they walked out onto the floor. He put his arms around her waist, and she draped hers around his neck. They swayed precisely to the beat and it was as if they had melted into one. The song's emotion swirled around them as they danced.

Samantha dared to steal a glance at him. He was by far the most handsome man that she had ever laid eyes on. There was a special innocence in his eyes and a gentle reassurance that she was sure could console her on her worst nights.

The song flowed on and on. Samantha didn't want it to end, but as every slow song must come to a soft conclusion, so did this one. It was at this end that the most unexpected, yet amazing, thing happened.

Soon they were in the midst of a delicate first kiss.

When the song ended, they gazed at one another and smiled gently. Samantha was so enthralled with him that she couldn't speak.

They barely spoke on the way back, and they were outside of the Hextons' house sooner than Samantha wanted to be.

"I really wish this didn't have to end," she whispered.

"Me too. Samantha, can I be serious with you for a minute?" Luke asked.

"Sure." She shifted in the passenger seat as they gazed into each other's eyes.

"I feel like I've really connected with you tonight. I

guess what I'm trying to say is that I like you, and I can't wait to see you again."

She blushed. "I feel the same way. I don't know if this means anything, but I felt something incredible on the night of the wedding. When I heard you sing… you were singing directly to me no matter the song. Maybe that just means you're a captivating performer, I don't know. Either way, it seemed like I *had* heard you before, even though I hadn't. It seems like I've known you forever."

"You know," Luke said as he thought, "I felt the exact same way when I looked at one of your photos, the one with the blue boardwalk leading to a dock. I felt like I'd been there before, like the picture was meant for me."

They fixated on each other for a moment, beaming. This wasn't a coincidence.

"Call soon?" she asked.

"Definitely!"

As she watched him drive off, her heart sank a little. Luke had touched her in a way she hadn't thought possible, and she didn't want him to leave.

She had had only a few boyfriends. Most had never amounted to much, save one, but he had hurt her tremendously. Foolishly, she thought that it had been love, but it became apparent that he only used her. He deserted her for someone else who was more attractive and more sophisticated. And more richer. The wound had never fully healed, and the scar normally ached and haunted her whenever she would even think about moving on with someone new. Maybe that's why she always felt so insecure.

No. Tonight was completely different. She wasn't afraid of Luke. He didn't come off as the sort of guy who went around breaking hearts. She needed someone like him in her life to brighten the dark, someone to fill the void.

Upstairs in her bedroom, she got ready for bed. The only problem was that, every time she closed her eyes, sleep didn't come. It kept getting interrupted by a guy named Luke Cavarelli. His hopeful smile, light eyes, and gentle voice floated around in her head. Dreams can come true.

* * *

When Luke opened the apartment door, he was submerged in complete darkness. Well, all except for the colorful television lights that projected onto Ryan's tired face.

The door slammed shut, bringing Ryan up, alert and eager to ask Luke about his date with Samantha.

"Would some light kill you?" Luke threw his keys on the kitchen table and flicked on the light switch.

"I'm a vampire, don't you know?" Ryan squinted, trying to get his eyes adjusted.

"I bet the ladies love that. Suck blood often?"

Ryan chuckled lightly. "So, how'd it go?"

"Great!"

Ryan turned around to look at his best friend. "Just 'great'?"

"It was! I really like her. I just don't know if—"

"Don't know if what? Dude, I can see by the expression on your face that you have a crush on her big time. Stop doubting yourself! Don't let this girl get a—Lucas Michael Cavarelli, are you listening to me?!"

"No, Ryan Cornelius Delhart, I am not!" Luke yelled jokingly.

"Hey, don't you ever use my—that—name again!"

"That bad, huh? You want to gag yourself with a spoon? I'm getting closer to the spoon drawer." Luke moved towards the sink.

"Who gives a kid that middle name? It's horrible, disgraceful, embarrassing—"

"Wasn't that your great-grandfather's name?"

"I—uh—hey, stop distracting me! We're talking about you here."

Luke's face flushed, and his eyes darted away.

"Oh… you kissed her already!" Ryan exclaimed.

"How do you—"

"It's written all over your face, dude." He smirked. "That's wicked. That's a new extreme, for you!"

"Don't tell anyone!" Luke pointed at him. "It just happened."

Ryan scoffed. "That's what they all say."

"I mean it, Delhart!"

"Okay! You have my word."

"Thank you. And by the way, no, I don't plan on letting her get away. I'm holding on for dear life."

"Good," Ryan answered simply. "Now get over here before the movie ends. I know you're a sucker for *The Empire Strikes Back*.

But Luke couldn't focus on the movie. Instead, he replayed the night's events in his mind. He had liked Samantha from the start, but their dance moved him in a way that he hadn't thought possible. This girl didn't simply attract him. She was a pure sweetness that he had never known, someone who actually understood the way he felt and made him feel at ease, like he could be himself. He hadn't planned on kissing her, but he couldn't contain the moment any longer. The more he thought about her, the more he couldn't quench the burning desire in his heart to make her happy.

Chapter 10

Ghost from the Past

The Hexton wedding was long over, and the business card that Mr. Hexton had given the boys ended up on the table with the stack of mail. When Luke sorted through the huge pile (because Ryan never remembered to do it) he came across the note with the name and number scribbled on it. He hadn't completely forgotten, but thoughts of Samantha had been occupying his mind as of late.

"Why don't we record new demos on Saturday morning?" Luke said. "We can get the band together early, before we go to the club at night."

"Alright, cool. I'll call the others and let them know."

On the following Saturday, the band assembled their equipment in Tyler's basement, where there was more room and no one to disturb. All they had to do was decide on what tracks to play, record them, and send them off with a cover letter.

"We can record four songs on one tape with the Portastudio," Ryan said.

"'Forever Mine' for sure," Luke called out.

"How about the new version of 'Music Man'?" Ryan said.

"Yeah, that's good. What about two of the covers we did for the wedding?" Joe said.

"Sounds good. I think a couple of them came off pretty strong."

"Okay, we'll go in that order. When I turn it on, count us off, Joe."

"One, two. One, two, three, four…"

They spent their morning recording on a Portastudio, a recording device that translated the songs onto cassettes. Luke watched Ryan perform post-production magic on the recordings, so that the songs would sound the way the band desired.

"I'm pretty sure this is the button we want." Ryan carefully pushed the buttons.

"Please try to not mess anything up," Luke said.

"Look, I don't know everything about this machine. I only know what Jeff taught me, and his directions were scattered anyway!"

"Um, I don't think that control is supposed to be that loose," Luke pointed out.

"What in the Geddy Lee—"

Tyler rolled his eyes. "Ryan's using Rush members as swear words again."

"Listen, if we don't return this thing in tip-top shape, we can kiss all our record label dreams goodbye." Ryan groaned.

Luke had several record labels in mind, including Sforzando Records. The band had sent off demos before, so he was familiar with the process. After writing out the cover letters, he and Adam sealed them each in a manila envelope along with a cassette. Fingers crossed, Luke hoped that someone would approve this time and dish them out a record deal—if only it were that easy.

Time seemed to drag on. Sometimes Luke felt anxious for an answer. He started to think that one would never arrive, but he maintained his patience and clung to hope. Luckily, he had Samantha to distract him from his worrying.

One Friday, he brought her over to the apartment after their lunch date. The band didn't have a gig that night because Luke had to work later, and Samantha had managed to get a much-needed afternoon off.

"Hey, babe, how are you?" Ryan greeted, like usual.

"Fine, thanks. And I'm not your babe."

"No, she's mine," Luke said.

Ryan shrugged. "It doesn't matter; I have my own girl-friend."

"You do?" Luke raised an eyebrow.

"I—I'm working on it."

"Well—" the phone rang and Luke rushed to answer it. He cleared his throat. "Yes, I'm Luke Cavarelli from The Steel City Boys."

Ryan and Samantha turned excitedly to look at Luke.

"Okay. Mm-hmmm. Oh. Okay, well, thanks for taking the time to review our demos. We appreciate it. You too. Bye."

Expressions of sheer disappointment wiped away Ryan and Samantha's smiles.

"I take that as a no," Ryan said.

"Yeah." Luke sighed. "They said that we're good, but they're afraid that our songs won't make the charts. We're more of a cover band."

"That's not true!" Ryan shouted. "We barely do covers. We only put two covers on that demo!"

"I know. Everyone's a critic."

"I'm sorry, guys," Samantha said as she rushed over and hugged her boyfriend.

"It's alright." He held onto her tightly. "We still have three more to hear from. Mr. Hexton's guy is still on the table." In the meantime, Luke tried to be optimistic. He went to work that day and did his best not to think about it.

Luke worked at Chill, a popular cafe downtown. The place was quite small, compared to the area's other offerings:

Silva's Place and The Edge of Town. The counter stood only about three feet from the doorway, yet it stretched almost the length of the room. The kitchen was behind the counter and could be accessed through a narrow door. A dozen tables were lined on the surrounding floor, and there was a huge, violet booth in the back corner that curved outward, providing plenty of seating for a group of customers.

The interior flashed a bright ambiance, and the cafe served as a great hot spot for Pittsburgh's young adults, especially those under 21. Sticking with more of a creative theme, the majority of it, all except for the chalky walls, was decked out in neon. From the outer casings around the lights to the chair cushions, it had the ability to attract even moths thanks to its luminescence.

Luke rarely worked the Friday night shift because of gigs, but one of the other employees had called in sick, so he had agreed to fill in. He mostly stayed behind the counter, handing out steaming hot coffees and other popular beverages.

Ryan had conjured up the other three members of the band, and they followed Luke there.

"Hey! Okay, I need my coffee black with a bit of milk. And, could you load it up with sugar, Mr. Barista?" Ryan announced proudly as he pranced through the door.

Luke laughed. "Have I ever told you that I hate you?"

"You tell me every day!"

The guys settled down onto stools at the counter. Joe, Adam, and Tyler shouted out their orders too, which only made Luke shake his head and continue working.

"Can't you turn this music up, dude? Come on, let's party!"

Luke rolled his eyes, but he wasn't really annoyed. The guys were his homeboys, so that made the bossy commands just fine. The cafe began to grow a little crowded. Thanks to Ryan's stash of change, the stereo was pumping synthesized beats from the jukebox in the corner of the room.

* * *

Later in the evening, Emily persuaded Samantha to head over to the cafe.

"You need to get out," Emily said.

"I'd rather be taking snapshots," Samantha said.

"You have a boyfriend now. You have to actually get out and try to have a life."

"We went out to lunch this afternoon," Samantha said. They were walking on the sidewalk, approaching Chill.

"I'm sure he'd love to see you again," was the reply.

"I'm just glad we got out of that place for the night," Samantha said. "Let the Hextons fend for themselves. Maybe Charlotte and Sara will learn to do something."

"And Gina," Emily added.

The bell tied to the door chimed when the girls stepped in the building.

"Hey!" Ryan shouted and lifted his cup in the air. "It's Luke's girlfriend!"

"Man, you didn't spike that, did you?" Joe whispered to Luke.

"Believe me, you wouldn't have wanted me to." Luke was glowing now that he had Samantha in his sights again.

"And *who* is *this*?" Ryan said seductively as Emily passed him by.

"Wouldn't you like to know." She shot him a little smirk before claiming a back table.

Samantha paid Luke for their order and then joined Emily. The table was far enough away from the bar that the boys couldn't overhear their conversation.

"So, how's college life?" Emily leaned back in her chair after Samantha handed her a sweetened iced coffee.

"Fine, I guess. I just wish it was over. I'd rather be raking in a better income instead of watching it fly out the window."

"Yeah, but the education's helping you, right?"

Suddenly, Samantha's mind wandered. Right behind the table on the wall hung a piece of abstract art. It looked like an artist just swirled a couple of pale red and blue stripes on a canvas and declared it art.

"Samantha, where's your mind at? Clearly, it's not on your dreamy boyfriend 'cause you're looking in the wrong direction."

"What if I shouldn't be a photographer?"

"What on earth are you talking about?"

"Maybe I'm wasting my life. I'll never make any money at it."

Emily's eyes grew wide. "Seriously? Are you out of your mind? Photography's been your passion for years. Why would you give it up just for a couple extra dollars? Besides, you're talented. You're great!"

Samantha looked down at the tabletop, quiet for a moment in thought. She shook her head. "You're right. I don't know where my mind went."

Emily sipped her coffee, considering that she could see the steam pouring into the air like a huge ghost taking off to haunt its prey. "Speaking of photography, shouldn't the gala be coming up soon?"

Samantha nodded. It was once again that time of year when her college held its annual art and photography gala. The gala featured artwork from selectively chosen students, both current and alumni. Samantha had been lucky enough to have several of her photographs selected to be in the show throughout her college career. At the end of the night, some of the students' pieces were awarded and others had the potential to be auctioned off. The event was open to anyone and everyone.

"You're coming with me again this year, right?" Samantha said.

"Huh-uh. Not this year, girl."

Samantha scoffed. "What do you mean you're not coming?"

"I didn't say I wasn't coming; I'm just not going as your wingman like I always do. You have a date for this year."

"Absolutely not!" Samantha's eyes flew over to Luke, who was laughing at something Ryan had said. She folded her arms and stared at her friend. "I can't take Luke as my date."

"And why not?"

"You know I can't. Nick's parents help sponsor it every year, and I can't chance it. He's always there. It's just awkward. Plus, he won't pass up the opportunity to ridicule me."

Emily pursed her lips. "Does it still hurt that much?"

"I wish it didn't," Samantha tried to soften her voice, so no one else would hear, "But all he did was use me, and I can't get that out of my head. That's why I didn't even want to start a relationship with Luke, in case he was the exact same way. They all start off perfect, you know."

"Well, now you know that Luke isn't like that, so it shouldn't matter."

"Still, I don't trust Nick. Who knows what he might start while we're there. I mean, I gave that guy my heart and my savings. My parents worked hard for that money and had good intentions when they gave it to me. I wasted my money on traveling and—" it was difficult for her to get the words out "—him. He always said that he believed in me and my photography." Samantha shook her head again. "He never loved me. He just came along for a free ride, even though he had his own money."

Then, Emily took hold of Samantha's hand. "It'll be fine. I promise." She made sure to gulp down one last shot of caffeine before demanding, "Come on."

"Where are we going?"

"To ask Luke out."

"No." Samantha glared at her.

"It isn't a choice." Emily pulled her by the arm and dragged her over to the counter. The crowd had cleared a bit, so Luke was talking to the guys.

"Hey, it's you again," Ryan said when he realized that Emily was standing next to him.

"Keep dreaming," she said. She focused her attention on the guys while Samantha talked to Luke.

Samantha rested her arm on the counter.

"I must be lucky." Luke stole a quick kiss. "I never get to see you twice in one day."

"You said before that you were good luck. Maybe you're just getting a taste of your own medicine."

"So, what's up?" he asked as he refilled Emily's coffee

and then Tyler's.

"Where are you going to be on the 26th?"

"Uh…" he set the coffee pot back on the coffee maker. "We have a gig. We finally managed to schedule one at The Edge of Town. It's really hard to book there."

"Oh." Samantha tried to hide her disappointment.

"Why?" He tilted his head and looked at her curiously. She explained to him about the annual gala and how much it meant to her. She took extra caution to make sure that she didn't tell him anything about her ex-boyfriend. The less he knew, the better.

"Hmmm." Luke thought for a moment. "Maybe I have the date wrong. Ryan, what day are we playing The Edge?"

Ryan waved his hand and ignored him. He was too busy trying to flirt with Emily.

Luke turned to look at the calendar behind him. "The more I think about it, it definitely is the 26th." He glanced up at her apologetically. "Hey, Ryan? Ryan. Ryan!"

"What?" An annoyed Ryan Delhart flashed Luke the death stare.

"Can you cover for me that night? I know it's a big night, but Samantha needs me."

"Whatever."

"He'll come around," Luke said. "I'll work on him. Don't let him fool you. He loves to be the lead singer. All of that attention goes straight to his head." Luke winked, which caused Samantha to smile even wider.

* * *

"Does this look okay?" Samantha was frantically trying

to insert an earring. She was sitting in her bedroom in the Hexton Mansion, staring at her reflection in the mirror.

"You look amazing, girl. Luke's going to be blown away."

"Let's hope I can slip past Nick unnoticed."

"You really think you can get away with that?"

"No." Samantha shook her head. She stood up and smoothed the wrinkles out of her dress. "It's just wishful thinking."

"But at least he'll see that you're able to move on from his games," Emily said.

Samantha grinned after blotting her cherry-red lipstick. She hadn't considered that she would prove to Nick that she could both look glamorous and at ease with a fabulous man.

It certainly was a black tie event. She wore a long, short-sleeved evergreen dress with a sweetheart neckline and a tulle bottom. She accessorized with a matching bulky green bracelet and a diamond necklace. Emily had crimped Samantha's hair and then used a generous amount of hair-spray to seal the deal.

"You'll be fine. You look totally awesome. Who cares what Nick thinks? You've found a fine man in Luke, that's for sure. Just go, have fun, and be proud of yourself. You've come a long way."

"Thanks." She picked up her purse and started for the door. They walked downstairs, her heels letting the whole mansion know that she was coming. "See you there."

Luke offered to meet her at the mansion, so that way they could enter the gala together. Emily said she'd come on her own accord when her shift ended.

Samantha stepped out into the blistering summer heat,

thinking about her life. This was a milestone night for her. She was thrilled that she had the chance to celebrate her own work with a guy that made her feel a lot more than just special. Even if sometimes he had little faith in himself, he always had enough energy to encourage her. He was a dreamer like her. He was smart and amusing. He knew how to draw the depression out of her weary body and light up her soul. That guy was Luke Cavarelli.

She began her descent down the driveway when she spotted the Firebird crawling up the road. Her skin felt warmer than usual, but she couldn't tell if it was because of the heat or her anxiety. The hot flash seemed to control her whole body, and her tongue clung to the roof of her dry mouth. It wasn't Luke, though, that she was worried about. There was another man lurking in her mind.

She slid into the passenger seat with a soft "Hi."

"You—you look great," he said as he shifted the car into reverse and turned around.

"Thanks." She glanced over at Luke. It surprised her to discover that he had on the same pastel colored suit he had worn for the Hexton wedding. He looked amazing in it, she had to admit, but did he only own the one?

"Only one suit?" she asked once they got onto the main highway.

He frowned, scanning his body while trying to keep his eyes on the road. "Do I need more than one?" He produced a half-smirk.

"A little variety wouldn't hurt." She smiled back.

"I don't have the extra money."

"I'd buy them for you."

Luke cocked his head and gave her a sideways glance.

"Do you have the money?"

She shrugged. "Does it matter?"

"Kind of."

"Well in that case… No, I don't have the money. But hey, you got to give a girl credit for caring, right?"

"Right." He reached for the radio dial and turned up the Billy Joel song.

The gala was held at a convention center downtown. While it may not have been as swanky as the Hexton reception hall, it still had enough class for the artists that were gathering there that night. It had three floors, but the gala was held on the first floor, where side rooms branched off from the main area. For the most part, the center room attracted the majority of the attention and contained the most pieces.

"So how does this thing work?" Luke said.

"Just follow my lead; it's actually pretty boring."

"What am I, your entertainment?"

"No, you're my wingman. But if you get bored, feel free to bring out a microphone."

He laughed. "Will do."

She stopped before the door and looked up at him. "Thanks, Luke, really. You've no idea how much this means to me. I know you'd rather be with the band tonight. I appreciate it."

"It's my pleasure." He put a hand on her arm. "I want to be here with you, and don't you doubt that for one single second."

Samantha walked into the building, and a middle-aged woman greeted her.

"Hello, Samantha! You look lovely tonight."

"Thanks, Professor!" Then she introduced her college professor to Luke, whose cheeks reddened when Samantha referred to him as 'her boyfriend.'

"It's nice to meet you." The woman shook hands with Luke. She turned towards Samantha. "They've already hung up your pieces. Let's hope by the end of the night someone buys them. You've worked hard this semester. Enjoy the night. You deserve it."

"I will." She took Luke's hand. "Are the Ansons here yet?"

"They're floating around here someplace. Say, don't you know their son—oh, what is his name?"

Luke squeezed Samantha's hand, but even Samantha wasn't sure if Luke could ease her anxiety about her ex-boyfriend.

"Nick! That's it." Samantha's professor lit up when she remembered the correct name. "Don't you know him?"

"Mm-hmmm." The sound barely came out. Why did her professor bring it up? She didn't want to be here. She just wanted to shrink into nothing; and pray that no one would notice she was gone. What was she expecting? Of course Nick Anson would have a presence at the gala. He made a showing every year because his parents were two of the big-shot sponsors. She could still remember her first gala when he agreed to be her date freshman year.

"You okay?" Luke asked, as they moved into the center of the building.

"I'm fine."

"Do you really know this guy, whoever he is?"

"Yeah. He's no one important, just an old friend."

"Can't wait to meet him."

Her stomach churned. The last thing she needed was for Nick Anson to meet Luke Cavarelli and vice versa.

It didn't take long for her to locate her photographs. All five of her pieces were arranged on a wall adjacent to each other. She gasped when she saw them, taking a minute to admire her pride and joy.

Luke's response was just as appreciative. He stared curiously at every picture, as if he were tracing each little fine line and detail that she had purposely incorporated into each photo. He exhaled. "These are amazing, Samantha."

"You like them?" She grinned, feeling as though she were floating on a cloud of pure sugar.

He nodded, still entranced by the photos.

She put her arms around Luke, resting her head on his shoulder. She didn't want to let go. She was on top of the world, and she would have stood there forever. She didn't want the night to end, but she quickly changed her mind when she heard the voice that she had been dreading: "I see you've made it here again this year. Doesn't get old for you, does it?"

Samantha jumped and instantly pulled away from Luke. "Nick." She ran her eyes over her ex-boyfriend disapprovingly.

Nick Anson folded his arms over his chest and stared at Samantha with his arrogant eyes. He ran a hand through his dark hair, which he had always styled in a mullet, and smiled that same charming smile that forced Samantha to remember why her foolish young self had fallen in love with him in the first place.

"Why wouldn't I be here? You know I do this every year. I'm actually trying to make something out of my life, unlike you."

"Face it, you only loved me for my wealth."

"And all you do is sponge off your parents. Have you ever written a check in your life?"

"You haven't changed at all. You're still feisty and always talking about money."

"And I'll bet you're still hanging out at parties every night of the week."

Nick scoffed. "Oh, come on, you weren't any better." He looked over at Luke. "Who's this, your new boy toy?"

Samantha started to fume. She could feel her body temperature rise. She felt hotter than Texas on a good day. "For your information, Luke is the first guy I've been serious with since you made a fool out of me. Let me guess, you're not even with *her* anymore."

"Oh, no, I'm not." He stretched out a hand to Luke. "Nick Anson."

"Luke Cavarelli." He cautiously shook back.

"Why do you sound so familiar? What do you do?"

"I'm the lead singer of The Steel City Boys."

Nick raised his eyebrows. "So, you're the singer of that band? Well, I have to admit, you ain't half bad."

"Thanks, man."

Nick took a step closer to Luke, but Samantha could still feel his hot breath as he whispered, "She'll bleed you dry. She ain't worth the time or the energy."

"Hey! No one talks about my girl like that—"

"Samantha Denvy!" A tall older lady with a fur coat (despite the summer heat) rushed over to where they were standing.

"Mrs. Anson," Samantha said matter-of-factly.

"It's so good to see you! Apparently, you've already met up with Nick again. It's great to see you two together. How long has it been since we've seen each other?"

"Last year… At the gala," Samantha muttered under her breath.

"I think your pieces will do very well this year." Mrs. Anson put on a pair of glasses as she wandered over to examine the photos. "It's a shame you two aren't still together. You made a good pair." Then she looked at Luke, whom she just realized was there, and said, "But that's not to say you're not a fine young man." She patted his arm on her way past and called to her son as if he were a dog: "Nick, come along."

Once the Ansons were out of sight, Luke exclaimed, "I hope you're not still friends with him! I can't believe how rude he was to your face!"

Soon the gala was underway, and a flood of spectators was crowding into the hall to get a glimpse of each piece. Waves of laughter, small talk, and clinks of wine glasses hung in the air. Everyone who stopped to check out Samantha's work offered hearty compliments.

Luke stuck by her side throughout the night, not regretting that he didn't go to The Edge of Town. Samantha was radiating happiness. She absolutely took his breath away. She talked to each guest with such a friendly poise; it was refreshing.

"I had tranquility in my mind when I took the photo, but I'd love to know what you see in it." Samantha had a conversation with every visitor and genuinely listened to comments and feedback.

Later, Emily showed up to support her best friend. Samantha truly couldn't have asked for much more. Her bubble felt so comfortable, she couldn't even fathom having it burst. But, when the night was almost over, Emily had to leave, and it was almost time for the actual auction to begin. Any and all potential buyers would end the night by fighting over which pieces they wanted.

Samantha's photographs were to be auctioned off last. In the downtime, she and Luke had to wait it out. She headed over to the refreshment table that had been set up along the back wall. Out of the corner of her eye, she spotted Nick strolling over while she busied herself ladling fruit punch into two plastic cups. Now that she saw him approaching, she wished that she had hit up one of the waiters for a glass of wine.

"So, how've you really been?"

"You know you don't care."

"You blame me for our breakup, but it was your fault."

"How so?" Her pulse quickened. Why would he even suggest this?

"You're the greedy freeloader. All you care about is money, yet you go spending it until you have none."

"That's not true; you spent it all too. You freeloaded off of me. You have the money. Besides, you still cheated on me." She furiously dumped the red liquid into the cup, which resulted in some of it sloshing onto the table.

"Maybe so, but you deserved it." His eyes flicked over to Luke, who was talking to someone. "Does he know what you're actually like? Does he know how much of a slut you really are?"

In an instant, she flung the cup upwards and stained his smug smile with fruit punch.

He blinked rapidly and felt around for a napkin on the table. He didn't say another word.

She couldn't stand the sight of Nick, nor deal with the flurry of emotions. She had to get out of there. With the uncontrollable hot tears streaming down her face, she tore off out of the hall and into the muggy night.

Luke noticed immediately. "Samantha!" He chased after her and found her sitting on a bench just outside of the hall. Sobbing, she had her face buried in her hands.

"Hey." He put his large arms around her and drew her close. They remained like that for a few minutes with him stroking her, saying it was going to be okay.

"You want to tell me what's going on? I have a suspicion it has to do with Nick Anson."

She tried to sit up a little, but she still kept her head against his chest. His touch was soothing and cool on her already-heated skin.

"Do you remember when I told you that, before college, I traveled and attempted to make my photography work? I wasted all of my money? Well, he was my boyfriend at the time, and he came with me. We were reckless. We spent that money like it was water. We went out, had a good time, and didn't look back. He prides himself on wasting other people's money and not spending a dime of his family's or of his own. He blames me for everything." She paused to fight the urge to cry again. "But the thing is, he encouraged it. He did the drinking. I was more like his arm candy. Then, the next thing I knew, I was broke, and he dumped me for some hotter girl who was much better than me."

"Samantha, you're amazing. Believe me, she couldn't have been better than you."

"But she was. I—I really loved him. I thought we had something unique and special. I thought he was the love of my life. Turns out I was dead wrong. He was with so many other girls behind my back. He calls me a slut because he thinks I stayed around him just to sleep with him. That's not true. We never went farther than a kiss." She shook her head. "I know this is cliché, but he only used me and then tossed me aside after he was done with me, like I was a plastic bag."

He hugged her tighter. "You know I'll never do that to you."

"It's all my fault. I let him walk all over me."

"It's not your fault. You were just young. We all did stupid things a couple years ago, before we really knew what we were doing. Look at you now, getting ahead in the world, working on making your dreams come true. You have so much to be proud of and happy about. He's in your past. Let him go."

She shifted on the seat. "I love you so much."

They both paused and stared into each other's eyes. This was their first "I love you."

Taken aback that she said it first, Samantha felt the need to justify. "I didn't mean for it to be so sudden—but I do. Because you're amazing."

Luke squeezed her hand. "I'll always love you, no matter what happens. You may not think that you're perfect, but you're still my angel."

Gently, his lips brushed hers, and she had no energy left to fight the kiss. Once their lips met, she grew tingly with excitement. Their connection felt so natural. She so desperately tried to make the moment last, not wanting to let him go. She felt like he was the only one who truly understood her. The sweetness of the kiss and the feeling of just being in their own serenity made Samantha feel safe. Before today, no one had been able to console her following her ugly breakup with Nick.

Suddenly, Samantha's professor came running outside. "There you are! Samantha, all five of your photographs just sold for $3,000!"

Samantha pulled herself off of Luke, pushing him back teasingly. She jumped to her feet and hurried into the building. "You are a good luck charm!"

* * *

Luke watched as Samantha rushed inside with her professor to meet the buyers of her work. He continued to stare at the doorway, even after she slipped inside. He just couldn't peel away the image of her in his mind. How was it possible for her to become more radiant each time he laid eyes on her? After the Nick debacle, he was glad to finally see that her smile was back in full force. *That's the smile I want to see. God, she's gorgeous. And you're letting me have her?* Life was sweet.

Chapter 11

Career Crescendo

Slowly, the months passed by, and the other record labels responded. The next one denied them too, which really disappointed the guys. Luke began to doubt everything. He constantly thought about his future. Music meant the world to him, and he couldn't just relinquish his life-long dream.

The next label sent a letter explaining that they were interested in the band, but had not yet written up a potential contract due to the fact that they had been recently overwhelmed with a surge of new clients. It would be some time until they got back in touch with the boys; if they actually decided to accept them.

In no time, Luke was a complete wreck. He didn't want to eat. He didn't want to sleep. He didn't want to go to work. He didn't want to sing anymore. He even kept some distance from Samantha. If Luke Cavarelli wasn't meant to be a singer for the world, then who was he supposed to be?

"Don't worry," Ryan comforted him. "We still have a couple more to hear from, including Hexton's guy, Karl Deimos."

"If the smaller labels won't accept us, then what makes you think Sforzando Records will? Ryan, aren't you the least bit worried? Our dreams could flatline and we'll be left with poor-paying day jobs and no college education!"

"Chill, dude. Do you realize how many record labels are out there? We just have to find one willing to take us on. And if you're that worried about it, why don't you pray, or do whatever that religious mumbo jumbo is that you do. We can use all the help we can get."

"God isn't a genie, you know. If He was, I'd have been out of wishes years ago."

"That's not the impression I get."

"You don't have a clue." Luke did choose to take Ryan's advice, which, for once, made sense. *God, if this is meant to be, then let one of these last record labels come through. Let Your will be done.*

The band continued to play on the weekends. They tried to book some gigs at different venues, ones that would rake in a bit more money and get their faces out there. The ritzier locations took kindly to them, and it worked out. Or, it did in the beginning, before the record label rejections prevented Luke from even leaving the apartment. Ever so quickly, the high-paying gigs slipped away from the band, and they were replaced in a heartbeat. Ryan could only sing so much, and the audiences preferred Luke.

At first, Luke was angry with himself for giving up to the point of not performing. He paced around the living room and stared out the window, wondering whether or not it was worth joining the band for the night's gig. He would pace and stare until the busy road below was full of glowing headlights. In the end, he would fall down on the couch, weary from the mental exhaustion this decision required. If he went to the club, he'd wake up the same unknown singer tomorrow; if he didn't go, then he'd still wake up unknown, but now less himself.

Eventually, the anger subsided into apathy. He curled up on the couch in self-pity. He turned the lights out, stashed away the TV remote, and sulked. Who was he supposed to be?

"Do you realize that the entire crowd chanted your name last night?" Ryan asked one night. "Now, are you coming to Silva's tonight or not? Luke, we can't do this without you. You're the face and voice of this band."

"I'm not going." Luke shook his head while sitting slumped on the couch. "I gotta rethink my life. You should too."

Ryan sighed. "Fine. I'm going regardless, but I don't know where the hell it's going to get us without a lead singer. I can do it, but they don't want me as much as they want you." He picked up the car keys along with his guitar case and exited the apartment. Then, he popped his head back in and added, "I thought you loved music. I thought you wanted to entertain and make people happy. I thought you wanted to connect with others through the power of song. What happened to the Luke Cavarelli I used to know? Sure, he was a pessimist, but he didn't pass up the opportunity to sing his heart out, even if it was just for a crowd of careless drunks."

Luke shook his head. "How long are we supposed to wait, Ryan? It's been almost five years since we started searching for a record deal."

Ryan frowned. "So what if we never make it out of this town? A local following is better than nothing."

"But we're not growing!"

"Sometimes you only see what you want to see," Ryan shot back. "I know you want us to be famous like Bellano and The Leather Heartbreaks, but we don't have to rush. You won't even try to enjoy the good we have going for us."

"I always thought we were on the same page," Luke said, crossing his arms.

"We're on the same page, Luke. You think I don't want to be a bigshot guitarist? We both know that you can sing like Bellano, and I can shred like Ace, but we have to wait our turn. We're not leather; we're steel, and we can go a lot farther than the Leather Heartbreaks. It just takes time for steel to temper."

Luke felt the guilt rise in his stomach. Ryan was right. Instead of enjoying what they had as a band, Luke had sunk into greed and jealousy.

After a minute of silence, Ryan said, "Well, if you're not going to say anything or change your mind…" He slid out the door.

"Ryan, wait!" Luke hurried to put on his shoes and then he slid down the hall into his bedroom where he picked up his guitar case. He rushed out and made his way to the car.

Ryan was already in the Firebird.

Luke pulled the passenger door's handle. It wouldn't budge. "Ryan, let me in, dude!"

"Promise me you'll stop being all doom and gloom?" he asked.

Luke rolled his eyes. "Come on, man."

"I mean it. Promise me, or you're not getting in this car."

He thought for a moment. When did Ryan Delhart suddenly become mature? It was scary that everything Ryan said kept making perfect sense.

"Okay," Luke said finally, "I promise."

"Good." Ryan reached over and unlocked the door. "Welcome back, brother."

Just like any other night, the band performed phenomenally. The music behind him flourished and Luke, once again, felt the vibrations flow through his veins. His vocals leaped, and probably would've taken off out of the club and into downtown Pittsburgh, if only he'd allowed them the chance to get that far. It felt great to be back in action.

When they had finished, Mr. Silva approached them

onstage.

Luke thanked him for the money like usual. He opened the envelope as the old man walked away. Something wasn't adding up.

"Mr. Silva, you gave us too much."

"Oh, that's just an extra tip."

"For what?" Luke was confused, though anyone else would've kept their mouth shut.

"It's just one last thank you for playing here for the past few years."

"But we're not leaving."

"Aren't you?" Mr. Silva glanced over at a center table which occupied three grave looking men. He shot Luke a toothy grin.

Luke watched the men stand up and meander their way over to the stage.

"Ryan." Luke hit his friend gently on the arm.

Ryan had just successfully lit a cigarette. "Oh boy, men in suits. I hate fancy clothes. This must be serious. Hey, isn't that Mr. Hexton?"

The men were traipsing up the stairs onto the stage. The rest of the band gathered around Luke and Ryan.

"Y—you're—" Luke stammered as the stranger in front of Mr. Hexton shook his hand.

"Yes, boys, my name is Henry Langderate, and I'll cut right to the chase: I think you guys have tremendous talent. I've worked with a lot of excellent performers in my day, but you put a fresh perspective on music. We'd like to know if you're interested in becoming part of the Sforzando Records family."

Ryan nearly choked on his cigarette smoke. "You want

to give us a record deal?"

Mr. Langderate nodded. "Why don't you guys come down offstage? We have a lot to talk about."

The Steel City Boys eagerly joined the men at a long table. They sat across from them and Mr. Hexton put himself on the end.

The other man introduced himself as Mr. Karl Deimos. He was from the legal department, while Mr. Langderate was the A & R man who discovered and worked with new artists.

"Now, I understand that you two, Luke and Ryan, are the front men?" Mr. Deimos asked.

"Yes," they said.

"Okay. You two can still be the main focus, but we don't want to make you guys look like just another duo. There are too many of those out there right now. What would be the point of you other three if we did that? Besides, your sound is what it is thanks to all five of you. Am I right? We've already drawn up a contract," Mr. Deimos continued.

He pulled out a manila envelope from his briefcase and pushed it over in front of the boys. "We'd like to sign you for two years to start. We want to see how you do with one album and a tour; if you're very successful, then we'll go from there."

Mr. Langderate decided to jump in. "We're asking that you move out to LA, though. That's where the record label's headquarters is as well as our in-house studio. We offer our artists their own individual recording studio, which is why we only sign a limited number of clients."

They talked for an hour or two. The topics varied, but they mostly dealt with music. By then, the club was beginning to empty.

"Well, Henry, I think we ought to get going," Mr. Hexton said.

"Richard, thank you for hooking me up with this fantastic band. I think they're going to go far. I look forward to working with them."

"I have to get going too." Mr. Deimos stood up. "I have to catch the next plane to California. What are you doing, Henry?"

"Oh, I'm staying with Richard for the remainder of the weekend. We have a lot of time to make up for." Then Mr. Langderate glanced at the men gathered around him. "By the way, is there a Catholic church around here by chance?"

Luke thought he heard wrong at first, but then he jumped at the chance to answer: "Yes, actually. There's one about five blocks away from here."

"Wonderful!" Mr. Langderate said. "I'll make sure to head over to Sunday Mass tomorrow."

"Wait," Luke said, barely believing his ears. "You're actually Catholic?"

Mr. Langderate nodded. "I am. What, you think people in the music business can't be religious?"

Luke grinned. "No, sir. You don't know how much that means to me, because my faith plays an important part in who I am and how I present myself."

Mr. Langderate winked. "See, I knew you there was something special about this band."

Then Mr. Deimos turned towards the guys and shook hands with all five members. "I couldn't have said it better myself, Henry. There are a bunch of singers and bands out there, but you guys are rare, a true gem. Honestly, I'm not just saying that. We wouldn't be here if that were a lie. We only take artists who we believe are capable of growth, and you are outstanding. If you ask me, the other labels don't know what they're missing. So look over the contract, think about it. Let me know what you decide. Don't throw away this chance."

The three men left together, looking more like FBI agents than two music nerds and an entrepreneur.

The band wasted no time in celebrating after the men were out of sight, whooping in delight and disbelief.

"We're going to be recording in the same studio as Tony Bellano and The Leather Heartbreaks," Luke said. "I'll finally get to meet my hero. This is surreal."

"But it's what we wanted. Why didn't you pray sooner?" Ryan said.

"How do you know if that's what caused it?"

"Because I know you, and you're pretty strong in your faith. You may be a pessimist, but when it comes to religion, you trust in it."

Luke grinned. "We've known each other for way too long."

Ryan laughed. "Wouldn't have it any other way." He stared off into the distance. "Wait a second…" His facial expression twisted into worry—unusual for Ryan Delhart—and he looked at Luke. "Do you think we can get Ruby out there?"

"Ryan, I'm not driving from Pittsburgh to LA!"

"I know, but what am I going to do with her?"

Luke huffed jokingly. "I still can't believe you named the car."

"Hey, I had to—Mr. Hexton?"

"Mr. Hexton?" Luke had been facing the other way, so he didn't see the man come back into the club.

"Can't get far without these," Mr. Hexton found his car keys sitting on the chair that he had made himself comfortable in. "Must've fallen out of my pocket when I stood up."

"Sorry, we didn't see them there," Luke said.

"That's okay," Mr. Hexton said. "You have a lot to celebrate, a lot to think about." The keys jingled softly in his hand. "But, uh, just don't leave that sweet girl back at my house waiting. She loves you, you know. Go tell her the news."

Before Luke could respond, Mr. Hexton had strolled back out the door.

Suddenly, his joy had vanished. It had washed off like an enchanted spell that ends at midnight. He felt sick to his stomach. "Samantha."

"Aw, dude." Ryan put a hand on Luke's shoulder.

"I can't leave her." His eyes shone in the club lights. His voice started to break. "I want this so bad, but how do I leave Samantha behind?"

"I don't know," Ryan said softly.

"I don't want to have to choose. I—I just—"

"You love her." Ryan tried to smile comfortingly. "It's okay. I'm sure she'll understand."

"Ryan, we have to follow this dream, but my other dream is to be in love and live a good life."

"Go. Go to her, you big softie. Go on. Take Ruby."

"How'll you get home?"

"I'll hitch a ride with Joe and the guys. Don't worry about me, I'll be fine."

"Thanks, man." Luke took off at once.

"Uh, Luke?"

Luke whirled around.

"Keys?" Ryan smirked as he held up his key ring. He slipped off his house key and shoved it in his pocket. The keys became airborne, and Luke caught them swiftly with one hand. Then, he was out the door.

On the way to Rigby Mansion, he couldn't help but let all kinds of thoughts swarm around in his brain. If Mr. Langderate was staying with the Hextons, then maybe she had already heard. No. He knew her too well. Even if she had heard it, she'd want him to tell it to her in person. Career or girlfriend? Those were the worst two choices. He knew he couldn't ask her to stop school and jump on a plane to LA. *She's going to hate me! No! Calm down. You know she's not that way. Ryan's right—how many times can I say that in one night? She'll understand. She just has to.*

Despite the internal bickering and the rehearsing of how he was going to explain it to her, when he found himself standing on the Hexton's stoop, he also found that his mind had gone completely blank. He rapped on the door anyway.

Charlotte Hexton had just so happened to be going by the door. She thrust it open and then stood there, glaring at Luke with her sharp, judgmental eyes. "Who are you, and what do you want at this late hour?"

"I'm here to see Samantha Denvy."

"You're that kid; you're that trashy singer."

Man, Samantha wasn't kidding when she complained about this lady. Luke cleared his throat. "Yes, I'm Luke Cavarelli, and I'd like to speak with Samantha."

"She's asleep. You'll have to come back another time."

"Please, ma'am, this is urgent."

"Are you dying?"

Luke's brow furrowed. "No."

"Then come back tomorrow."

"Let him in, Charlotte," Mr. Hexton said as he passed through. "It is pretty important."

Charlotte took a step back and let Luke in with a scowl on her face.

Mr. Hexton winked. "I'll take you upstairs."

Luke eagerly followed him.

"Here you are, son. Good luck." Mr. Hexton headed downstairs and left Luke alone outside of Samantha's bedroom.

He took a deep breath before gently knocking on the closed door. He had to repeat the ritual several times. Still, there was no response. Tired and disappointed, Luke turned to go.

"Luke?" she said in a hoarse voice.

"Hey!" he exclaimed energetically.

Immediately, she could decipher his nervousness through one word. "What's wrong?"

"Nothing, everything's fine. Actually, it's more than fine. Well…" He rambled on and on.

"Luke, slow down. First, come on in. There's no point to you standing in the hallway."

She pulled him in and shut the door. She went over to the nightstand and switched on the lamp. Satisfied, she flopped herself on the edge of the bed. She patted the vacant space beside her. "Sit."

He only stared at her.

"You know you can tell me anything, right?"

"Yeah," he said shakily. He steadied himself and met

her gaze.

"Well?"

"Haven't you heard?"

"No. Heard what? No one tells me anything around here. Is everyone okay?"

"Yes, yes! It's nothing like that." *Come on, just tell her. It's not like you're breaking up with her. It may feel like it, but you know that's not what this is.* "Samantha—"

"Oh no," she got to her feet. "You're breaking up with me, aren't you?" she asked flatly.

"NO!!"

"Luke!"

"The band got a record deal tonight,!" he blurted out.

He watched her lips twitch and form a huge smile. "Really? Why didn't you just say so? That's awesome! You guys are going to be famous! Luke, your dreams are finally going to come true."

He fixed his sight on the ground and didn't say a word.

"You can't be upset over this."

"Samantha, The Steel City Boys have to move to LA"

It was her turn to be in shock. "Oh. That explains a lot."

He took her hand and looked into her sparkling eyes. "What's going to happen to us?"

"What do you mean? You're going to fulfill your dreams. I'm more than happy for you. I'm ecstatic!"

Luke shook his head. "But you can't drop everything and come with me. I can't ask you to do that. I don't know if you realize this, but I love you with all my heart and mind. I can't get you out of my head. You understand me more than any girl I've ever been with. Maybe I'm just young and naïve—"

"Stop. Luke, I really fell for you too. You're my best friend, and we fit each other perfectly. You know how to fill the hole in my heart, the one that all of those other meaningless boyfriends made bigger every time they hurt me.

"I want you to follow your dream. I have another semester of school left, so we'll see what happens after that. Look, I've managed on my own before. You might not believe it, but I've been alone a lot."

He sighed. "Samantha, you are the one I've been waiting for. I'm such a pessimist when it comes to how I treat myself, but you give me hope and confidence." He scoffed. "I can be good to you, but I can't be good to myself." He stayed silent as he contemplated what to say next. What could he say? "I can't believe this is happening."

"Then embrace it. You know this won't be the end of us. If other people can pull off long-distance relationships, then I'm sure we'll be just fine." Samantha hugged him. "Just don't worry about it."

"I still can't believe this."

"Me neither. My boyfriend's going to be a superstar."

They laughed nervously.

She walked him down to the front door. Before he ventured out into the cool night, she kissed him.

"Well, I love you too," he said reassuringly.

With the first challenge over, he retreated back to Ruby. His mind was still racing, so he couldn't leave right away. No girl had ever made him feel the way Samantha did. The feeling was so powerful that it was difficult to put into words. All he knew was that it was magical. Meanwhile, Samantha trudged upstairs slowly and almost painfully. She propped herself upright on the bed and leaned against the head-board. Her emotions couldn't be leashed. The bitter tears softly slid down her cheeks.

The last thing she wanted was for Luke to leave. Luke, the only sunshine that had come into her life after a couple stormy years. What if they both followed separate paths and those paths never dared to cross again? What if they couldn't make a long-distance relationship work? Or, even worse, what if he found another girl out in California, one even better than her?

"Do I even love him?" she asked herself in the pitch-black darkness that was her bedroom. "Yes, and I can't lose him. I just can't do it. I can't go through that heartache again."

She slunk down and eventually situated herself under the covers. It took a while, but she did drift off to sleep. The final thought she recalled before falling into unconsciousness was: *I wonder what rock stars' wives do with all their money.*

Chapter 12

This is Not Goodbye

The next few days rolled by in a blur. Their first plan of action was to hire an attorney to review the contract Mr. Deimos had given them. The attorney found a couple of small discrepancies, and the band negotiated the terms with the record label. In the end, it was decided that Luke and Ryan would be the producers of the music along with Mr. Langderate.

"Okay, I'm ready to sign my life away!" Ryan said before he signed the contract.

"You may as well sign in blood." Luke grinned. "I know how you are; you hate binding agreements, and that's exactly what this is."

"Hey, this is different. I'm cool with it." Ryan signed his name. "It's official! We're real musicians." He looked at Luke. He could tell that his best friend was still struggling with his emotions. "Luke, you're going to be fine. We got this."

Luke nodded. "I know. I'm ready."

Ryan actually believed that Luke had gained some much-needed confidence. It was about time.

People had to be notified, meaningless day jobs had to be abandoned, and things needed to be packed. The final rent payments were set up with the landlord, and all that was left to do was move out and fly to dreamland.

Because Sforzando's brand relied on valuing both the music and the musician, the record label paid for the move, but the guys had to arrange their housing ahead of time. Luckily there were plenty of apartment buildings near the studio. The advance payment for the band's album was also a plus!

On the day of the big move, Luke took one final walk around his city. The temperature was frigid and the air crisp.

The people were bustling about on the streets like ants pushing to get to a single piece of bread. Then he realized how much more congestion there would be in the City of Angels.

He sauntered through downtown, the downtown that held so many fond memories of his teenage years: the restaurants, the clubs, the theaters. How can somebody just pick up and move away from everything they've ever known? But, as scary as it was, Luke knew it was right. He couldn't deny his longtime desire. Maybe change was a good thing.

Just at that moment, he passed by Silva's Club. But then again, it wasn't just any plain old club. It was *the* club. The one that really started it all for The Steel City Boys. Luke couldn't imagine what would've happened if the band had never played there. He had spent so many Saturday nights there wondering if it was going to get him anywhere. At least the nights hadn't been in vain.

A little farther down, he walked by the club that he had taken Samantha to on their first date. He sighed. Samantha. No, she was right. He had to embrace this and build up some confidence. *Samantha needs a man, and the band needs a leader. Everything will work out.*

At about lunchtime, he made it to the Catholic church on the corner, a few blocks down. This church meant the world to him. It was where he grew up, where his faith was formed and strengthened. Red bricks built up the tall and voluminous foundation. The steeples strived for heaven, and the stained-glass windows sparkled.

Mass was not going on at the time, so he went straight in. His body shivered, adjusting to the heat. He closed the door slowly and soaked in the beauty of the place: the marble pillars, the golden altar, the ceaseless rows of wooden pews in front of him.

Going up to the very first pew, he knelt down on the padded kneeler and prayed: *I just wanted to say thank You for this opportunity. I know that my prayer life has been a little distracted lately. I won't disappoint You, and I'll never abandon You.*

Instead of leaving right away, he took a few moments to take in the scenery. The altar was adorned with an assortment of flowers, especially poinsettias left over from the Christmas season. The devotional candles flickered in the corner, and the ivory altar cloth, decorated with tiny crosses, swayed lightly thanks to the central heating system. Luke's eyes darted over to the shiny oak podium where the cantors sang for Mass. Luke had grown up singing psalms and hymns from that very spot. Now he could hardly believe he was leaving it behind to fulfill the ultimate dream.

He got to his feet and slowly left the church. Before he passed through the doorway, he stole one last glance over his shoulder. One look at the ornate crucifix on the wall compelled him to grin almost foolishly. A gushing sort of sensation dispersed throughout his body like he was a champagne bottle ready to explode. For once, he felt proud to be who he was. He wasn't ashamed; he was a bit anxious, yes, but mostly excited.

Back outside, he sat down on the cold, concrete steps of the church. Exhaling, he watched his breath seep out and float carelessly into the air. It reminded him of smoke drifting off of one of Ryan's cigarettes. He asked Samantha to meet him at the bus stop near the church. He wanted to walk back to the apartment with her before he departed later that day.

He almost couldn't believe his eyes when he found her sashaying down the street wearing the same green dress that she wore for the gala, but this time she had a sweater on with it. His heart skipped a beat, maybe two. On one hand, he felt crazy lucky to have her, but, on the other, he was crushed to know that he wouldn't see her again for a while.

"Too dressy?" She beamed.

"No," he said as he stood up and wrapped his arms around her waist. He kissed her tenderly. "It's perfect." He absorbed her image, then looked down at her and frowned. "But it's cold."

"I'm fine."

"It's January." He slipped off his jacket and draped it over her shoulders. "And it's snowing." He tilted his head up to watch tiny pieces of glitter fall innocently around them.

"What're you complaining about? It's warm where you're going." She hooked her arm through his, and they headed back towards the apartment.

Luke tried to slow his pace, not wanting this precious memory to end. He started to feel the cold now that his coat was off, but he didn't mind. It was worth every second of it. "It'll be cold without you."

She punched him jokingly. "You sound tacky, like Ryan."

"Me? Hmm. That's going to have to change."

"Sure you don't share DNA?"

He laughed out loud, letting out another stream of white mist. "Not a chance!"

By the time they got to the apartment, they had talked about everything, just as they did on their first date. They did indeed make the moments last.

Ryan was throwing boxes into the car, fighting to make everything fit in the trunk. His back was turned, so he was oblivious to Luke and Samantha, who had come up behind him.

Luke separated himself from Samantha and laid a hand on the top of the trunk. All the while, Ryan kept swearing under his breath. Luke started to move the top of the trunk downward over Ryan, who now had his head buried even further inside. Just when Luke pulled it down, almost to Ryan's neckline, Ryan shot back and stood up as straight as a pool cue.

"Hey! Who do you think you—" he stopped, glaring at Luke. "You! Where've you been? Did you think Ruby was going to pack herself?" His eyes slid over to Samantha and they softened instantly. "Oh. Hi, Samantha." He rubbed the back of his neck nervously, as though Luke had really hit him with the trunk lid. "You look nice."

"Thanks."

"Are we ready then?" Luke asked, feeling a little queasy, since he knew what had to happen next.

"We're ready. The guys left about two hours ago. That leaves you and me, bro."

"Okay," he whispered. "Give us a minute?"

Ryan looked at Samantha. "Yeah. I'll go back up and check to make sure we got everything."

Once Ryan was out of sight, Luke took Samantha by the hand. "I guess this is it."

"It's not the end," she reminded him and smiled.

"No, but it'll be a while until we actually see each other again."

Her smile faded as quickly as it came. "I know. I'm not happy about it either." She turned her head so that he couldn't see the tears welling up in her eyes.

But, Luke couldn't be fooled. He pulled her closer. "Come on, don't cry." His voice was soft and not the least bit condemning. "I won't trade you in for a newer model. I promise."

The smile switched back on. Her eyes shone brightly, and she laughed. She flung herself around him and buried her head on his shoulder. "You better not," she whispered. "Just promise me you'll use the phone. They made the long-distance feature for a reason."

"You can bet on it."

They shared one last kiss before Luke decided it was time to pull away. It was sweet, and it seemed like time had frozen, like they were the only two in the world.

Ryan perked up when the passenger door slammed shut. He flashed Luke a faint grin and shifted the car into reverse. "Let's get out of here."

Luke and Samantha waved at each other. Before they knew it, the boys were off to the airport. By nightfall, they had successfully left the Steel City. There was a new band on the rise in the music industry, and the two front men were prepared to give it all they had. A group called The Steel City Boys and a car named Ruby (thanks to a car shipping company), arrived in LA, ready to make it big.

Chapter 13

Blue Skies and Palm Trees

The band began recording right away. They had barely enough time to settle in and become familiar with LA. Fortunately, Luke and Ryan's new apartment was only a few blocks away from the studio, so they had an easy walk.

At the first glance of his new, blue-skied and sunny paradise, Luke could only gape in awe. None of it seemed realistic. The warm breeze outside reassured him like a fuzzy blanket comforts an anxious child. He was floating through a dream. Right?

On their first day at the colossal studio, Mr. Langderate gave the band the grand tour. He led them through corridors filled with individual recording studios and offices. Every door had a lighted sign above it bearing the name of either a singer or band. Luke felt his heart flutter when they passed the door labeled *The Leather Heartbreaks*.

"Here it is," Mr. Langderate said as he stopped in front of a door at the end of the hall on the third floor, "Home of The Steel City Boys."

The five guys stood dead still. Hanging onto each other like schoolboys, they admired the name on the wall. Every letter was big, black, and spaced perfectly. It was official.

Luke traced each letter with his eyes and exhaled. "This is it."

Eagerly, the band fought their way to the door, tripping over each other to be the first in the room.

"Now remember," Mr. Langderate said as he walked in behind them, "every once in a while, musicians from other labels will come in and use our studios, so you may have to share a bit. Just because your name is on the door—"

"—doesn't mean you own the thing." A voice from inside the room crescendoed. A chair in front of the recording controls swiveled around, revealing a hefty man wearing a business suit. He was older than the boys, but significantly younger than Mr. Langderate. His hair wasn't even the least bit gray yet. "Mark Arrowitcz, your manager." He extended his hand.

The guys took turns introducing themselves, shaking his hand.

"So, you're Luke Cavarelli." Mr. Arrowitcz shook Luke's hand last. "I look forward to working with you." His beady eyes jumped back and forth between each band member. Looking down his crooked nose, he said, "I see a lot of potential in you. Just do as I say, and you'll make it far."

"As we say," Mr. Langderate corrected him.

"What?" Mr. Arrowitcz glared at him.

"We both call the shots around here. It's not just you."

"We'll see about that." Mr. Arrowitcz got up out of the chair and left the room, slamming the door behind him.

Mr. Langderate shrugged. "You'll get used to him. He's great with new artists. He's actually not hired yet, he just acts like he is. It's up to you. Do you want him as your manager?"

The boys glanced at one another.

"What's his rep like?" Ryan asked.

"Well, every band he's managed has made it to the top of the charts within their first year or two and has done remarkably afterwards. He's done numerous side projects with musicians who've gotten onto the charts. He's great at conserving money."

After talking it over, they agreed to have Mark Arrowitcz as their manager.

They checked out the rest of the studio; it consisted of three smaller rooms. There was the recording booth, the control room on the other side, and a wide area with a table and a few chairs. No, this area was better than that. It had its own mini kitchen on the back wall.

Within the first couple of days, they started working on their first album. Writing and recording filled most of their days. Luke absolutely loved every minute of it, and he couldn't imagine being anywhere else. After hearing the first recording, even he was surprised at how extraordinary his vocals sounded.

It was early in the afternoon when the long-awaited meeting took place. Luke had to take a break from the studio work. His head was still buzzing after complying with Mark Arrowitcz's barked and choppy orders. If anything, it seemed more like sheer mismanagement, but he and the band kept giving Mark their undivided attention. In fact, the band had nicknamed him Maniacial Mark. Between Mark and the actual recording of the songs, Luke needed a walk to clear the fog from his brain.

His mind traipsed off though, wandering back into work stuff as he meandered down the carpeted hallway. *Do we want this song in A-flat major or concert D-flat major? We'll probably want it in A-flat for the lower pitches.*

Thud.

"Hey! Watch where you're going, doofus," a voice in front of him said. *Wait a second,* Luke thought. *This voice sounds familiar.*

Luke's gaze had been transfixed on the hallway beyond, so he hadn't been paying attention to the guy who had just turned the corner.

"Sorry, man, I—" Luke's eyes clearly absorbed the man. All of a sudden, he couldn't speak. "Tony Bellano?

Tony 'The Buff' Bellano from The Leather Heartbreaks?"

"Do I know you? Only my friends can call me The Buff."

Luke stepped back. "Not personally, but I'm a huge fan of your music."

"Fan club meets out back, sister," he said flatly.

Bellano tried to move past, but Luke used his body as a blockade. "Is that how you treat all your fans?"

"Maybe. What're you gonna to do about it?" Bellano cocked his head.

Luke was in shock. It was an honor to meet an inspiration, but to be insulted by him was a completely different story.

Yet, there he stood: *the* Tony Bellano. When it came to Bellano, it was apparent that he ranked high on the 'Ladies' Man' spectrum, casting Ryan Delhart down to the bottom of the totem pole. His towering figure made him both intimidating and manly. The greasy, charcoal hair on his head matched the shine of his tight, leather jacket. His eyes glowed spitefully, though he was as compelling to look at as a show of magnificent fireworks: complete perfection.

Luke's mind churned, thinking about what to say next. He had dreamed of this moment for years. The two-dimensional superstar from the album covers stood before him in the flesh. He admired Bellano for his voice and musicality. He wasn't sure what to think or do. The voice in his head pleaded with him to cower, keep his mouth shut, and then run back to the studio. But, another voice in his head wasn't ready to give up. He prepared to release his witty comeback right after it popped in his head when, just then, Ryan found them.

"There you are. So, I was just thinking—" His eyes stumbled on Bellano. "Tony Bellano?"

"Who's this, your bodyguard?"

"Am I missing something here?" Ryan said.

"What's there to miss? Your buddy here is gaping at me like I just shot J.R.!" Bellano snapped.

Luke scoffed. "I used to look up to this guy, but it turns out that he has no respect for his fans."

"Is that so?" Ryan was amazed.

"No way! Who do you two think you are?" Bellano folded his arms across his chest.

"The Steel City Boys," they said proudly in unison.

Bellano shook his head. "You're that new pop/rock band that just moved in?"

"Hey, hey, hey! Watch it, buddy," Ryan pointed at him. "Our style of music is just like yours. We've looked up to you for years."

"You think you're gonna make it out there in the real music world? You two don't stand a chance. You've gotta fight and claw your way to the top. It's no easy ride; I've been there. I can tell you're too soft. You look like quitters. Good luck gettin' nowhere." Bellano pushed his way between Luke and Ryan, storming off down the hall. "And don't think you can conquer The Buff," he called back. "No one can."

Luke covered his face with his hands.

"That was pleasant," Ryan said.

"This is my whole high school career all over again. Look at me, I'm just as weak now as I was back then. So much for being a man."

"Hey." Ryan put a hand on Luke's shoulder. "Real men are many things, and let me tell you, he is none of those things. You're more of a man than he is, dude. Don't sweat it. It's hard to talk to people like him." He paused. "What do you say? Want to go blow him out of the water? Want to go prove him wrong?"

Luke looked at Ryan, the anger building up. "Let's go. I'm ready."

The Steel City Boys: Boys of the Night only took a few months to produce since the band had some songs already written.

Mr. Langderate firmly believed that "Music Man" was the perfect song to release as a single. It had an attractive upbeat and a catchy chorus line, giving it potential for dance club success.

The band gathered at the studio to listen to "Music Man" air on the radio for the first time.

"I got popcorn and Cheez Balls!" Tyler said, scattering packages on the conference table.

"Dude, not this microwave popcorn again," Joe whined. "It's cool and all, but it's sorta sketchy."

"Tyler, the song is only three minutes long," Adam pointed out.

Tyler waved his hand and tore open a flat package of popcorn. "We gotta live a little; this is our first single!"

Like usual, Ryan took control of the radio dial. The boombox was placed in the middle of the table, its long cord stretched all the way across the table to reach the corner out-let.

"You're listening to WJET 99.4, LA's Freshest Hits straight from the sound booth and into your speakers. This is Jeff Lentz with today's newest singles…"

Qrrrrk. Qrrk. Qrrrrrrrrk.

"No, no, no!" Ryan shouted and started pounding the

radio, as if hitting it would eliminate the static. He turned the dial frantically and played with the antenna.

Luke's grin faded as he realized that they could miss the big moment, so he tried to think quickly. "Ryan, the Firebird!"

"Luke, this is no time to talk about Ruby, I—Luke, you're a genius! Everyone, to the car!"

The Steel City Boys raced and slid down the hallway, laughing and teasing each other as they went. Tyler made Adam and Joe carry the snacks while Ryan, the fastest of them all, hurried to the stairs. They had no time to wait around for an elevator.

"The last one to the car has to pull a prank on Maniacial Mark!" Joe yelled as they all raced to be the first one in the car.

Ryan found his way to the driver's seat and turned over the ignition while the others clamored their way in. Joe managed to claim shotgun, leaving Luke in the backseat between Tyler and Adam.

"I hope we didn't miss it," Ryan said under his breath.

The Leather Heartbreaks had recently dropped a new song called "Déjà Vu," and it blasted through the car speakers.

"We can hear Tony Bellano anywhere," Tyler complained as he tossed more popcorn in his mouth. Then he started chanting, "SCB! SCB! SCB!"

Ryan, Adam, and Joe joined in, but Luke was a bundle of nerves. He hoped they hadn't missed their song, but he was more concerned with Bellano. This was the first Leather Heartbreaks' song he had heard since the encounter with Bellano. He still didn't know what to think about it all.

When Bellano's rough voice faded out with the guitars, the entire car went silent as Ryan and Tyler's first chords of "Music Man" resonated through the speakers.

Luke felt a chill as he heard his own voice. It was so surreal. As he fought the urge to sing along with himself, he forgot about Bellano. This was the moment he'd dreamed of for so long. The world was finally going to know Luke Cavarelli.

As expected, "Music Man" entered at the bottom of the song charts, but it gradually climbed its way towards the top and finally settled comfortably at number eight. For a newly-signed band, the boys were allegedly doing "alright." After a couple of weeks, the song really soared, making it an absolute favorite in America. Slowly, but surely, it spread globally, making them a household name and number one on the charts.

But, everything changed with "Forever Mine." Mr. Langderate loved the song to pieces. When he suggested that the band release that song next, Mark Arrowitcz was the first to jump in and protest. "It's too slow. It'll never sell. We just gave these guys a name with a dance song. That's what the audience craves right now." He looked at Luke and Ryan. "I'm telling you, if you throw that in their faces, you can kiss this dream goodbye!"

Mr. Langderate wasn't about to give up the fight that easily. "Mark, get off of my ground. We have a strong back-beat, and we've added a guitar solo for Ryan, not to mention a romantic sax part and a trumpet part. Luke's vocals will make this song skyrocket. What else do you want?"

"This isn't the '70s ballad scene!" Mark retaliated. "We want upbeat, something we can dance to."

"It has a jazzy background to it. Just listen to the lyrics! It's supposed to be graceful and heartfelt; that's the point! I don't know if you've noticed, Mark, but saxes are all the rage these days."

Mark backed off and plopped himself in a chair, defeated. Then he looked up. "What are you doing?"

The band was sitting at the table, and Ryan had just lit a cigarette.

Once he realized Mark was staring at him, Ryan took the cigarette out of his mouth. "What?" he said, confused.

"Get that addiction stick out of here!"

Ryan furrowed his brow. "You never told me not to."

"Well, I'm telling you now! Smoke outside or not at all."

Ryan glanced at Luke, and Luke shrugged.

On the way out the door, Ryan mumbled, "The dude literally smoked half a pack in here yesterday."

Despite Mark Arrowitcz's irrational need for control, "Forever Mine" made its entrance into the music world and onto the radio. Mr. Arrowitcz laughed when the song started off stuck at the bottom of the charts. Actually, it was reluctant to make it on the charts at all. Then, to everyone's surprise, it rose, eventually knocking The Leather Heartbreaks out of the number one spot. When Mr. Arrowitcz learned that it had reached number one, his eyes practically fell out of his head. The song stayed at number one for nearly a month. Mark Arrowitcz never again questioned the releases.

Meanwhile, Luke, at first, didn't like the fame. After years of watching Bellano make a fool of himself by letting the fangirls go to his head, Luke knew that, in the fame department, Bellano was the last person he wanted to be.

The MTV video for "Music Man" exploded in viewers' homes. It began with Luke sifting through vinyl in a record store, and then he and the band shifted scenes as the song continued, going from a 1920's jazz scene and a 1940's big band room to a disco and a neon stage. Once "Forever Mine" hit the airwaves, The Steel City Boys were recognized on the streets. Girls were asking for Luke and Ryan's autographs almost every time they went outside their apartment or the studio. However, one day, Ryan insisted on stopping in a record store to admire their own handiwork.

"What if someone notices us?" Luke asked.

Ryan waved his hand. "Publicity, Luke, publicity. We're in that business now."

They went inside and browsed a bit. When Luke rounded the corner near the register, he saw a boy, who looked to be about thirteen, holding a copy of *Steel City Boys: Boys of the Night.*

Luke grinned. His music had already reached a new generation of listeners, which is what he had always wanted, ever since he first pinned a poster of Bellano to his bedroom wall. Then he wondered: should he talk to the boy?

He headed toward the register and tapped the boy on the shoulder. "Excuse me? How would you like to have that album autographed?"

The boy's eyes lit up, and he pushed his hair out of eyes. "Luke Cavarelli! You're the best new artist of the year! Will you really sign this?"

Luke and Ryan both signed the album and talked to the boy for a few minutes. That was the day Luke realized that fame didn't have to be an overwhelming burden.

Around this time when the band's popularity grew, Luke and Samantha's phone calls were long and frequent.

They'd spend the evening hours chatting and giggling away. Luke couldn't have asked for anything more.

Their album had earned them the privilege of going on tour. But, Mr. Arrowitcz claimed that, since they were a new band, money was tight and they couldn't afford to do a solo tour. The band would have to serve as the openers of each show. The boys weren't overly thrilled about it, but they were still getting the chance to perform in front of real crowds.

The decision of who The Steel City Boys should tour with quickly became a nerve-racking affair. There were a multitude of megastars that year, and the band could've easily performed with any of them. It was just a matter of who offered the better deal and how the financial situation would play out.

Mr. Arrowitcz sat at the table with a list of bands and singers. Frustratedly, he dialed phone numbers and crossed off names. Spots were filling up fast and, frankly, Mr. Arrowitcz's terms were a bit too demanding, bordering on totally unreasonable.

"I got it!" he exclaimed as Luke and Ryan strode into the studio that morning. "We've got you in on the 'Tough as Nails' tour."

The boys looked at one another.

"You mean… with The Leather Heartbreaks?" Luke asked.

"Yeah. It's a perfect fit. Two pop/rock boy bands together will drive the fans wild. Ticket sales will shoot through the roof."

They glanced at one another again, as if to say, *I'm not telling him. You do it.*

Luke took a deep breath. "Mark," it came out shakily at

first, "We can't tour with them."

Mr. Arrowitcz's rare grin vanished, and he glared up at them. "And why not?"

"Um…" Luke nudged Ryan with his elbow while he tried to think of the right words.

"Tony Bellano isn't exactly our biggest fan," Ryan chimed in.

"What do you mean by that?" He leaned back in his chair like a tyrannical king on a bejeweled throne.

"We had a run in with Bellano a couple of months ago. It wasn't pretty," Luke continued.

Mr. Arrowitcz huffed. "What do you want me to do, schedule you with the Pink Diamonds? Wouldn't that just look great." His voice grew louder. "If you want to keep this dream alive, then you're going to have to compromise!"

"Bellano will never approve. He'll torment us for half a year!" Ryan protested.

"Suck it up! You're touring with The Leather Heartbreaks and that's it, end of story!"

"I'd rather tour with the Pink Diamonds," Ryan mumbled under his breath, "Might score a hot one."

It was settled, and there was no doubt about it. What else could the band do but try to avoid The Leather Heartbreaks while on the tour? The Steel City Boys rode in a separate tour bus from Bellano, and, when Luke could manage it, he'd have all five band members squeeze into one green room. The last person that the band needed to derail their chance at fame was Tony Bellano.

Meanwhile, Luke was still in shock that Bellano wasn't welcoming. He had waited so long for the moment when he would meet Bellano, but now it was all turning nightmarish.

Still, Luke knew not to cause trouble where he wasn't want-ed, so he planned to stay away from Bellano.

Once again, everything washed by in a blur. Before they knew it, Luke and Ryan were in the green room that they shared, waiting to open for their first concert.

"Do I have to wear nice pants?" Ryan whined.

"Well, jeans are off the table. We're trying to stand apart from Bellano, remember?"

"Look, Luke, it's not the clothes that are bothering me."

Luke buckled his belt. "What is it, then?"

"We've never played for a crowd this big. I'm nervous."

"Me too, dude." He slumped himself in a chair. "Good thing we're not the main attraction yet."

"One day, though…" Ryan smirked.

There was a knock on the door. "You girls in tune?" Bellano jeered in the doorway, having too much fun.

"More in tune than you'll ever be," Ryan shot back.

"Really?"

"Yeah, considering you lip-sync." Ryan walked over towards Bellano casually, until their faces were only inches away from each other.

"You think you're so smart? You think you can intimi-date me by saying that? You know it's a downright lie."

Ryan shrugged. "So what if it is?"

Instantly, Bellano grabbed Ryan violently by the shirt and pulled him even closer. Ryan felt every puff of hot breath that came out of Bellano's mouth.

"That crowd out there ain't for you. They're here for me and my boys. You're just here to look pretty and to give my vocals a break. You ain't nothin', and you're never gonna be. Just stay out of my way and you won't get hurt."

"You call two top ten hits nothing? We pushed you out of the number one spot."

Bellano stopped talking. He was beginning to fume. "That was just a fluke."

Ryan's cheeks started to turn bright red. Suddenly, he drew his fist back and punched Bellano straight in the face.

Bellano stumbled backwards, disbelief written on his face. He clutched the doorframe, which helped him to not double over. A trickle of blood streamed from his lower lip. He touched it and frowned.

By the time he steadied himself again, the members of both bands were already gathered outside of the green room to get a glimpse of the action. The Leather Heartbreaks encouraged Bellano, but The Steel City Boys watched, not wanting to make matters worse. This time, Bellano took a swing at Ryan, but Ryan ducked just at the right moment and managed to straighten up uninjured. Bellano wasn't going to give up, though. He tried again and successfully pushed Ryan to the ground.

Luke couldn't speak. He knew that he had to help his best friend, so he didn't give himself much time to think. In mere seconds, he jumped in the middle of the brawl and put himself in between the two guys so that Bellano couldn't take another shot while Ryan was on the floor.

Bellano just stood there gawking at Luke. "Finally grow a pair, Cavarelli?"

Luke didn't move.

Bellano prepared to strike, but a roaring voice in the doorway forced him to stop. "Don't even think about it!"

Bellano spun around to lay eyes on The Leather Heart-breaks' manager. "Who? Me?" He pointed at himself dumbly.

"Who else would I be talking to? Step away from them. They're doing you the courtesy of opening the show. The least you can do is show them a little respect. Don't make me regret taking you on." The large and stern-looking man waited for Bellano to step away.

On his way out, Bellano laughed. "Boring fight anyway. If Ace were still alive, he'd have flattened you into pancakes by now. Come on, boys." He summoned the rest of his band and then started singing Adam Ant's "Goody Two Shoes."

"Please don't push his buttons," the manager said wearily. "I've been in this business for 20 years, and I've never seen a moodier rockstar. God, I wish Frankie Pierce would've stuck around. I hear he's the only one who kept this band sane." Then the manager stalked out of the room.

Luke stared at Ryan for a moment while he let all of that chaos sink in. He sighed and stretched out his hand. "Hope no one tells Mark about this. He'll flip."

Ryan gladly clasped the proffered hand and pulled himself to his feet. "Thanks, man." He went over to the dressing room mirror and ran his fingers through his hair.

"But I didn't do anything."

"That's not true." Ryan fixated on his appearance.

"I just stood there."

Ryan came away from the mirror. "Hey, it's a start."

* * *

At the first glance of the massive crowd, Luke went completely numb. He wasn't even sure if he could pick up his foot to move out onstage. But, when the familiar downbeat of "Music Man" drifted into his ears, his nervousness dissipated immediately, and he felt like himself. He could dominate this stage, create enough energy to electrify the thousands of people waiting to be invigorated by music. He took center stage with microphone in hand. Ryan was by his side, strumming all the way.

My days are hard and my nights are long,
Only one thing, though, can help me hang on.
All I know is that I can't live without it,
Some people say that I'm just
over-dramatic...

Out of nowhere, the crowd's excitement seemed to disappear. What's happening? He was singing his heart out like usual, but the response wasn't as extraordinary as he'd expected.

The stage lights were strobing down in rays of purples, greens, and blues while a fog machine poured its contents over the floor. This ambiance was to depict the mood of The Leather Heartbreaks' opening song. The Steel City Boys, though, were to have yellow lights, regular stage lights, and no fog whatsoever.

The crowd couldn't see any of the band members' faces. All they could do was hear them. This mysterious vibe matched The Leather Heartbreaks style, but "Music Man" didn't fit. Something was wrong.

Suddenly, Luke's mic gave out right before he hit the chorus. He didn't know what to do, so he kept going. The show must go on, right?

> But what can I say?
> It feeds my soul,
> It's who I am!
> Oh, don't you know it?
> Don't you know I'm just a music man?

Things were getting worse. He sounded far away, and he was annoyed at how dark it was. Not wanting to stop, he proceeded to the second verse:

> Give me a beat, don't forget the bass line,
> That sweet surrender that makes me feel fine.
> Oh that melody that gets stuck in my head,
> It never leaves me holding on by a thread.

By the time he went into the chorus again, he could feel that all of the crowd's pent up energy had definitely vanished. Luke quickly looked over his shoulder while he sang. He could've sworn that the curtain that separated the main stage from the wings had been rustled. He knew it shouldn't have distracted him, drawing him away from the crowd as he carried on, but he looked again anyway. This time, in the midst of the strobe lights, the shadow of Tony Bellano's smug face was poking out from behind the curtain with a large, satisfied grin planted on it.

Luke couldn't say that he was totally shocked. Of course Bellano would try to embarrass the band during their first performance. A bout of anger came over him, and he felt a hot sweat rushing over his skin. He tried to put it out of his mind and finish the song. Stopping the song would only add to his embarrassment. He looked back again and, this time, Bellano had disappeared, though there was a good bit of commotion going on behind the curtain.

He just made it to the last repeat of the chorus when, miraculously, the correct lights shone from above and the mic boomed back on. The concert hall came back to life, and Luke's voice exploded:

Oh, don't you know it?

Don't you know I'm just a music man? Oh!

It's who I am!

Don't you understand?

A music man is who I am,

It's what I need.

I am forever... a music man!

The audience roared again, the excitement building up once more. Luke ended the song strongly, smiling from ear to ear. He imagined The Leather Heartbreaks' manager backstage shouting, "For God sakes, would somebody turn the lights on for the poor boy? And turn that mic back on!"

The fans applauded like crazy while Luke announced that they would perform "Forever Mine." The girls went absolutely wild. The band didn't think that the thunderous applause would ever end after the song was over.

After a quick break to adjust equipment for Bellano's band, Luke introduced his favorite music act. "Ladies and Gentleman, The Steel City Boys are proud to welcome to the stage… The Leather Heartbreaks!" Luke hung on to the words even though it broke his heart that Bellano didn't care about him.

The stage setting reflected the new band accordingly. Bellano strode out onto the stage like he was the ruler of the world. He moved to the edge of the stage and held up his arms, taking in the crowd's enthusiasm.

Backstage, the boys huddled up, bouncing up and down.

"That was amazing!" Joe exclaimed.

"More fun than at Silva's," Tyler said.

"Cool job, Luke." Adam held up his hand for the lead singer to high-five it.

Ryan guzzled down water like he had been wandering in the desert for days.

"Do you think Bellano rigged the lights?" Luke said suddenly.

Ryan wiped his mouth with the back of his hand. "Probably, but when they were turned back on, let me tell you, you rocked that stage."

"I swear I saw his face sticking out from behind the curtain."

"Doesn't mean he was trying to sabotage us."

Luke crossed his arms. "You think Bellano wouldn't?"

"I know he'd do it," Ryan said calmly. "Look, Luke, I don't want to worry about it right now. It's bothering me too, but let's try to enjoy the rest of the night, okay?"

The night concluded on a high note. However, that all changed when the bands had to deal with each other backstage.

Trying to be the bigger man, Luke told Bellano, "You were awesome, dude."

He rolled his eyes. "Flattery won't get you anywhere, fan or no fan."

Luke scrunched up his face in confusion.

"I don't like you, it's as simple as that. You ain't that great. I've heard better. A lot better."

"That crowd loved me. They weren't just out there for you," Luke got defensive.

Bellano waved his hand. "If that's what you tell yourself at night, honey."

This got to Luke. "You think I didn't see you sticking your head out from behind the curtain? I know you rigged the lights to embarrass us. You wanted the audience to get a bad impression."

"You know, you really got to get these bogus fantasies out of your head." Bellano glanced back at his gang behind him. "You might crack up before you get your own tour." He laughed, "Besides, you won't see any more number one hits."

"You know, I can't stand it that some days you're just not in it for the music. Some days all you care about is being famous: spending late nights at parties and having girls fall all over you. What about the time you said in an interview that the songs mean nothing to you?"

Bellano scoffed. "Dude, I was drunk outta my mind in

that interview! Any idiot could see the beer bottle glued in my hand."

"That's my point! Where's your passion and devotion? All you care about is having a good time and getting laid. Some days, I can't tell why you deserve to be a revered musician." Luke stepped so close to Bellano that he could've spit on him. "You don't know what music is. You don't know what it's like to be a real musician, so who do you think you are telling me I can't make it to the top?"

"Whoa, back up, man." Ryan tugged Luke back.

But Luke continued. "You were supposed to meet me three years ago in Pittsburgh. I won the Leather Heartbreak Songwriting competition, and you didn't even hold up your end of the bargain."

Bellano nodded to himself. "So that was you, eh?"

"Yeah," Luke shouted, "That was me. But you clearly didn't care."

"You wanna know what I think, Mr. Goody Two Shoes?"

Luke's voice grew outrageously loud. He didn't even recognize it. Nothing logical registered in his brain. He just wanted sweet revenge. "No, I don't give a da—" His mouth became dry, and he couldn't speak. He shot Bellano an evil look before scurrying away to find solitude in the dressing room.

As he took off, he heard Bellano say aggressively, "What the hell was that?"

There was a pause. "He won't swear. He's Catholic," Ryan said softly.

Chapter 14
Long Distance Relationship

Luke never let the attention from the screaming girls in the audience get to him, unlike Ryan. He only had one girl on his mind, and she danced across it whenever he sang "Forever Mine." Every time, he couldn't help but let his lips form a grateful smile. But, at the end of the day, Samantha Denvy had no way of knowing if Luke even thought of her.

She had thought of him every day since he left. She kept to herself and devoted her time to the large amounts of work she had piled up. Her classes were almost finished, and she would graduate soon. After that, she could leave and finally get to making her dreams come true like Luke.

In the beginning, they talked almost every day. But, as the band got busier, the habit broke and he regularly called every Sunday. Though she understood that his line of work demanded a great deal of time, she wanted to talk to him more often. There were a few times when he only called twice a month. She would call too, but sometimes he didn't answer, or he said that he was busy or that he couldn't talk for long. He said that it'd be easier for him to call her since his schedule was so unpredictable. Often, he claimed that he was tired and it had been a tremendously long day. Not that she could blame him, but she felt that they were more distant than they'd ever been. She herself was busy, between her schoolwork and the Hextons.

One Sunday night, she was in charge of clearing off the dining room table and washing the dishes. Being the only staff member in the house during the night and weekend hours meant that she didn't have much of a choice, and Emily had left for the night after cooking dinner. Free time? What free time?

She tried to go about her job quietly, so that she wouldn't

be noticed. She was carrying a stack of the expensive chinaware to the kitchen when she heard a voice echoing from the parlor, a voice that immediately caught her attention.

The entire Hexton family, including Jake and Sara (who had decided to live in the mansion after their marriage), were gathered together with all of their eyes glued to the television.

Samantha stood in the archway, peering in to see the screen. The others were so transfixed by the show that they didn't even realize that she was there.

The large screen bore a live account of an interview that was taking place on *Entertainment Tonight*. The camera shifted smoothly from the big-haired interviewer to none other than Luke Cavarelli and Ryan Delhart.

She crept a bit further into the room so she could get a good glimpse of his face.

"The Steel City Boys really stand out from any other artist we've seen so far this year. Most new bands don't see one song from their first album make into the top ten, but you guys have seen two rise to fame in a short time frame. How does it feel?"

Ryan jumped to answer. "Honestly, this all feels like a dream. We imagined it, but we never believed that it would become a reality." He put a hand on Luke's arm. "Okay, I thought we could make it, but this guy over here…" Ryan shook his head and both boys laughed. "We're thankful for the fans who have jumped on board so quickly. This is just what we do, and we love it."

"Now," the camera swung back to the woman interviewing, "What can you tell me about 'Forever Mine'? Where did it come from? I mean, the song has become so explosive, and it's a complete contrast from your first song, 'Music Man'."

It was Luke's turn. "Actually, at the time I wrote it, our band was asked to play for a wedding. I kind of made the song fit the occasion. But," he shifted in his chair, "That's not to say that it has no meaning to me. The song shows how I wanted to feel back then in terms of a romantic relationship."

"Do you not feel that way now?" The interviewer attempted to dig deeper.

"Oh no, I still do. Shortly after I wrote the song, I fell in love with a girl who fits the song to a tee. I found that she was the girl I wrote about in the song. She's the one I've been waiting for."

Back to the interviewer. "Luke, you may not be aware, but did you know that there are rumors that you're in a relationship with a girl at Sforzando Records?"

She watched his face drop into shock. "No! Absolutely not! I don't know where the rumors came from, but they're completely untrue."

Instantly, Samantha blushed, though no one knew except her.

"I love Samantha with all my heart," Luke continued. "There's no room for anyone else."

The clatter of plates on the hardwood floor forced five wealthy heads to snap away from the television. Their focus turned to Samantha. The dishes were scattered in sharp, razor-edge pieces on the ground.

"Look how clumsy!" Charlotte cackled. "I told you, Joanne, you should've fired her long ago. That's at least $400 in plates right there!"

Sara cuddled up closer to Jake and mocked, "No, she's

just worried about her rockstar boyfriend. If you ask me, he can't sing to save his life! Didn't even want him to sing for our wedding."

"Sara!" Jake shot up on the couch and glared at her.

"Guys, please," Mr. Hexton raised his voice. "Did you forget that I helped those boys get to where they are right now? Look at them, they're doing fantastic." He stood up from his chair and bent down to help Samantha pick up the plates.

"Thank you, Mr. Hexton. You really don't have to do this. It is my job, you know. I shouldn't have been so careless."

"No, it's okay. Don't mention it." He gently laid the broken shards on top of the rest of the pile that she had in her hands. "Why don't you call it a night when you're done?"

She headed to the kitchen, successfully making it there this time. The TV blared on with the interviewer rambling away: "So, you guys are still on tour with Tony Bellano and The Leather Heartbreaks. What is it like touring with a band that you've always looked up to?"

After cleaning up the mess in the kitchen, she stifled a yawn and began her nightly ascent up the stairs. As she did, Mr. Hexton's deep whisper flowed from the parlor, compelling her to freeze halfway up the steps.

"Cut her some slack. She does her absolute best here. She does everything we ask of her and then some. She goes the extra mile, even if we don't ask her to. She's a sweet, hard-working girl, and she has a lot of potential." Mr. Hexton's voice drifted as if he had got up and moved across the room. "She's worried about Luke. She cares for him. She loves him. I can see it in her eyes." He sighed heavily. "I'm ashamed to have such a judgmental family! Do you think you're better than her? Big deal, we have more money. Is that cause for insults? If you have no respect for her, then you have no respect for me."

She heard his footsteps padding out of the room, so she tiptoed up the steps hurriedly and got herself out of sight. Once she made it safely to her room, she locked the door and leaned against it, feeling its coolness on her already-heated skin. She exhaled, trying to let all of the nervous tension go.

Her brain was still buzzing from the chaos. Nothing picturesque was going on out her window, but she sat there daydreaming, contemplating what both Luke and Mr. Hexton had said. She held on tightly to every precious word of Luke's.

He loved her. He hadn't given her up, at least not yet. That deserved a sigh of relief. Everything had remained the same, despite the fact they were miles apart. She could sleep easily.

A few weeks later, she received a letter from him:

Dear Samantha,

I'll start by saying that you know I miss you every single day. So far, everything out here is great. We just finished shooting the music video for "Forever Mine," and it'll air on MTV next week! When you see the video, don't worry. I wasn't particularly fond of the model they hired. I didn't think she fit the "Forever Mine" mold, especially since the only one who can fill those shoes is you.

We're keeping busy with the tour, but Tony Bellano is a handful. Other than that, we're having an awesome time. The tour we're on is actually coming to Pittsburgh. So, instead of just opening for The Leather Heartbreaks, we get to play more of our songs since it's our hometown.

She couldn't allow one inkling of doubt to pass through her mind. There he was, pouring out his heart to her. She sighed in relief and then eagerly pulled the tickets out of the envelope. While she studied every word, she wondered if she was dreaming. Not only did Luke still love her, but she was going to see him for the first time on the big stage.

The days dwindled down little by little as she impatiently crossed them off her calendar. When the concert was only a few days away, she couldn't refrain from smiling randomly at nothing every once in a while. Could time crawl by any slower?

Finally, the night arrived, and she couldn't have been more ecstatic to see him. She hung up her apron after helping Emily in the kitchen, and then she set off to get ready. Much pondering left her with the decision of whether to wear the same denim skirt and black shirt that she wore on their first date. Maybe she shouldn't have criticized Luke for only owning one suit after all.

The concert started at 8:00, and they planned to leave around 7:00. She hurried down the stairs at 6:45.

Emily was already leaning up against the doorframe, looking bored. Her eyes popped when she saw Samantha tramping down the steps. "Lookin' good, girl!"

Samantha smiled. "Not looking bad yourself."

Even though Emily had on a pair of jeans, her tall and slender figure helped her pull them off stylishly. She tossed her wavy, strawberry hair, revealing her huge hoop earrings. "I'm a natural."

"Any sign of Gina yet?" Samantha put a hand on her hip.

"Nope." Emily sighed, annoyed. "I know she was supposed to change here after her shift, but you know how flighty she is."

They waited until quarter after 7:00. Emily rushed for the door.

"You're not missing your famous, hot boyfriend because of that nitwit!"

"Wait, wait! I'm coming!" Gina practically slid down the steps.

She met them at the door, but before they could make their escape, another voice from upstairs shrieked: "They're gone! My diamonds! My precious diamonds! RICHARD!!!"

Charlotte Hexton.

"I stole them," Gina whispered proudly.

"You what?!" Samantha and Emily said simultaneously.

"Yeah, I figured we could trade them in for some extra cash. We can finally quit this place!"

"What?!"

"Don't tell."

"Are you insane?" Samantha couldn't believe it.

"We have to get going or we're going to be late," Emily

said.

"No one's going anywhere." Mrs. Hexton seemed to appear out of thin air.

Samantha tried to play the fool. "Why? What happened?"

"Someone stole the valuable diamond jewelry set that Charlotte's father gave her before his passing."

"But Mrs. Hexton," Emily jumped in, "We're going to the concert tonight. We're already running late as it is."

"Not now, you're not. No one's leaving until those diamonds and the culprit are found. You'll be fired if you leave. Charlotte's orders."

Samantha's heart sank like a stone in water. "But, I have to go and see Luke!"

"Sorry, girls. I hope she's just overreacting. Maybe she misplaced them."

Charlotte flew down the stairs, even though her legs weren't what they used to be. "I want to question all of the servants! I know one of them has to have done it."

Mrs. Hexton and Charlotte walked into the parlor. Just after their backs were turned, Samantha tried to tell them the truth, so they could get out of there and she could see Luke. Before she could get a word out, Gina clapped a hand over Samantha's mouth.

"Don't! Like, we'll sneak out the door."

Charlotte's ears weren't as old as the rest of her. She whipped around suddenly, and her hawk-like eyes glared at the girls. "It was one of you!"

"Gina did it!" Emily blurted.

Mr. Hexton's sister was a nuclear bomb ready to blow. She grabbed ahold of Gina and began to shake her aggressively. "Where are they?"

The girl grinned deviously. "I hid them."

Emily rolled her eyes. "There, Gina did it. Now, can we please get out of here? We're never going to make it in time. The roads will be jam packed."

"NO ONE leaves until they're found!" Charlotte stormed off to hunt for her diamonds.

"Just stay here," Mrs. Hexton said. She stood by the girls the whole time as if she were a security guard.

Emily kept shooting Gina dirty looks, and Samantha's eyes remained glued on the clock on the mantel. Time just ticked away carelessly. It didn't care that not allowing her to see Luke was like twisting a knife in her heart. But she couldn't lose her job.

"This is ridiculous," Emily mumbled.

It was already pushing 8:00 when the masters of the house lined up and asked the girls to step into the living room, serious and indignant.

"We found them," Mr. Hexton said.

"In Samantha's camera case," Sara sneered as she entered, the black case swinging from her fingers.

Samantha thought that she was going to be sick. "WHAT?!" She looked at Gina. "Why would you do this to me?"

"Ha! I knew she was involved. She was an accomplice." Charlotte was too cheerful.

"No, I would never—"

"Samantha wouldn't steal anything," Emily backed her up.

Mrs. Hexton shook her head in disbelief. "Samantha's trustworthy and loyal. She'd never do something as deceitful as this. Richard, it can't be the truth."

Sara's grin faded as quickly as it had come on. "But the camera case! There's proof!"

"I put them there," Gina croaked.

"How do we know? You're all friends. You're all probably in cahoots," Charlotte said. Then she pointed at Gina. "You're fired. Get out of here."

Gina gasped like she didn't think it could happen.

"You're done, Gina," Mr. Hexton said with a voice filled with both discipline and compassion.

"Like, omigod," she whined. "I can't believe this. Like, seriously?"

"Totally," Sara perked up and mocked her. "Like, take a chill pill and get out."

Gina shot her a nasty look and stormed out, slamming the front door behind her.

Charlotte turned towards Samantha. "Her. I want her out of this house too."

"Wait," Mr. Hexton intervened. "I don't believe she had anything to do with this. I'm not firing her."

"I don't trust her. I never have. You at least owe it to me, Richard, to remove this girl from our house. I don't want her living here anymore."

"That's not nec—"

"Now, Richard!"

Mr. Hexton sighed. He gently took Samantha by the arm and led her out into the hallway. "I know you didn't do it—"

"Thank you."

"—but once my sister gets something in her head, it's unchangeable. Look, I won't fire you. You don't deserve that.

However, I'm afraid I have to ask you to move out."

Samantha nodded sadly. "Okay."

"You can stay with me. The offer still stands." Emily stepped out of the parlor. "I could really use a roommate."

"Great. Thank you so much."

Emily waved her hand. "No prob. So, do you want to go to the concert and then come back for your stuff?"

"We'll never make it in time. We're already too late."

"But Luke gave you V.I.P.—"

"You heard Charlotte. She wants me out as soon as possible."

"Alright," Emily whispered, not wanting to argue.

They packed up Samantha's stuff and hauled it to Emily's car and then to her apartment across town.

"Come on, come on!" Emily tried to hurry Samantha, but Samantha didn't care about the concert anymore. He had been gone from her for so long that she had given up hope of getting him back in her arms.

After they got all of her belongings safely inside the apartment, Emily asked her if they should go find Luke.

"We can worry about the landlord and rent later."

"Do you think he'll still be there?"

"Totally. It's worth a shot."

They rode in complete silence. When they arrived, they found that the whole parking lot was completely dark. The lights in the concert hall had been extinguished, and any trace of screaming fans had long since disappeared.

"Are they staying in a hotel tonight?"

"I don't know." The knots in her stomach pulled tighter.

"They should still—"

"Emily, he's gone. He's gone, and I didn't get to see

him!" Even Samantha was surprised at how hostile she had become.

Emily put the car in park in the middle of the lot. She turned to look at Samantha, putting a hand on her arm. "I know. I'm sorry. I really wanted you to see him too."

Samantha was crying, not knowing how to stop it. "I can't stand being this far away from him all the time. He's famous now, which means all the girls want him. I haven't even seen that music video, and I'm sure I don't want to!"

"Wait, the 'Forever Mine' video? Look, girl, that model wasn't nearly as beautiful as you. Besides, the camera angles didn't exactly catch her good side. The wind covered her face in hair, and she had a snarky attitude, like she was the greatest thing since MTV aired. Even as Luke was belting out his lip-synched lyrics, I could tell that they didn't mesh. Seriously, like no chemistry. She may have been all over him in that pool lounge chair, but he's too focused on the song."

"You've seen the video?" was all Samantha could ask. Everything else she tried to say came out as gibberish. Did Emily truly know how she felt? As much as the model bothered her, she was still too upset about not seeing him, especially when her heart was so set on it. What would he think of her for not showing?

"If it makes you feel any better, I secretly wanted to see Ryan Delhart."

Suddenly, Samantha looked over at Emily. "What?"

"Yeah, you heard me."

All the tension dissolved and the girls sat there laughing almost hysterically.

"I'm exhausted. Let's get outta here." Emily began to drive again.

Samantha sighed. "Yes, please. I'll write to him in the morning."

"He'll understand," Emily reassured her. "Everything will be fine."

After that, Samantha kept quiet. She wrote to Luke immediately and explained what had happened. She knew that he wouldn't be back in L.A. for a while because of the tour, so she had no way of knowing when she could call him.

Work dragged on and she just focused on what she had to do so that she could get out of Pittsburgh. She barely smiled anymore. She didn't glance twice at Charlotte or Sara.

College finals approached quickly. Her nights were filled with endless studying, and, in the end, her final results reflected the hard work that she put into her photography studies. Finally, she was prepared to fulfill her dreams.

Following graduation, though, she had to find another job so that she could make ends meet. Rent and college tuition sucked up her money. She wanted to rake in as much as she could to keep up with her debts. During the summer months, she juggled a waitressing job, along with her photography work and the Hextons.

On the flip side, her mind wandered a lot to Luke. Not talking to him was like being strapped down to a pendulum and waiting for the blade to claim its prize. She longed for him, and she wanted to make sure that he wasn't mad at her and that he understood.

Maybe she should've been careful of what she wished for. When she heard The Steel City Boys' new single on the radio, she felt the pendulum at last make its first slice into her heart.

What have I done to you?
Why do you treat me so cold?
I've given all my love to you,
Is this what I get in return?
Oh tell me, please tell me:
Have you moved on?
I just gotta know
If you've found someone new,
Am I still in your heart?

Although it had a bit of an upbeat, she knew instantly that Luke had written it for her. He wanted to know why she stood him up. Hadn't he received the letter? The band was definitely back from the tour. She had her new number enclosed in the letter, and she was hoping that he'd have called. She tried calling him a few times, but there was no answer. Did he move on without her?

The next few months were agonizing. Samantha, confused by Luke's lack of response, had no choice but to continue moving as she neared her college graduation. She was already miserable at the Hexton house, thanks to Gina and Charlotte, and she had to compile her final portfolio, find a job, and worry about Luke, all at the same time.

Chill was a sense of comfort for Samantha. Even though the café felt empty without Luke's presence, she'd sit in a back booth and arrange photos or comb newspapers for job ads.

One day, when she looked up from her newspaper and glanced up at the counter, she caught her breath at the sight of a man around her age who was running the register. For a split second, the gold hair and gentle smile made her think that the man was Luke. She stared at the young barista, watching his hair fall into his eyes. Would it be easy to move on from Luke? She didn't know where they stood anymore, and she wanted nothing more than to land a job in LA where she could be closer to him. She wasn't ready to lose him, and she wouldn't.

Right before graduation, Samantha's professor gave her a list of potential employers nationwide. When she scanned the list, Samantha stopped dead at a studio in LA who was searching for a photographer. The business loved highly detailed shots of the ordinary; they wanted a photographer who could draw out the essence of anything. Samantha's photography style matched the criteria. She didn't just photograph a few bridges and skyscrapers, but she captured the texture and life within each object or person. Sara Hexton's wedding dress was a testament to beauty and luxury, just as Pittsburgh wasn't simply a city; it was a city rising from ashes; it was hope, and it began to build the foundation of Samantha's relationship with Luke.

She was shaky the day that she mailed her application at the post office, and she was still shaking the day that Mrs. Hexton handed her the telephone.

"It's for you, dear." Mrs. Hexton handed over the phone with a huge smile on her face, as if she knew that there was good news on the other end of the phone.

"Miss Denvy?" a warm female voice said through the speaker.

"Speaking." Samantha closed her eyes, thinking more about Luke than the job. What if this were her last chance?

"Your work is absolutely stunning, and we think you'd make a great asset to our team here in L.A. We'd like to discuss a contract."

Samantha had to fight the urge to start jumping up and down while still on the phone. For a few seconds, she didn't even pay attention to what the woman was saying about the job. All she knew was that her future with Luke Cavarelli still had a chance to exist.

With that, she packed up all of the belongings for the third time in the past year. She didn't regret saying goodbye to the Hexton household. On her last day, she nearly skipped down the driveway, beaming, the wind was ready to sweep her off to wonderland. She couldn't leave soon enough.

Chapter 15

Forever Mine

Luke had never received the letter. He waited backstage anxiously after the concert for Samantha to arrive. Every time Ryan told him that they had to leave, he said, "Just another five minutes. She'll be here. I know it."

He tried calling her that night when they were at a rest stop, but Charlotte answered the Hextons' phone.

"Can I speak to Samantha, please?" he asked desperately.

"She's no longer living here," Charlotte answered sternly and hung up.

Luke couldn't believe his ears. What just happened? Did that mean that Samantha lost her job? Did it mean that she moved out of the Hexton mansion? Both? How could he ever get ahold of her?

He couldn't understand what was happening. In order to get the emotions out of his system, he had to write the song. In truth, the heavy cloud of sadness that inspired him to write that song never really left, even after the song was recorded. He even considered flying back to Pittsburgh.

But, his main focus stayed on the music. The Steel City Boys were doing better than ever. Their songs seemed to grow bolder and more compelling. Things were looking up in the money department. Although the record label had to pay back everyone who worked for the band, fans devoured the first album, boosting sales. Frequent airplay boosted royalties, giving the band members a nice-sized income. But now, the second album had to blast the first out of the water.

As challenging as it was to both compose and sing the songs, Luke dived into each new project with endless energy. His vocal coach agreed that his voice had improved and had the potential to soar higher. There was talk that he might actually surpass Tony Bellano's vocal range.

Out of everything the band had to do, photo shoots were by far Luke's least favorite requirement. Performing in front of thousands of fans: wicked! Getting pictures taken for the band's second album cover: gag!

Mr. Arrowitcz totally immersed his unneeded managing skills in the entire affair. His crooked nose was involved so much that he should've been the cameraman. "We have to beat The Leather Heartbreaks on album sales."

"What'd they do for their last album cover?" Ryan asked.

"For the *Tough as Nails* album? They kept their jackets open and acted like they were going to go set the world on fire!" And so Mr. Arrowitcz's sour mood for the day began.

"I'm not taking my shirt off," Luke said angrily. The mere mention of Bellano made his blood boil. Ever since their last encounter, Luke had great animosity towards Bellano. It wasn't something he actually comprehended, though. Luke Cavarelli didn't normally get mad, plain and simple.

"It's not a big deal," Ryan said, trying to keep the peace.

"I'm not about to lose my dignity. I want people to love my voice, not my body. I don't need the free advertising."

Ryan looked at Mr. Arrowitcz and shrugged. "There you have it."

"Oh, it's far from free." Mr. Arrowitcz crossed his arms and glared at Luke. "I make the decisions around here. If you don't promote this album right, you'll never have enough money to pay for everything."

Luke had had enough. "With all due respect, Mark, you may be our manager, but I still have some free will regarding what this band does. You think you run this show when, in reality, we have the power to fire you."

Mr. Arrowitcz shut up real fast, and the photoshoot got underway. The band finally did what they wanted, everything from the clothing to the backdrop.

Luke tried to pay attention to the cameraman, who seemed like he didn't have a clue what he was doing. Outside, in the hall, he heard Mr. Arrowitcz's bitter voice shout: "I don't care if you're scheduled to see Mr. Langderate. We're in the middle of a photoshoot, so go away!"

"What's going on here, Mark?" Mr. Langderate's gentle voice echoed.

"This girl says she's scheduled to see you."

"Ah, yes. Samantha Denvy, is it?"

Luke instantly unfroze himself from the position that he was trying to assume and sprinted out into the hallway, half-believing that he was only imagining things. To his surprise, it was indeed Samanth standing there, glowing like the light from a candle flame, the light that fills a dark room with immediate joy and hope.

At first, he couldn't speak. Instead of saying anything, he ran over to her, swiftly picked her up, and spun her around in the air. When he safely put her back on the floor, he threw his arms around her and didn't let go for what felt like at least five minutes. Then, he took her hand and led her aside.

"Wh—what are you doing here?"

"I got a photography job."

"Wait a second," Luke said, thinking. "Oh, man." His eyes widened as he said, "I missed your graduation! Samantha, I'm so sorry. I got so wrapped up, I was going to call—"

"Luke, stop. I'm the one who should be apologizing to

you."

His smile faded. "The concert. What happened?"

"Didn't you get the letter I sent you?"

"No. What address did you use?"

"The studio's. That's the address you used when you sent me the concert tickets. I figured it'd be more convenient than trying to call since you're so busy."

"Cavarelli, get back in there! We gotta get this photo-shoot done today." Mr. Arrowitcz stormed back over.

Ignoring his command, Luke jumped on him. "Did any mail from Pittsburgh come here addressed to me?"

"How should I know?" he snapped.

"You handle that stuff." Ryan came strolling out. "Hey, Samantha! You look great."

"Uh…" The sweat poured off of Mr. Arrowitcz's forehead. His eyes darted back and forth to each person huddled in the hallway. "I don't know. There might have been something."

"Has there been?" Mr. Langderate became skeptical.

"Okay! Yes. Yes, but I threw it away."

"Why would you do that?" Luke couldn't believe his ears.

"There's no time for distractions."

"That was personal. You had no right to do that." Luke was more than agitated.

"Maybe you should've thought of that before you used the business address!" Mr. Arrowitcz turned on his heel and headed back into the room.

Ryan rolled his eyes. "See you in there."

"I'll leave you two alone." Mr. Langderate left too.

He took her down to the end of the hall and sat her

down on a bench near the elevator, and she narrated the story of what happened on the night of the concert.

"It broke my heart when I heard that song. I knew right then and there that you didn't get my letter."

He shook his head. "I only wish I had." He draped his arm over her shoulder and drew her closer.

"Are we cool?"

"The coolest."

Their lips met blissfully for the first time in months. The passion was relit, and their love was rekindled, stronger than ever.

Then something unusual occurred. Luke had never felt this way before. He felt like he just wanted to kiss her forever, as if time had stopped indefinitely. The stars and the moon collided. It was a rush, and it was exhilarating. It was heaven until: "GET OUT!!" Mr. Arrowitcz boomed from the other end of the building.

Samantha looked up at Luke innocently.

He closed his eyes and sighed. He opened them only to be delighted by the sight of her. "Apparently, he just fired the photographer."

"Fun guy."

"You've no idea."

"Do you need a photographer?"

Luke perked up. "Would you? Can you? Are you allowed to with your job?"

"I don't see why not. I can call my boss. It's the kind of stuff we do."

"Awesome!"

"But he won't like it." Samantha pointed down the hall.

Luke dismissed it, waving his hand. "I don't think he

even likes music!"

They both laughed and the tension melted away. They were good.

After consulting with Samantha's boss, and carefully persuading Mr. Arrowitcz, she was permitted to complete the photoshoot for the album cover and other promotional materials.

Luckily, Mr. Arrowitcz didn't make a single comment. He watched her fluidity as she told the band what to do and clicked the camera with ease. She was done in no time.

When all was over, Luke and Ryan walked her to her newly-bought car. The sun sank lower, and the humidity had been replaced by a light wind. Luke kissed Samantha gently and then watched her back out of the lot.

The best friends liked to travel to the studio some days on foot, since the weather was always so beautiful and their apartment was within easy walking distance. They strode home alongside each other, moving in perfect harmony. "I'm glad she's back in your life, dude." Ryan grinned. "You two are great together."

They experienced a moment of silence, until Luke blurted out, "I want to ask her to marry me."

Ryan was furiously trying to light a cigarette, struggling against the warm wind. Luke's statement caused his thumb to slide off of the lighter, forcing the whole business to clatter to the ground. Even the cigarette fell out of his mouth and onto the pavement. "You want to what now?"

"You heard me. I want to marry her."

"Dude, what about the 'Young Guns' philosophy? Are you crazy? What kind of drugs are you hopped up on?"

"Really?" Luke cocked an eyebrow. "You're the one inhaling nicotine. Look, I don't care about being young and reckless. I don't need to go tear up the town every night. I love her completely, and she's my best friend."

"Gee, thanks."

"No woman could ever replace you, Ryan."

"Good, you know I'm irreplaceable."

"So, you don't care?"

"No, man, go for it! You two deserve each other. If you're happy, I'm happy. Besides, you were never like me when it came to girls. You took your time and got it right."

"Thanks. So… you're gonna be my best man?"

"No, I thought you were going to ask Mark Arrowitcz."

"Oh, you're the maid of honor then?"

"I'm pretty enough."

* * *

Luke may not have had many relationships, but he knew that Samantha was the one. Luke knew that most people doubt and criticize young marriages, arguing that they don't last. In this case, he couldn't have been more sure that this was the right choice. His plan had been set for days, yet last minute nerves kept trying to choke him.

He brought her back to his and Ryan's apartment after they went out to eat one night.

The new apartment was much larger than the old one. The halls seemed to wrap around endlessly. The interior shone bright in glimmers of off-whites and hints of blush-roses. The long and luxurious couches followed suit, and the lights only added to the cheerful vibe, radiating a sense of calm and familiarity. It wasn't Pittsburgh, but it was home.

"Do you care if I set these leftovers in the fridge?" Samantha asked when they stepped in the door.

"No, go ahead. Then meet me in the living room."

"You know it'll take me five minutes to reorganize your fridge. You two just throw stuff in there."

All he could do was produce a sideways glance at her.

He only had a few minutes to prepare his master plan. Hastily, he made his way into the living room and plugged in the huge stereo to the nearest outlet. "Now where'd I put it?" He rushed into his bedroom and swiped both a cassette and a cassette case. He slid the cassette into the slot on the radio and stood up just as Samantha walked into the room.

She sat her purse on the round table in the center of the area before sitting down on one of the couches.

He sat too, moving a fluffy pillow out of his way.

"Where's Ryan?"

"Why? Do you like him more than me?" He tilted his head to the side.

She snickered. "Is that a trick question?"

He smiled again, shining that smile that made her blush. Then he shifted, putting one leg underneath the other. While doing so, he handed her a colorful plastic case.

"The second album's done already?" she exclaimed once she held it in her hands.

"*Steel City Pride* is done, but it won't be released right away. We're releasing the first song in the meantime."

She turned the case over and over as she admired her own handiwork. The tiny print on the back corner proclaimed: *Photography by Samantha Denvy*. The dazzling grins of Luke and Ryan stared back at her gratefully. The image was clear, and the background sparkled while the rest of the band stood arched around the other two; they were cool and ready to take on the night. Turning it over once more, she scanned the track list.

Looking up at Luke, she started to hand the case back to him. Her arm stopped midway and her brow furrowed in confusion. She could've sworn something inside it moved from one side to the other. "Is the cassette in here?"

"Why wouldn't it be?"

"Are you going to make me open this thing?"

He threw up his hands in protest. "I'm not making you do anything."

She rolled her eyes jokingly. Slowly, but anxiously, she cracked open the case. To her surprise, there was no cassette tape resting in the grooved lining. Instead, it held a fine-looking, glistening diamond ring. Her mouth dropped instantly, and she was speechless. She picked it up with her fingertips like it was some fragile entity that would shatter if she grasped it too tightly.

"May I?" He said softly.

She glanced up at him and then back down at the ring. She didn't want to give it to him; it was too precious; but, she gently placed it in his palm.

Ever so smoothly, Luke slipped off the couch. He skipped a few tracks on the cassette he had put into the player until "Forever Mine" echoed through the speakers. He got down on his right knee, and took her hand. "Samantha, I love you. You're the most talented, heartwarming, and compassionate girl I've ever met. I want to spend my life making you happy. I want to see that reassuring and radiant smile when I wake up in the morning and right before I close my eyes at night. You're a breath of fresh air with a reassuring grin that can help me through a hopeless night. You give me confidence and make me feel like a man, even if I'm sensitive at times. I—" He laughed. "I want you to be 'Forever Mine.' That is, if you'll have me."

Her eyes found his, and she blushed. She didn't say anything, which made him even more nervous.

After what felt like hours, he couldn't wait any longer. "Well? Are you going to marry me or not?"

She nodded frantically as tears of joy began to well up.

In one swift motion, he had the expensive rock on her finger.

She flung her arms around his neck and kissed him eagerly. "I'll definitely be forever yours!"

"Is that the sound of happiness I hear?" Ryan walked through the door with a pretty model hanging from his arm. "So, I take it you didn't break his heart?"

"Nope." Samantha beamed. "And I'm not going to."

Chapter 16

Passion

They decided not to wait long to have the wedding. It didn't have to be as elaborate and complicated as the Hextons', but it had to reflect who they were. So, they chose to exchange vows back home in Pittsburgh because, after all, home is where the heart is.

A cozy nostalgia hit Luke when he entered the same church that he had said goodbye to not long before his rise to fame and fortune. Before everyone arrived, he had a few moments with his parents.

"Look how grown up you are!" Mrs. Cavarelli stood back to admire her son. Her blue, soulful eyes, the same color as Luke's, shone with tears. She wrapped him in a hug.

Mr. Cavarelli, who was just as tall as his son, stretched out his hand. "Congratulations, Luke. I'm proud of the man you've become."

Luke shook his father's hand, but, as he did, he thought about how much of a man he really was. His father would take back that statement in a heartbeat if he knew about the Bellano situation.

Mr. Cavarelli was a real kind of tough, not a cheap impression. He grew up during the Depression and knew what it meant to work hard. Sadly, he was laid off from the steel mill and had to go into an early retirement.

"Oh, you look so handsome!" Mrs. Cavarelli continued to dote. "My son, the rock star!"

The three of them stared at one another, not saying a word. Then, Mrs. Cavarelli decided to ease the tension: "Oh honey, it's not that we didn't think you could sing. It's just that we knew the music business wasn't easy. But now it doesn't matter, because you've made it, and we're so proud of you."

"I'm sure you're working hard," Mr. Cavarelli said.

"I am," Luke said with a confident nod. "I'm glad you guys aren't mad at me anymore because of my career choice." He hugged his parents and breathed a sigh of relief.

Meanwhile, Samantha was getting ready at her parents' house.

"Gorgeous!" Mr. Denvy peeked through the doorway after Samantha had her dress on.

"I'm not ready yet!" Samantha jokingly threw a shoe at the door.

"Sam, stop being impatient!" Mrs. Denvy shouted at her husband. "If you want to do something productive, go bring in the bouquets from the kitchen table."

Mr. Denvy followed his orders and brought back the flowers. "I'm glad your sister offered to make these."

Mrs. Denvy met him at the doorway and took the bouquets. "One less thing to pay for." She winked at him.

When it was that time, Luke tried to keep a straight posture, standing there at the head of the altar. Ryan proudly stood next to him, as giddy as ever. Luke scanned the pews and then leaned towards Ryan to whisper in his friend's ear, "There're too many people here."

"You invited them." Ryan smoothed back his already-slicked-back hair. "Come on, it's only a few friends and family. You can sing in front of a thousand strangers, but you can't profess your love for Samantha to the people who know you best?"

Luke smirked. "Call me a dweeb, then."

"I'll call you something…" Ryan headed to the back of the church for the procession.

Before Luke had a moment to process what was

happening or to change his mind, the bridal party began its procession down the aisle.

The bridal party consisted of the four band members and a few of Samantha's friends, including Emily as the Maid of Honor. Even though the wedding was small, they still stuck to a color scheme: a proud partnering of a pale teal and a sparkling gold.

Samantha's last promenade as a Denvy seemed to flash by in a second. Her dress wasn't too frilly, but it highlighted her natural elegance. It would've been a simple, strapless gown, had it not been for the flowery lace overlay. The lace on top covered from her neck to her mid-forearms. This feature gave the dress its sleek and stunning look. Her veil was long and flowing, and her wavy blond hair stayed tucked behind her ears. The guests had a good view of her diamond earrings, which her parents had been saving their money for.

When Luke got his first glimpse of her, he almost lost whatever self-control he had remaining. He couldn't fathom that, in only about an hour, the exquisite woman before him was going to be his wife, his other half. He'd have the rest of his life to hold her and love her.

The ceremony went without a glitch. At last, the priest before them proclaimed the magic words: "I now pronounce you man and wife. Luke, you may kiss your bride."

The reception was only a small party, but that didn't matter in the least. The party was still magnificent by its own standards: a group of family and friends who enjoyed each other's company. Ryan did the honor of singing "Forever Mine" for the newlyweds. Then again, it seemed that every radio station was playing the song that night in celebration of the lovable singer and his wife.

After a peaceful and food-filled honeymoon in Italy, it was time to finally settle down. Luke took a couple of weeks off following their return to LA so he and Samantha could get comfortable. Mark Arrowitcz wasn't exactly thrilled, but Luke didn't have a care in the world.

"Your eyes aren't closed!" Luke glanced over at her from the driver's seat of a rad silver corvette.

"How much longer?"

"We're almost there."

"You said that five minutes ago!"

He drove a little further up a hill on the outskirts of town. The bumpy road smoothed out at last, leading them to a dead end. "Okay, go ahead."

She opened her eyes and soaked up the grand view in front of her. No, this was impossible.

The huge mansion before them was a dream, enough to take a newfound breath away. Its cream-colored stonework and curved gray shingles gave it a palace-like feel. There were also many windows of varying heights and sizes. Two stone columns on each side led to a set of cement steps and, eventually, a porch and the door. Large and flowering bushes bloomed around the bottom border of the house itself.

"Luke, is this really ours?"

"Depends. Do you like it?"

"Well, I've only seen the outside, but—wait, do I have a choice?"

"Uh, not really, considering that I already signed the deed and started making payments."

She laughed. "I guess the guitar I bought you doesn't compare, huh?"

He parked the car in the driveway, and they emerged

from it. Samantha was eager to take it all in. Luke unlocked the door and let it swing open. He reached around the corner to flip on the light switch.

"After you."

They stepped into the hallway, onto the hardwood floor. The walls were absolutely bare, but Samantha could imagine photography being hung up every few feet. To the left was a room that Luke explained would be his private music studio. She peeked in to find that he already had his stuff moved into the big room. To the right of the hall was the living room, complete with a long-screen TV and dark furniture. Adjacent to this room was the first-floor bathroom, which didn't have a shower like the one upstairs. This didn't make much of a difference though, because it was painted a deep, oceanic blue and had a wide sink and bright bulbs attached to the mirror.

Across the hall, on the opposite side of the house, was a wide laundry room and an office space that seemed ideal for Samantha. Instead of turning left or right at the end of this new hall, one could go straight and come to an open space that served as the dining room. Just beyond, then, stood the kitchen.

The staircase that connected the two massive floors was located back over between Luke's studio and the kitchen. Samantha rushed up the steps two at a time, making sure that she'd arrive before Luke. She discovered the master bedroom, second-floor bath, and two guest rooms.

"Did you see what's in the master?" Luke asked as he came up behind her.

She was a statue in the bedroom, examining the bed at the left wall, the dressers, and not to mention the extra couch and TV that was set up in there as well. Then she saw it. "There's a balcony!"

There were two sliding doors near the bed that led to a small, but sturdy and fenced-in, balcony. Looking out over the edge, she observed the property and her eyes came across the in-ground pool directly below. Her hair blew lightly with the wind, and she felt Luke's warmth by her arm.

"Well?"

She shook her head. "I love it. I absolutely adore it."

"More than me?"

She turned around and kissed him at once, almost knocking him over. "Never!"

"Good. Let's keep it that way."

* * *

On the night before Luke went back to the studio to work on the band's next tour, he held Samantha in his arms down on the patio, right in front of the pool. The LA weather was working in their favor that night; there wasn't a single cloud in the sky, and the pink sun took its sweet time disappearing over the horizon. All was quiet and peaceful, until Luke turned the radio on.

"Trying to hear yourself?"

"Just trying to calm down. I'm paranoid about this next tour."

"Do you think your second album is that bad?"

He shrugged. "No clue. All I know is we have to top Bellano on the presentation front."

Samantha sat up and looked at her husband. "Why do you have to outdo Bellano? Can't you just be yourself?"

"The Leather Heartbreaks' video skyrocketed on MTV. Our last video wasn't nearly as clever or impressive. I'm trying to be myself, but it's hard. You wouldn't understand."

"What do you mean? Luke, I know all about competition! My photography suffered for years because of it."

He backed down. "I'm sorry," he said gently. "Our bands are so similar, it's like we have no choice but to try and beat each other." He pulled her closer.

"I thought you were a fan of Tony Bellano."

Luke sighed. "I am. I was. That is, until he made me feel like a fool." He stood up suddenly, leaving her alone on the patio loveseat. "He stormed right in and told me that I wasn't good enough, and that I never will be."

She kept silent for a moment, smiling faintly when the sound of Luke's hypnotic and euphonious voice belted through the speakers of the radio. The song had just been released, but, already, The Leather Heartbreaks moved up to the tenth spot on the charts while The Steel City Boys were pushed down to the fifteenth. Maybe Luke had a right to worry.

"But, you know he's just saying things to discourage you."

"What if that's how the audience sees me?"

"That's a downright lie, and you know it. If that were the case, you wouldn't have any fans or a second album."

Luke turned around to face her. "Do you know why I'm so pessimistic and insecure?"

She shook her head. "Tell me."

Cautiously, he sat back down, as if she would bite him if he drew too near. He stared at the ground for a minute, trying to think of the right words and how he could explain it in a way that wouldn't sound lame and wimpy.

"When I was in high school, I was an outcast. You know, the music nerd. The band geek. Don't let Ryan fool you, he clung to my side most of the time. He went back and forth from nerd to bad boy. Anyway, it wasn't praiseworthy to be the Catholic 'good boy.' I was constantly made fun of and thrown around. Ryan would stand up for me, but he couldn't always be there.

"Look, I wasn't going to go to senior prom, mind you. I would've rather stayed home and busied myself with a radio—"

"Did you have a date?" Samantha shot up, interested.

"Yeah, but we just went as friends. We went our separate ways after the Grand March. Anyway, the school asked the band to play a song or two. Everything went great. Afterwards, I offered to haul the equipment out to the car so the guys could enjoy the rest of the night—don't look at me like that! You know big dances aren't my thing.

"So, I went outside and the usual gang of bullies approached me. They backed me up against the car and verbally abused me. If it wasn't because of my religion, it was because I was a gay nerd who couldn't keep a girlfriend—but you know that it wasn't that I couldn't hold on to one, I just focused on my music—or it was that my songs were stupid. You get the gist. They beat me up so bad that day. I mean, the blood… I didn't come out of my room for three days, until all the swelling went down. I couldn't defend myself; there were too many of them. I tried."

"That's terrible! Didn't you tell your parents or a teacher or anybody?"

"I was too afraid. My old man would've called me a

coward for not standing up to them, and he never would've let me hear the end of it. I just couldn't retaliate. I didn't have it in me. If I told a teacher, well, then it would've cycled around the school and eventually to home. I didn't even tell Ryan because that would've shown how much I actually rely on him. I caught a bus home that night, and when people at school asked what happened, I said that I was tired and just left. To be honest, this wasn't the first time I had been beaten up by them."

"And you've kept all these insecurities with you through the years."

He looked up and laughed wryly. "Ryan is my bodyguard."

"That's not exactly a bad thing," she pointed out with a grin.

"Every time I feel a sense of pride or a glimmer of hope about myself, I end up shutting it out, and I let my inner critic control me. I know I need to change, but it's just so hard. I can barely talk about it, let alone manage it."

"You're talking to me, aren't you? That's a start."

"Yeah. I mean, but I've always felt comfortable with women. I'm not like other guys, so I don't know how to relate to them. Bellano isn't helping. Whenever I was at my lowest back then, I used him as my comfort. I could always pop a cassette in and be whisked away to another world. His toughness made me feel like I could be just like him, just as confident. Now my own idol is my bully."

Samantha hugged him tightly. "Sometimes people aren't who they appear to be."

They stayed there, watching the sun make its great escape. The water in the pool rippled slightly. For a moment,

Luke felt relieved that he had found someone who understood him completely. They really could tell each other anything.

Just then, a Leather Heartbreaks' song came on the radio. Luke couldn't deal with it. He didn't need his enemy following him to his home, a place where he was allowed to be himself with no harassments. Without a second thought, he got up and unplugged the radio. He edged closer to the pool and swung his arm out like he was going to slam dunk the radio in the water.

Samantha jumped up and dashed in front of him, blocking him from finishing his vengeful task. "Luke, stop!"

"Why should I?"

"Because it's only a radio! It's not Bellano himself. You're overreacting."

"But why can't he understand? Why can't he just leave me alone?"

"One day he will," Samantha said, a tremble in her voice as if even she didn't know what she meant by that statement. "Luke," she whispered, "Please stop."

Slowly, he dropped the radio to the ground, and he was trembling. "I'm a mess," he said through the tears.

"But you're one mess that I'm happy to help clean up." She leaned up and kissed him passionately.

In that moment, he remembered why he loved her so much. She was truly his angel. She was his; he had her.

Chapter 17

The Manager

"I can lend you the money," Ryan insisted.

"No, Ryan. I'm flattered, but I don't want you to spend your money on me. I can handle it," Luke said.

They were riding in the elevator to the third floor of the studio.

"Just get a mortgage."

"What do you think I did?"

Ryan shrugged. "But if I give you money for the mansion, then I'll have less to spend on myself, which means I can quit these things." He patted the box of cigarettes in his pocket.

"If you want to bad enough, you can pay for the housekeeper." Luke laughed. "Better yet, you could be the housekeeper for all I care!"

Ryan shot him a dirty look. "You realize that I haven't cleaned the apartment once since you moved out, right?"

Luke didn't have a chance to respond because when the elevator chimed and the doors slid open, Mark Arrowitcz was there, practically trying to drag the guys out.

"Where've you been?"

"What do you mean? We're not late," Ryan said calmly.

"No, but we have to finish this song!" He stormed off down the hall and into The Steel City Boys' studio.

Luke and Ryan sat down and worked on the song that they had been composing. They stared intently at the piece of paper with the hand-written lyrics. They had some down time until the kickoff of the *Steel City Pride* tour, but, in Mark Arrowitcz's mind, it was never too early to start working ahead.

You don't deserve a boy like him,
He'll break your heart,
Right from the start,
But only if you let him get that far.

I watch him sweet talk his way straight
into your life,
Honey, that boy is not a man.
I'll never hurt you the way he will,
I got the time,
So let me love you for just a little while

And as the tempo grew faster:

If you don't like me
You can leave me
But I really think
You should give me a chance, babe,
'Cause he's just not your style

"The tempo needs to be dropped in the beginning. It needs to be slower," Ryan said.

"Yeah, but it can't be too slow. Let's hold 'deserve' out a little longer. Make that a dotted quarter note."

"Okay. How about we put a rest in between 'you' and 'for.'"

Luke thought for a moment. "I don't think we really need that pause, though."

"I guess. If that's what you think."

They continued on to the chorus line. Luke kept cutting lyrics and adding dynamic markings with a red pen. Before they moved onto the second verse, Ryan stopped him.

"Hey, Luke?"

"Hmmm?"

"Can I take the lead on this song?"

"Uh… I don't think that's such a great idea."

"Why not?"

"Ryan, no one's ever heard your voice. It might not go over so well."

"But—"

"It won't!" Mark Arrowitcz commented in passing, without even hearing the whole conversation.

"Look, this song is different. It'll give me the chance to show the fans what I can do. I can do it. Besides, why can't I have more vocal parts?" Ryan protested.

"Ryan, you're so much better on guitar. I'm not nearly as good. If you take the lead, what am I going to do?"

"You'll get a glimpse of what it's like to be in the boring world of backup." Ryan was getting agitated.

"Ryan—"

"Luke! Come on, dude, you know I can do it."

"I—"

"You think I can't sing, is that it?"

"No! You know that's not it."

Ryan sighed. "Just give me a fun guitar solo, then."

He stood up abruptly and started for the door.

"Ryan, don't leave! I'm sorry. I'm just used to being the lead. You can have it. I'd be honored if you took it."

"You're lying just to make me feel better."

"You know I wouldn't do that to you."

The best friends locked eyes. Without saying a word, they read each other. To Luke, Ryan's typical optimism had vanished and was replaced by a desperate, pained look. The moment took Luke back to the days when Ryan looked out for him, and when he kept Ryan from being completely reckless. What were they doing? Fighting wasn't in their nature.

"You can sing it," Luke said. "The song actually fits you."

Ryan nodded. "Thanks, dude. I appreciate it."

"You know," Luke continued, "Maybe we could add in that rest you were talking about."

The boys' little tiff went unnoticed, and they didn't discuss it at all. Ryan would have the lead on the new song. Meanwhile, preparations continued for the band's tour. The excitement was building as the dates grew closer. The new song would be released as a single, a floater without a spot on the second album, and it would be performed during the tour's sets.

One Saturday morning, only two weeks before the tour, Luke got an unsuspected call from Ryan.

"What do you mean, Mark Arrowitcz quit?" Luke couldn't believe it..

"Mr. Langderate told me he just walked into the studio, said, 'I'm done, I quit' and then he packed up his stuff and left."

"Now we don't have a manager and the tour is two

weeks away! I know he wasn't the best, but still. And, no offense, but why didn't Mr. Langderate call me?"

"You didn't give the studio your new number at the
mansion. You only gave it to me."

"Oh."

"Anyway," Ryan went on cheerfully, "Mr. Langderate
also said not to worry. He'll help us find a new manager. I
think he already has someone in mind."

"Okay." Luke paused for a moment, remembering that
it was the weekend and for once they didn't have a concert.
"Thanks for calling, man. Wanna come over tonight?"

"Sorry, dude, got a date."

"Seriously?" Luke suddenly became interested.

"Why does everyone think…"

"Well, considering I thought that Ruby the Firebird was
your girlfriend, I guess we just don't know what to expect
from you. Besides, you mostly specialize in one-night stands."

"Not this time. She's real, I promise."

"Good luck with that." Luke hung up the phone.

"Everything alright?" Samantha walked into the hall
where Luke was standing.

"Mark just quit, and now we need a new manager."

She shook her head. "Why'd he quit?"

"I don't know. Probably because we wanted too much
control."

Samantha moved past him and headed for the door.
She opened it and let the sunlight flood onto the floor.

"What are you doing?"

"Delivery guys are going to be here soon. I ordered new
patio furniture."

Luke looked at her oddly. "What's wrong with what we
have?"

She shrugged. "It doesn't really match and," she whispered the next part, "It's not very comfortable."

Luke left it at that and went outside to grab the mail, hoping that he could forget Ryan's phone call. When he got back inside, he flipped through the stack, mostly junk. The credit card bill caught his eye, so he tore it open.

"Samantha," he called. "Why is our credit card bill so high?"

She took the bill from him and skimmed over it. "Well, we needed a few things to spice up the place. And, I figured I should add to my wardrobe in case we get invited to fancy parties, and—"

"Honey, look, I don't mind you spending, but we need to save, too. I don't want to spend all the cash just because we have it."

Samantha shook her head. "Luke, we're rich now. We don't have to watch every dime like we used to."

He frowned. "No, but I'd rather make sure we have enough to donate to a few charities."

"And we will. I'm not going to spend it all." She laughed.

Luke thought for a moment. "I guess you're right. Besides, you always had to worry about money back in Pittsburgh. You do deserve to spend a few bucks."

Samantha slipped on shoes so that she could go out to greet the delivery truck driver who had just arrived. "Exactly! That's my point. Hey, when did you get so careful with money?"

"Being a married man makes you think," he said with an accompanying smile. How could he be mad? Samantha did deserve the best.

In almost no time at all, Mr. Langderate announced

that he had found a superb manager who would be more than thrilled to take on the boys as clients. Luke offered to host a dinner at his house for formal introductions. He invited Mr. Langderate, the new manager, Tyler, Adam, Joe, Ryan, and Ryan's girlfriend, who had yet to be seen.

"I should've called Emily." Samantha was trying to tend to the chicken that was in the oven while the timer went off on the microwave.

"You're not a bad cook." Luke entered the kitchen, hoping he could be of some assistance.

"Looks done to me." She set the meat plate on top of the stove before turning off the oven. "Can you take those two bowls and set them on the dining room table?"

"I got it. Do you want these candles lit, babe?"

"Yes, please." She finished setting the table.

The doorbell rang and Luke rushed to discover Ryan and the guys at the door first. "Hey, boys!"

"Hey! Luke, I'd like to introduce you to—"

"NO!" Samantha had just come back out of the kitchen and happened to glance up to see who was at the door. "Not you."

"Wait a second, have you two met before?" Ryan was confused.

Sure enough, Samantha's old roommate was standing in the doorway, hanging all over Ryan.

"Natalie was my roommate before I had to move in at the Hexton mansion. What are you doing in LA?"

"I'm an actress now." Natalie tilted her head to the side.

"Sure you are."

"I am! Look up my agent if you don't believe me. And just what are you doing in Luke Cavarelli's house? You know, the singer?" She said it like she was talking to a child.

"Missus Luke Cavarelli!" Samantha flashed her wedding ring. "You don't watch TV?"

"I had no idea."

But before Samantha could spit out another nasty comment, the doorbell rang again. This time, Mr. Langderate was there, holding a bottle of wine.

"I hope you don't mind; I brought the missus." He smiled at the white-haired lady next to him.

"Not at all. Come on in," Luke said.

Mrs. Langderate stepped into the door, dressed to the hilt, as if it were book club night at the Ritz, furs and all.

"And now, I'd like to introduce you boys to your new manager—if you'll have her. This is Miss Jennifer Mignonne."

There was no need to conceal it: Jennifer Mignonne was an absolute goddess. She was approximately thirty, but not a day older. She whipped her ebony hair out of her sharp, sapphire eyes. The eyes! They somehow illuminated her even and perfect silhouette. One second, they transformed her into a naughty sex symbol, and the next, they made her a sincere angel. Truly, she could bring any man to his knees, young or old, and, when she spoke, her voice projected out like pure velvet.

Her heels clicked rhythmically on the floor as she shook hands with each of the band members. She smiled widely when she shook Luke's hand.

"It's a real pleasure to meet you," she said simply.

The rectangular dining room table was massive enough to accommodate all of the dinner guests. Luke, Samantha, and Tyler sat on the side nearest the kitchen, while Ryan,

Natalie, and Adam were across from them. Mr. Langderate made up his mind to put himself next to Jennifer at one end of the table, leaving poor Joe to be mentally picked and prodded at by Mrs. Langderate on the other end.

It was an awkward dinner party. Luke and Ryan conversed heavily with Jennifer and Mr. Langderate, while the other three band members joined in only occasionally. Samantha didn't even look up at Natalie. Mrs. Langderate kept blabbing on about anything and everything. It may have started out with the weather, but it soon turned to the foolishness of the youth, and then it easily became centered around the old woman herself.

Samantha smiled and answered politely, but she kept a watchful eye on Jennifer. Something about this manager made her feel uneasy.

"People doubt my managing skills because I'm so young, but I have a lot of experience in the music business."

Mr. Langderate leaned forward. "She used to be a singer."

"Oh," Ryan said. "Then why did you become a manager?"

Jennifer started for her wine glass. "Well, I wanted to help other bands and singers make it to the top. I guess you could say I wanted to get on the business side of things. Besides, you can't get crazy famous when your stage name's Velvet." She took a sip of the white wine. "I see so much potential in you guys. You've made it so far, but I think I can take you even farther."

Luke rolled his eyes. "You better be prepared to deal with Tony Bellano."

"I think I can take him," she said matter-of-factly.

Ryan laughed. "Now that, I'd like to see."

"Don't laugh," Jennifer said. "I know what I'm doing. You think I can't handle an arrogant singer like Bellano?"

"Good luck!" Ryan stabbed a piece of chicken with his heavy fork. Clearly, Samantha had bought the best silverware.

Mrs. Langderate kept running her mouth. She looked over at Joe. "Why do rockstars keep insisting on long hair that makes them look like girls? I can give you the name of Henry's barber."

Joe's eyes popped. He stared down at his plate, unsure of how to reply.

Samantha tried hard to stifle a snicker, but her efforts were fruitless. The smirk on her face didn't last too long, though. She glanced over at Jennifer just in time to see her trying to come on to Luke. At least, that's what it seemed like.

They were only inches apart from each other, Jennifer moving closer every minute. The menacing glow in her eyes remained fixated on Luke.

Suddenly, Samantha elbowed Luke under the table. In a mere second, he snapped out of his daze and was welcomed back to reality.

After dinner, Luke took Jennifer and Mr. Langderate on a tour of the mansion, which ended in Luke's private studio with the rest of the band, except for Ryan.

"I'll help you clean up." Ryan stood up and pushed his chair back.

"Thanks." Samantha began gathering up the plates.

Meanwhile, Mrs. Langderate started condemning Natalie's choice of fashion and her overall appearance. This pleased Samantha greatly, but she turned away to the kitchen so that no one would notice.

"Ryan, I'm telling you, you've got to get away from her," Samantha whispered. "She will use you."

"Ah." Ryan scoffed. "She seems fine to me. She'll be an awesome manager."

"Not Jennifer, Natalie. Do you know how many one night stands she had in our apartment?"

"Hey, I'm a one-night-stander. Not my first rodeo."

"But you're not malicious and sneaky about it. You're at least open to a longer-term relationship. Ryan, the only difference between her and a prostitute is that the men don't pay her when they leave. How'd you get hooked up with her anyway?"

Ryan shrugged. "She was an obsessed fan who had a backstage pass to see me after a show. I thought she was hot, so I went with it."

Samantha shook her head. "Bad move, Delhart."

"Now you sound like your husband."

"I'm just warning you. I don't want you to get hurt." She put the stopper in the sink and let the water run. "And, speaking of my husband, did you see Jennifer try to make a move on Luke?"

Ryan took a minute to think. "She did a little, but I wouldn't worry about it. He didn't seem interested."

Once the dishes were done, Samantha emerged back into the dining room. To her surprise, Mrs. Langderate was admiring her framed photographs hanging on the walls of the hallway. She was gaping at the photo of the blue board-walk that had captured Luke the moment he saw it.

"Where did you buy these?"

"I didn't buy them. I'm a photographer."

Mrs. Langderate lit up. "Amazing."

"Would you care to see the rest of the house?"

"I don't want to impose."

"Oh no, I insist."

Samantha started, and then stopped. She looked at Natalie, who was sitting all alone at the table. She sighed. "Come on."

Natalie looked up. "I don't wanna be in the way."

"Get over here, before I change my mind."

Natalie hurried over next to Mrs. Langderate.

Before the beginning of the tour, Samantha grabbed her wine glass. She was going to need it. Thank goodness she was finally of age.

"The furniture, this artwork, incredible…" Mrs. Langderate said.

It felt good to have someone gawk in admiration. Then again, the Langderates had money too.

Natalie couldn't believe her eyes. When they finished the tour and ended up back downstairs, she just stood there, dumbfounded and jealous. She crossed her arms and kept sighing.

Samantha played it for all it was worth. "I love this new life. It doesn't get any better than this."

Natalie shot Samantha an evil look and stormed off to go find Ryan.

Soon afterward, the dinner party guests had filtered out, leaving the Cavarellis to peace and quiet in the bliss of their home. They put themselves in front of the television. While channel-surfing, Luke stumbled across MTV and found one of the band's music videos.

Luke was immersed in it as if he had never seen it before. Samantha watched carelessly at first, but then became engrossed in the content.

The video included live clips from several of the band's concerts. The camera whooshed past hundreds of screaming fangirls who were all attempting to catch the boys' attention. One even shouted, "I love you, Luke!"

She let this sink in for a moment. It was evident that Luke's life was full of women. There were thousands of pretty fans, plus a sexy manager, and, well, her. Where did she fall in the spectrum? How was she to compare herself to someone like Jennifer Mignonne?

"You okay?" He touched her arm, and it startled her.

"Do you really love me?"

Luke was taken aback. "O—of course. Samantha, you know you're the only one I love. Wait, where is this coming from?"

"Nowhere. Just double checking." She made herself comfortable on his shoulder. "I love you too."

But, after that night, Samantha didn't feel the same about their marriage. It seemed to take longer and longer for Luke to come home each night. Every time she looked at him, he seemed further and further away. Some days, he didn't even talk to her. He would just say that it had been a busy day, and he was tired. Samantha twisted and twisted everything in her mind. *What if he doesn't love me?*

Chapter 18

Light 'em Up

Ryan Delhart smoked about three packs of cigarettes a week. Luke couldn't remember how old Ryan was when he started. No one in the band's group of friends smoked, so the fascination didn't originate from there. Somewhere along the way in high school, Ryan did it so he could join the cool kids and not always be one of the band nerds. Then again, Luke remembered a pretty girl who needed to be impressed. Unfortunately, he ended up stuck with the nasty addiction. Ever since the Surgeon General's warning about the dangers of cigarettes, Luke pushed Ryan to stop; Ryan didn't care.

Unlike Bellano, however, Ryan didn't let his smoking become a part of the band's image. Sure, it may have reflected on him personally, but it didn't define The Steel City Boys. Luke knew that there was a part of Ryan that wanted to quit smoking, but there was another part that said no. So, Ryan remained undecided and promised that he'd reconsider quitting after the launch of the new album.

"I've smoked for this many years," Ryan said. "I highly doubt if a few more months are going to kill a young guy like me."

Steel City Pride went off with a bang, thanks to Jennifer. So far, it was the band's best album, and the fans were eating it up like ice cream on an August afternoon. Money streamed in, and their songs seemed to be everywhere, even in television commercials. Almost half of the album charted, but some songs failed to make it to number one, peaking at two or three. The artists in the music industry were hot that year, spicing up the competition.

The boys were looking forward to their first tour as actual headliners. The first couple of months for them were extraordinary. It was so hard to believe that all of the thrilled and screaming fans were there for them. They rocked the stage every night, mostly to crowds of young girls who were excited to see their heartthrobs.

But, it wasn't just the music; Luke and Ryan's stage presence attracted attention. Wherever one was, the other wasn't too far away. They had an energizing fluidity that kept fans fascinated on every performance. There was a confidence between them, a bond that was irreplaceable. Their friendship was truly authentic, with smiles that couldn't easily be feigned and stage quirks that made their relationship even more lovable.

Luke and Ryan had a perfect blend of sound. When Ryan let loose on an improvised guitar solo, Luke had a knack for vocalizing to match the solo. Likewise, Ryan could figure out chords to play while Luke improvised and repeated lyrics. Their ability to listen to each other made them a sensation on a live stage. Sometimes Luke would let Ryan finish singing lines so that, by the end of the song, they were in harmony.

They were also known to be hilarious storytellers on stage. Tyler, Adam, or Joe could suggest something dumb that happened in the past, and Luke and Ryan would continue the story, cracking up the audience.

One night, Luke and Ryan finished getting ready in their joint dressing room.

Luke rolled up the sleeves of his white shirt. "You ready to take lead?"

Ryan sat before the mirror, staring at himself intently.

"Dude, are you alright?"

Ryan brought the cigarette to his lips and, before inhaling, he murmured, "How long have you known me?"

"Long enough to know that you're definitely not alright." Luke's image grew closer in the streaky mirror.

"How'd you get so lucky?" Ryan asked in a trance.

"What do you mean?"

"Look at you: you love your job and you're happily married to the woman of your dreams."

Luke folded his arms. "Oh, c'mon. You love your job too, and you know it. Is this about your girlfriend?"

"I don't know. This relationship just isn't going how I hoped."

"How is it go—"

The door swung open so hard that it hit the wall, causing both boys to jump.

Jennifer stormed in. "You're still in here? It's five after eight. Get out there!"

Luke took off and, as he did, he heard Ryan mumble, "I just want to be loved."

The concert started off strong, with an upbeat and dance-friendly song called "This is Us." After the audience was pumped up, the band set up for "Love You for a Little While."

Nerves threatened to bring Ryan down, but he carried on and did extremely well with the first verse of the song. Surprisingly, the fans took kindly to the change in voice. But, by the time he was halfway through, his voice had disappeared and had been replaced by an evil coughing fit. His throat was dry and he could feel it trying to close up on him. He doubled over and tried not to be noticed, but that was impossible because the band had stopped playing and all eyes were turned to him. It just didn't want to let up, so he waved them on and rushed offstage to find water.

Luke jumped in and started where Ryan had left off. Ryan eventually made his way back, and the boys finished the song in a smooth-sounding duet.

The applause thundered after the song, leaving the band to bow and smile.

All of a sudden, the applause faded and an annoying, incessant buzz filled the room. It was the fire alarms.

The massive crowd dashed for the exits as if the auditorium were a mall on Black Friday. The shrill screams bounced off the walls.

"Head for the side door!" Jennifer struggled to yell over the noise.

A chaotic scramble left thousands of fans and a bewildered band outside in the parking lot, wondering what was going on. There were no visible flames or the presence of smoke from the outside. Soon enough, though, blaring sirens approached and the investigation was underway. Meanwhile, security had to block the fans from bombarding the band.

Luke shook his head. "I don't understand."

Ryan remained silent.

"We're gonna have to pay for any damages," Luke continued.

"Not if it wasn't our fault," Jennifer said, arms folded.

Ryan sat on the stone steps. A look of worry came over him, and he buried his face in his hands.

"Ryan?" Luke put a hand on his friend's shoulder, then he thought about it for a moment. "No. No, Ryan, please tell me it wasn't."

Ryan nodded, head down. "The cigarette must've fallen from the ashtray in the dressing room. I guess I didn't put it out, and the ashtray was on the edge of the dresser."

Jennifer raised her eyebrows. "It was carpet, not hardwood."

"We were in a hurry, and—and—" Ryan's voice began to break. He couldn't hold it in any longer.

"I can't believe this," Luke kept repeating, pacing back and forth.

"I'm sorry, I didn't mean—"

"I told you, you should've quit."

"I want to, but—"

"But what?" Luke's voice raged, and some of the fans were starting to gawk. "Was this worth it? Our fans could've been hurt or even killed. We've put them in harm's way. Now we have to pay for this because of your stupidity. We may as well give up. The band's done. The media will kill us."

"Not on my watch," Jennifer interrupted.

"I'm sorry!" Ryan moaned.

"Stop saying that! And don't tell me you're sorry for that coughing fit earlier too. The concert almost ended there. You're just lucky I could fill in for you. You beg me for the lead and this is what I get in return? You don't deserve the lead! Suddenly 'guitar boy' doesn't seem so bad, does it?" Luke let the anger flow through him. He didn't care anymore. He was tired.

Ryan jumped up and started moving towards Luke. "You think you're so great. Well, all hail the mighty Luke Cavarelli! Do you think you're the best singer there's ever been? Fine, I made a mistake, I own that. God knows I'm not the only one with a flaw. Is this the thanks I get for helping you stand up to Bellano? You act like a little girl every time he walks by! All you do is tell me to quit smoking. Can't you see I have a problem, and I can't help myself? Do you realize how difficult it is? If you were so worried about me, friend, then maybe we wouldn't be in this situation! And what's so wrong with wanting to take lead? You just need to be in control of everything! You didn't even let me write the song the way I wanted! What am I even here for? You don't need me."

By this time, Ryan was so close to Luke that he hit him roughly on the chest. Luke almost lost his footing, but he caught his balance.

"I'm done. I quit," Ryan shouted. "I want outta the band. I'm tired of being screwed over."

"You're still under contract for another few months," Jennifer explained. "You can leave after that, unless you want to pay the fees."

Ryan groaned.

Luke pointed at Ryan. "Promise me you'll put on a game face until this is over. Promise me you'll at least act like we're friends. It's for the fans."

"Fine," Ryan answered while looking at the ground.

Luke and Ryan's relationship didn't get any better during the rest of the tour. They talked to each other when they had to, and they each spent more time with the other band members. Ryan gravitated toward Joe, while Luke felt better talking to Tyler and Adam. Luke needed space. He just couldn't forgive Ryan's carelessness. Not yet.

The report came back that a cigarette had fallen onto the carpet and began smoldering. The band did eventually have to pay for the damages, and for the fact that the remainder of the concert was canceled. It swallowed a good chunk of money, and Luke preferred not to think about it. The media exploded with the fight. Fans had seen the brawl, so it couldn't be denied. Some tabloids even tried to argue that Ryan purposely knocked the cigarette down when he went offstage to find water.

When Luke returned home from the tour, all he wanted was to be consoled by his one and only true love, the only friend that he seemed to have left.

She sat on the couch with him while he poured out his heart.

"What did I do that was so wrong? Am I that bad of a front man?"

"No, it's just—" Samantha paused to find the right words.

"What?" The pain in his eyes was apparent and striking.

"You never want to give Ryan a chance."

"That's not true! I gave him a chance, and he blew it."

"You need to help him and work with him. Smoking may not be his real problem."

"He also said he didn't feel loved."

"It's Natalie, isn't it?" She looked up at him.

"Probably. But I should've helped him. I need to help him. Do you think it's too late?"

"Ryan's soft, despite his tough guy vibe. Believe me, he doesn't want to lose you any more than you do him."

Luke sighed shakily. "It'll take time, but I have to do it."

"I know you can," she said. "Luke, smoking is like any drug addiction—no matter how much Ryan wants to quit, he isn't strong enough to do it himself. It's a disease he'll be fighting for the rest of his life. He needs someone like you to support him."

They remained quiet for a moment in each other's arms, absorbing the moment.

"Luke?"

"Hmmm?"

"I missed you."

"I always miss you."

"Do you ever wonder?"

"About?" He sat up, alert and ready to change the subject.

"If you hadn't met me, what would your love life be like now?"

"I don't get it. What do you want me to say?"

"Well, would you be with a fan like Natalie or with someone you work with like… Jennifer?"

"Whoa, whoa, whoa!" He laughed. "A fan, maybe, but Jennifer? Samantha, if I wouldn't start a relationship with a music video actress, then why would I hook up with my own manager! Why are you asking me this?"

"Well, you've been with her a lot lately. She's attractive and, uh, you seemed interested when we first met her."

Luke couldn't believe this. "I'm not—Samantha! Hey, if you think I would ever cheat on you, then you're so far beyond wrong."

"Okay," she whispered. "I'm sorry. It just looked like she wanted to make a move. That's all."

"I'll see to it that she won't." He kissed her.

"Thank you, Mr. Cavarelli."

"Anytime, Mrs. Cavarelli."

Ryan never made any real indication that he was going to quit the band. One day, not long after the tour ended, he walked into the studio (alone because Luke stopped coming to work with him), and Jennifer sprang on him.

"Contracts are up soon. I gotta know: you in or out?"

Luke came out of the recording booth and stumbled

across Ryan.

"I'm in!" Ryan said automatically, as he sat a box of donuts on the table. He looked at Luke. "Can I talk to you for a minute?"

"Sure." Luke followed Ryan out the door and into the hall.

"Let's walk," Ryan said. He had to prepare himself, so he took a deep breath before diving into it. "Luke, I really want to apologize for that night. I said some things that were way out of line—"

"They weren't, actually," Luke admitted.

"It doesn't matter. I shouldn't have been so blunt. I hurt you, and I'm sorry." They got to the end of the hall. "Let's go outside. You know what I need to do."

The elevator chimed and they waited for a band called Totally Viva to step out.

"Hey, how you doing?" Ryan greeted a tall brunette that stalked out.

The blond beauty behind her made eye contact with Luke and flashed him a wide smile.

"I'm married," Luke answered quickly while trying to catch the elevator door.

"Look," Ryan got serious again. "I never wanted to leave. I just want a little more involvement. Sometimes you're too controlling."

Luke sighed. "I know, and I'm sorry for that."

"What do you say? Can we move on like nothing ever happened?"

"For sure."

It was a sunny, perfect Los Angeles day. Ryan leaned up against the wall and sadly pulled out his cigarettes and lighter.

Luke watched him as he pathetically tried to light it. His heart just wasn't in it. "Wait." Luke put a hand out and snatched the lighter from Ryan. "Why don't we try this?" He tossed the lighter into the nearby garbage can.

"I can't," Ryan groaned.

"Just try it."

Ryan stopped and attempted to talk about something else, but he didn't stray far. "You know, I've been thinking about it for a while." He paused. "I don't think my cigarette started it."

"What?" That caught Luke off guard.

"I thought that maybe I didn't put out the cigarette because we were in a hurry, but I always make sure I do. Even if I did forget, I don't think the ashtray was on the very edge. The more I think about it, it couldn't have tipped over by itself."

"Why didn't you say something before we paid the damages?"

"What evidence did I have? There were no cameras in the green room."

Unfortunately, Ryan was right. They couldn't have proved it.

"I put my money on Bellano," Luke said matter-of-factly.

"That's crazy. Besides, they were on tour too." Ryan let Luke's idea digest for a second. "Maybe it's not so crazy. Their first concert was the day after ours, and they would've had to pass through where we were. They were only a state or two away."

Speak of the devil. Just then, Bellano came marching

towards the door with his boys lagging behind. "Still lightin' 'em up, eh, Delhart?"

Ryan hadn't realized that he still had the cigarette clenched in his fist, half of it sticking out.

"Here, I'll get that for you." Bellano pulled out his own pocket lighter and clicked on the flame.

"No!" Ryan jumped back, letting the cigarette fall from his hand.

"A little jumpy, are we? That's what happens when you set a place on fire."

"I didn't do it," Ryan defended himself.

"Just keep on telling yourself that."

"What do you know about it?"

Bellano's lips twitched. "I know a lot about it, for your information."

"Yeah? Like what?"

Bellano laughed and turned to the door. His obnoxious guffawing echoed in the lobby.

"What do you know?" Ryan called after him. Getting madder by the second, he started to follow.

"Stop!" Luke tugged him back.

"There's our proof walking through the door."

"Let it go," Luke cautioned. "He could be bluffing. We don't know he did it. We're just making up stories to hear what we want to hear."

But, Ryan Delhart didn't let things go when he could control them. That night, he sped up the driveway to the Cavarelli mansion. He was on a mission.

The sky had grown dark by the time that Luke flung open the door and found Ryan standing there, anxious and excited.

"What's up?"

"Come on, we're going out."

"Who?"

"The band."

"What are we—"

"Just come on!"

"Samantha, I'm going out with the guys!" Luke shouted into the house. He grabbed the keys and headed for the Firebird.

"Hey, guys," Luke said as he squeezed in between Adam and Joe in the backseat.

Ryan started the car and took off.

"Where're we going?"

No answer.

It felt like they were driving to infinity, but finally Ryan steered the car into a large bus lot.

"To your right," Tyler directed from the passenger seat.

Into their view came a gigantic white tour bus with tinted windows and a painted black leather heart, making it obvious. Luke knew instantly who it belonged to: the only person who could demand a unique tour bus and actually get his way; the only one who would put it on display rather than lock it up in the garage.

"Tha—that's Th—The Leather Heartbreaks'," Luke stammered.

"And this is spray paint." Joe shoved a can in Luke's face.

"NO! We are not doing this." Luke couldn't believe his boys would stoop that low.

"Gonna take all four of us down?" Ryan pulled the can away from Luke since, clearly, he didn't want it.

"We're better than this!" Luke protested. "We can't prove he—wait! Guys!"

The guys didn't hear him or think twice. They each got out of the Firebird and took a can of paint before making a beeline for the tour bus.

Luke's mind raced in a frenzy of thoughts. He couldn't stop them, and he couldn't deny being there. There had to be cameras. A sick wave rolled up in his stomach and came crashing down as he watched his boys graffiti The Leather Heartbreaks' tour bus. The colorful lines stuck gleefully to the sides of the exterior.

Suddenly, though, his thoughts shifted to his inner hatred of Tony Bellano. As much as he agreed that The Steel City Boys' foul play was a childish overreaction, he couldn't help but hear Bellano's snide comments in the back of his head:

I've heard better. A lot better… You're too soft. You look like quitters… Don't think you can conquer The Buff—'cause no one can… You ain't nothin', and you're never gonna be. Just stay out of my road, and you won't get hurt… It was just a fluke.

In that moment, Luke felt like he was a volcano ready to explode. All he ever wanted was to be like Bellano, and now even that was a crime. Tony "The Buff" Bellano was absolutely nothing like that awesome and imposing poster image that Luke had had plastered on his bedroom wall. Bellano wasn't an inspiration anymore; he was a rival. He was like a hatchet, methodically attempting to break up the band.

Luke emerged from the car and picked up the last can of paint. He moved himself in front of the tour bus, and his finger pressed down on the nozzle, his skin feeling the tiny ridges of the plastic button. He really wasn't aware of his actions. It was like he was walking through a rainy mist or a dream. Luke Cavarelli had no presence. The harder he pressed down on the trigger, the more satisfied he became. The volcano erupted and the lava flowed almost endlessly. All the anger was released.

After the can was empty, Luke stood frozen, hypnotized.

"Luke?"

His arm slowly fell down to his side. He turned to face Ryan and the guys, who were staring at him with horrified expressions.

"You okay?" Adam asked.

Luke, coming back to his senses, nodded and trudged back to the car. They drove home in silence. When they made it to the Cavarelli mansion, Ryan didn't let Luke leave right away.

"Are you sure you're alright?"

"Never been better." Luke strode onto the porch and into his house.

Chapter 19

No More Mr. Nice Guy

"You just had to vandalize their tour bus, didn't you?" Luke hollered over the buzzing of coffee shop gossip as he and Ryan gradually followed the line to the counter. He didn't want to admit that he had taken any part in the action. Besides, it was simpler to blame Ryan.

"Did you forget that you were there too?" Ryan began shifting from one foot to the other, urgently craving his dose of caffeine. He could've also used a cigarette.

"Don't remind me." He stole another glance at his watch. Jennifer was by no means Mark Arrowitcz, but he had a feeling that the previous night's escapade wasn't going to make her jump for joy. The last thing they needed was to be late.

"Do you think she'll yell at us?"

Luke faced his friend. "Ryan, we're not five; it'll be worse! And could this line move any slower?"

"Uh, sir?"

"What?" He felt his face flush as he noticed that it was their turn. "Oh. Sorry."

After they received their order, they advanced out of the chilled building and into the rising L.A. heat. They started their daily commute to the studio, Luke's pace quicker than Ryan's.

"Here, hold this." Ryan shoved his coffee cup in Luke's free hand. He dug out a cigarette and light from his pocket, and he got to work on killing the desire.

Luke scoffed. "You never learn, do you? What happened to quitting cold turkey?"

"I need something else. That's not going to work."

They passed a bus stop, and Luke tossed both half-filled coffee cups into the garbage. "Let's get this over with."

Trudging into the studio, Luke prepared himself for the punishment. To his surprise, The Leather Heartbreaks were sitting around the table with Jennifer perched on the edge of it. When she laid eyes on him, she slid off and hurried over to meet him, her heels clicking all the way.

"Get back out there." She pushed him out of the door and into the hall. Ryan had just arrived.

"I'm ashamed of you! How could you do that to them?"

"It's their fault we had to pay the fire damages," Ryan said.

"Bellano's trying to rip us apart!" Luke added, though he still wasn't sure if it was just speculation.

Jennifer leveled her shoulders and glared at them sharply. "Maybe so, but you can't touch their property. Do you want to lose the profit from your last tour?"

"Of course not," Ryan said.

She nodded, her mouth a straight red line. "That's what The Leather Heartbreaks' manager and I decided. They're not pressing charges, and neither is the bus company."

"So, why are they in there?" Luke pointed at the door.

She smiled proudly. "The Leather Heartbreaks and The Steel City Boys are going to do a collaboration, and your royalties will pay off the tour bus damages."

Both guys stood there, speechless.

"Hey, guys!"

The other three members from the Steel City made it on the scene.

"We're doing a song with The Leather Heartbreaks?" Adam asked.

"Yeah, and both bands are writing the song," Jennifer said.

Luke rolled his eyes. "This is ridiculous."

There was an awkward silence so, to ease the tension, Tyler said, "And did you hear about this new cherry cola thing?"

"Just get in there and play nice." Jennifer opened the door and motioned for them to step inside.

"Oh look, the girls are back." Bellano leaned back in the chair, forcing it to hold his weight on two legs.

Luke stomped into the room. "Wipe that smug grin off your face. Writing a song ain't easy."

And just like that, the songwriting process was underway.

Luke knew that Tony Bellano was by no means a songwriting expert, but he also knew that Bellano would still care about this song they had to create. After all, the song had to fit Bellano's image. Scribbling lyrics in a notebook, Luke tried to ignore Bellano. Every time The Leather Heartbreaks' singer threw in his opinion, one of The Steel City Boys would shoot him down. From key and meter to instrumental interlude and back-up, he barely had a say.

"Hey, is someone going to tell me what's happening? I have to sing this song, too, ya know." Bellano crossed his arms and stared at Luke, who still had his head down, writing.

"I'm thinking about bouncing back and forth between our personalities," Luke said calmly.

"That could work," Bellano agreed and uncrossed his arms. He leaned on the table and looked at Luke with interest. Meanwhile, his band members sat around looking bored. Two of them were throwing a ball of paper at each other.

Luke's voice may have been calm, but his mind was

restless. Why hadn't Bellano blasted him about the tour bus? He just sat there, more cool and collected than usual.

Either way, the man was no help when it came to writing the song. Luke took it over himself. He knew what he wanted, so he made it happen. When he was finished with the first draft, he handed the lyrics to Bellano and sang a few lines for the boys around the table so they could hear what it sounded like. He was satisfied, but it wasn't his feelings that mattered.

Bellano carefully read the lyrics. He drummed his fingers on the tabletop and mouthed the words, taking them in. He sang a few of the lines and slid the paper back over to Luke, grinning oddly. "This is good."

"Sure it is." Luke doubted everything that came out of Bellano's mouth. It should've been an honor to write a song with his inspiration, but this was a nightmare. This isn't how he dreamt the moment would be at all.

"No, man, I mean, like, for real. This is awesome!"

"You don't have to sugarcoat it for my benefit." Luke started to stand up, but Ryan kicked his shin underneath the table so that he'd sit back down.

"Dude, I'm not insulting you. I can't wait to sing this. You're very talented."

"Thanks."

"It's pretty good, Buff," one of the band members said, standing up.

Bellano nodded. "It's better than I expected coming from you. I have to admit, kid, you really know how to capture my style. How long did you say you've been a fan?"

Luke cleared his throat, trying to keep confident. "For years."

"Well, man, maybe I shouldn't be so hard on you. Let's go see what this song will sound like!"

Bellano led his band to the sound booth, and Luke just sat there, looking at the rest of The Steel City Boys. He couldn't believe what had just happened.

* * *

"Does this dress look okay?" Samantha stood in front of the bathroom mirror and meticulously applied her eyeshadow.

"Babe, you look gorgeous," Luke answered as he took a minute to figure out which tie he wanted to wear.

"You haven't seen me yet!"

"I know what you look like."

She walked out into the hallway to admire herself in the full-body mirror that she had just bought. Turning from side to side, she checked to make sure that the new sapphire dress fit perfectly.

Luke came up behind her, wrapped his arms around her waist, and sat his chin on her shoulder. "Can't you wear this dress all the time?"

"Can't you go to the Grammys all the time?"

He was silent as he thought about it. "Never in a million years did I think we'd make it this far."

"Are you nervous?"

"I'm going to be on national television, live, singing with Tony Bellano. What could go wrong?"

Samantha rested her head on his, feeling his body heat on her cool skin. "I love you," she whispered.

He didn't answer.

"You okay?"

Suddenly, he took her hands and spun her around so that he could look into her sparkling eyes, full of light and optimism. "You know I'll always love you." He kissed her before remembering that they had important places to be.

The L.A. sun shone joyfully in every crevice that it could find and refused to fade quickly. The temperature remained in the low 70s, and the night approached, even sleeker and more radiant than usual.

"Ryan's here!" Samantha called from downstairs.

"I'm coming." Luke rushed to the front door and locked it behind him. All of the wind was nearly knocked out of him as he watched his wife's hips sway to an unheard rhythm as she walked down the driveway. But, he instantly recognized her annoyance when she found her old roommate sitting in the passenger seat of the Firebird.

Ryan stepped out of the car wearing his white suit and designer shades. Naturally, he had a cigarette hanging out of his mouth. "Who would've thought?"

"Only Mr. Silva." Luke grinned.

Ryan laughed. "The old man ought to be proud." He held the cigarette between two fingers, knowing that he should get rid of it.

"You're not throwing that in my yard!"

"*Your* yard?" Ryan stared at the cigarette. "Wouldn't dream of it, rich guy. Come on, dude, we got an award show to get to."

Looking as sharp as Crockett and Tubbs, they hopped into the Firebird with Natalie in the passenger seat and Luke in the back with Samantha. Ryan drove down the hill and, as soon as they got onto the main road, he flicked the cigarette out the window. It wasn't helping him calm down anyway.

Samantha refused to talk to Natalie. There was nothing to say. Luke and Ryan tried to contain their excitement; they blasted the radio and sang along. It was a wonder that the whole state of California didn't hear them.

The other boys followed Ryan in another car. Tyler couldn't wait to show off his new girl, and Adam invited his younger sister. Joe ended up flying in his mother all the way from Pittsburgh. Mrs. Bassly was bubbling from top to bottom. She felt so honored that her son chose her to tag along to the biggest music show of the year. Her delight was evident, and she rambled on that evening, commenting on everything from the seats to the huge, dangling chandelier.

Ryan hesitantly surrendered Ruby to the valet. "Don't scratch her," he said before getting out and handing over the key.

Both Luke and Ryan helped their girls out of the car and exhaled anxious, astonished breaths. They stood in front of the red carpet, amazed.

After the band gathered together, the atmosphere turned into complete chaos. Camera flash bulbs and booming microphones invaded their private spaces, while roaring fans from the sidelines shouted praise and obsessive appreciation.

On the red carpet, Samantha experienced a sense of enlightenment. Luke was on cloud nine, but she absorbed the moment on cloud ten, and not because she herself was a photographer. In those captured moments, she realized how on top of the world they were. Fame and money weren't just dreams anymore; they were reality. Luke was a celebrity, a household name, and she had the luxury of being his wife.

Her dreams weren't untouchable; they surrounded her everywhere she looked. New dresses and heels? Getaway weekends and bottles of wine? Her life now had no limits. Who says someone made of money can't be a helpful and decent person? When the night concluded, she would retreat back home to her glorious mansion with the man who loved her and continue living the good life. She was drunk on entitlement, and no one could snatch that away from her. She was a long way from her days of scrambling up every dollar and cent for survival.

Once they escaped the "new arrivals" clutter, they filed in amongst the rest of the stars. Interviewers roamed and bands socialized with one another.

Natalie hung all over Ryan like she had that day at the Cavarelli mansion. She giggled obnoxiously at everything that he said. She strutted around as if she were Madonna. One time, when Ryan was talking to an interviewer, she put her head on his shoulder.

Luke and Ryan were still in a state of shock just over being at the Grammys. Every one of their favorite singers and bands were all joined together, and now they were a part of the family.

"Please tell me I'm dreaming," Luke said.

"Dude, I think Whitney just winked at me," Ryan said while squinting.

"You just said that about Belinda Carlisle."

"What can I say? I'm popular."

"You have a girlfriend," Luke reminded him.

He frowned. "She's not who I thought she was."

They had taken a moment to step away from their girls and absorb the magic around them.

Then, the dream got even more fantastical. Phil Collins and the Boss himself both shook their hands, and Huey Lewis came over and laid a hand on Luke's shoulder, saying, "You're different; you're just what this industry needs."

Finally, Jennifer Mignonne made her grand entrance, not hanging on any guy's arm. How could a masterpiece from a Louvre exhibit show up alone to the Grammys? Sporting a simple red evening gown and matching stilettos, she clutched her handbag tightly and amicably hugged each member of The Steel City Boys. "You enjoying yourselves yet?"

"Yeah, but it's so crazy in here," Luke said.

Jennifer rolled her eyes. "Tell me about it. You get used to it."

Cue Tony Bellano. He led his boys down the red carpet like they were the main attraction. Like always, he had a girl on his arm. She was a dazzling, newly-acclaimed actress.

The first glimpse of Bellano disgusted Luke. "I need a drink." He headed for the bar as Prince nodded at him in passing.

"I'll come with you." Ryan rushed alongside him.

"He better not screw this up tonight." Luke downed his glass, not giving a hoot who was watching. "It's the premiere of this duet. And I heard that Huey Lewis is doing a cappella too."

Ryan shook his head. "I know. Let's just have fun with it."

"That's not up to me."

They stood there, still taking it in. Culture Club had just arrived with Boy George dressed as interestingly as usual, makeup and all.

"Do you think I can ever quit?" Ryan asked out of the blue.

"Smoking? Absolutely. I'm going to help you, Ryan. You're not alone in this."

"No, I meant being a one-night-stand kind of guy. But, thanks. I need help with that too."

"Is she that bad?"

"I don't know. It's just not as serious as I would've hoped. Hey, look! There's Duran Duran."

Soon, the time came to move into the auditorium. The band sat in the middle section of the massive room, and they were only two rows behind Bryan Adams; Foreigner was across the aisle, only five feet away.

"Seats are red—check. Seats are soft and plushy—double check. Could we get any more ordinary?" Ryan joked to kill the nerves.

Natalie giggled again, forcing Samantha to lean towards Luke. "It's going to be a looong night," she said in his ear. "You better sing your heart out and win a Grammy."

He looked at her out of the corner of his eye and they smiled.

"See you backstage in a bit, Cavarelli," a familiar, rough voice said.

Luke lifted his head and discovered Bellano standing behind him. Holding back his shock, Luke answered, "Can't wait."

Bellano flashed an almost harmless, toothy grin before meandering further down the aisle until he found his band's seats.

"What was that?" Samantha questioned.

"Devil in disguise?" Ryan suggested.

Natalie giggled once more.

"Shut up," Samantha snapped. "It's not funny! Shouldn't you be off worrying about your rent payments?"

Natalie didn't reply, and she remained quiet for a long time after that.

The host introduced the night with the typical bout of celebrity toasts and roasts. Awards were presented, and musical performances lit up the stage. But, the stage wasn't truly on fire until it was time for the anticipated duet.

"And now, to perform their new single for the first time, here are The Leather Heartbreaks and The Steel City Boys with '(I Want You) Next to Me'!"

At first, there were no lights. The stage gave off a mysterious sort of feel. After a few short seconds, the flourish of an interesting blend of voices filled the air. Luke and Bellano started the chorus of the song a cappella, singing together:

I don't know how long I've been here,

But I think I've been here all night long.

All I know is I've been staring at you, girl,

And I'm liking what I see.

I think I need you,

I know that I want you,

Babe, I want you next to me.

The multi-colored lights switched on and both bands lit up the huge stage. Since they didn't need two drummers, Joe was selected to do the honors. The acoustics in there were phenomenal, and the guitars amplified louder than ever. Bellano sang:

> Hey, won't you walk this way?
> You know how to keep me on edge.
> I'm a man of no commitment,
> No vows on my heart,
> So why am I still waiting for you?
> I can tell that you want me,
> Let's get outta this place,
> 'Cause, babe, I want you next to me.

They sang the chorus again together, then Luke, alone:

> Hey, i see you walking this way,
> Your eyes have locked onto mine.
> But I'm a man of commitment,
> Got a girl with my name, so why do you
> keep tempting me?
> I can tell that you want me,
> I need outta this place,
> 'Cause, babe, I want you next to me.

The crowd went insane at least two times during the song. Bellano's solo entrance earned applause, as did Luke's.

Bellano:

Every guy in here's got their eye on you,
But, baby, I am so much better.
(So much better)

Luke:

My baby's waiting back home for me,
Say, is the music getting louder?
(Yeah, it's getting louder)

In this portion of the song, though, something extraordinary took place. Luke was concentrating hard on belting out his part when he noticed Bellano gazing at him with a sincere smile spread on his lips. It actually scared Luke for a second. It was one of those trusting smiles, one that anyone could expect from a lifelong friend. Comfort and selfless pride were infused into it. No longer did Bellano seem hardened or even a "tough guy." He was compassionate and… almost like Luke. Luke couldn't help but think that his being on this stage was like being a member of The Leather Heartbreaks. Ace Holloway and Frankie Pierce may not have been onstage, but Tony "The Buff" Bellano was all Luke needed to finally feel welcome in this moment.

Bellano:

But I want you (next to me)

Luke:

I think I want you (next to me)

Bellano:

All night—

Luke:

Oh but, girl, you can't be mine!

Bellano:

Oh, this happens every time!

Both:

Wait, we've been here all night—

After two more rounds of the chorus, the song ended with a few strong guitar chords that resonated throughout the auditorium. The room shattered with applause, and there were over a thousand standing ovations.

Unexpectedly, Bellano threw an arm around Luke and waved his thanks to the audience. Stunned, Luke tried to pull away, but Bellano had no intention of letting go. Luke stopped fighting it and thanked the crowd.

"That was fun," Bellano murmured to Luke.

Luke nodded. "Yes. Yes, it was." And it wasn't a lie. He just sang with his idol.

The bands disappeared backstage and slowly worked their way back to their designated seats.

"Amazing, as always," Samantha said.

"Thanks." Luke smoothed his tie as he sat down.

The show carried on and more awards were dished out. The Leather Heartbreaks didn't win Best Pop/Rock Band, and Luke was a bit surprised. Bellano and the band had won this category many times; now Luke wasn't sure who he should expect to win Album of the Year. The Leather Heartbreaks had won this category several years in a row, but if they couldn't snag Best Pop/Rock Band, did that mean The Steel City Boys had a chance for Album of the Year?

"And the nominees for Album of the Year are…"

Samantha located Luke's hand on his knee and took it in her hand. Over the announcement of the nominees, she said, "Could be you."

Luke's mind wandered nervously. He wanted to win, but having Bellano as a contender made him uneasy. As far as he was concerned, Bellano could have the Grammy. The Leather Heartbreaks had more experience, and Bellano would be unbearable if he didn't win.

"And the Grammy goes to…"

Samantha clasped Luke's hand even tighter.

"The Steel City Boys!!!"

A fusion of shock, excitement, and worry overcame Luke and his mind raced. This couldn't be happening. Everyone in the band's row stood up while cheers echoed from all sides of the hall.

Immediately, Samantha kissed him and Ryan flung an arm around him, but they had to keep moving. The band strode proudly down the aisle, following their lead singer.

Luke dared to steal a glance at Bellano. No longer was Tony Bellano as giddy as a kid on Christmas morning. The frown on his face was threatening, and his eyes glared daggers at them, like he could've murdered all five of them with one stare.

"Music Man" blared in the background and the stage glowed welcomingly.

On stage, Luke gently accepted the golden award, afraid that he would drop it.

"I wanna talk," Ryan whispered.

The audience's splendor died down as Ryan spoke into the microphone. "We first want to thank our fans. We're more than grateful for your loving support. You help keep our music alive. Thank you to our families for being patient with us because, look, we made it!"

Ryan stood back and allowed Luke to take the mic.

Luke took a deep, shuddering breath. "We also want to thank Jennifer Mignonne and Henry Langderate at Sforzando. We have to give a special shout out to both Richard Hexton and Mr. Silva. Without you guys, we wouldn't be here today. And, finally, I'd like to thank my wife, Samantha, for always being there for me. I love you, and I wouldn't make it through the day without you!"

At last, the long night concluded and musicians flooded

out of the place, eager to seek out the afterparties. The Steel City Boys drove to a nearby party, but Luke wasn't in the mood to stay very long.

"Woo-hoo!" Ryan shouted as they rolled past gleaming street lights and motley billboards.

Luke shook his head. "Did you see the look on Bellano's face?"

"Who cares?" Ryan accelerated the car.

"Luke," Samantha said, "Don't worry about it. You guys won, and that's all that really matters. And thanks for the honorable mention."

"Wouldn't have said it if I didn't mean it." He leaned his head back on the seat and watched the night pass him by. He felt so alive. Once he pushed Bellano out of his mind, he felt pride and accomplishment. If this was what people meant by the "on top of the world" feeling, then he wanted to feel it every second of every day for the rest of his life.

Chapter 20

Heartbreaker

The afterparty was glorious, just as Samantha had dreamt it would be. She still couldn't absorb the fact that she and Luke were surrounded by the hottest celebrities. The club reserved for the afterparty was packed. All Samantha had to do was accidentally bump into someone and she could manage to get Rick Springfield's autograph!

Luke and Ryan were the real stars of the night. Just like before the Grammy ceremony, the band received a fair share of compliments from idols and peers alike. All except one.

Samantha sat on a barstool while Luke stood next to her, sipping his drink.

"I don't see Bellano anywhere," Luke said flatly.

Ryan strode over to them. "Maybe he's at home crying his eyes out."

Samantha couldn't help but chuckle. She could tell, though, that Luke felt miserable. "Luke, you won. Don't let him steal away the joy you deserve."

Luke shook his head. "All the tabloid interviewers keep asking me to comment on the performance, on winning Bellano's award. I don't know what to say! Even worse, they want to interview us together."

Suddenly, Ryan slapped his palm on the bar counter. "I got it! Where's Jennifer? She's our manager, so she can comment for us."

As much as Samantha didn't want to think about Jennifer Mignonne, she had to admit that Ryan had a point. Just as she looked up into the crowd, she spotted Jennifer fighting her way through.

"Here she is now!"

Jennifer pushed her bangs out of her eyes. "I'm so

sorry I'm late again, guys. Traffic was horrible." She grinned. "But we did it! You won!"

"Uh-huh, sure we did." Luke downed the rest of his drink.

Wrinkling her face in confusion, Jennifer said, "Of course you did! You're not worried about Bellano, are you? He's not going to do anything to you."

"Why don't you ask him?" Luke pointed at a group of people who were making a commotion near the entrance.

A few girls screamed the name "Buff" and then the icon came into view. The interviewers swarmed around him, and he wore the same smug smile as always.

"Here's the deal," Jennifer leaned in and whispered. "When the interviewers are done with him, I'll corner him at the bar. He can't go very long without a drink; it fuels his ego."

They waited for about twenty minutes. Just as Bellano started to come their way, Samantha began to lead Luke away from the bar so that they could steer clear of any confrontation, but her good intentions failed the minute they hopped off the barstools.

Bellano grabbed Luke by the arm and pulled him toward an interviewer who was trailing behind him.

"Hey there, Lukey, boy. This young lady over here would like to interview us together. What do you say?"

Samantha watched with anxiety as Luke left her and joined Bellano near the interviewer. She wished that she could help him, but what could anyone do with a guy like Bellano?

As she watched uncomfortably, she muttered to herself, "I hope he can pull himself out of this one without being a complete wreck."

Just then, Jennifer leaned toward her. "Don't worry, Bellano won't try anything stupid in public. For him, it's all about image."

"I don't care about his image," Samantha answered. "I care about my husband's image." The last thing Samantha wanted was to be talking to Jennifer; she felt uneasy. How could a woman so extravagant show up stag to the Grammys afterparty?

"Look," Jennifer whispered. "When the interview is over, either you or Ryan should distract Luke while I corner Bellano."

Samantha shot her a side-eye. "What exactly do you think you're going to say to Bellano? I don't think you can rough-up a guy like the Buff."

"Oh, I have my ways." Jennifer winked as she said Bellano's catchphrase. Then, she got up and moved to the other end of the bar.

When the interview was over, Ryan swooped in and threw an arm around Luke.

"He didn't tear us apart, did he?" Ryan asked.

Luke shook his head. "He acted like he wanted us to win the award."

Ryan simply rolled his eyes.

"Hey," Samantha said, with an ulterior motive in mind, "I'm going to use the restroom. I'll meet you back over here."

Lucky for her, the bathroom was in the back corner, near where Bellano was talking with Jennifer at the other end of the bar. She walked past them, hoping that they wouldn't notice her. Once she was safe, she eavesdropped by the bathroom entrance.

"It shouldn't have been theirs." Bellano slammed his glass on the counter.

"Maybe you should cut them a little slack. They sold more albums than you guys did this year."

"Don't mention that."

"You're Luke's inspiration. Shouldn't that make you happy?"

"Yeah, but my fanatic shouldn't be better than me."

"Face it, Buff, rock stars get older. There's always a new voice in the music industry, more heartbreakers for girls to drool over."

Samantha started thinking. Who was allowed to call him Buff? She remembered Luke telling her that Bellano got defensive when Luke called him that nickname. If Bellano only let close friends and fangirls call him Buff, then did Jennifer know him well?

Bellano began ranting. "I wish I could split them up by getting their record sales to plummet, or—"

"It'd never work," Jennifer cut him off. "Their friendship is too strong. They're up so high now, people would get skeptical if something like that happened."

"They are talented," Bellano said weakly.

"Arrowitcz already had them everywhere on the charts. There was no way to stop them like that without people getting suspicious. Besides, you think I'd let you wreck them that way?"

He raised his voice again. "The Leather Heartbreaks have to come out on top. There's no room for competition. I have to pulverize The Steel City Boys."

"Don't even think about doing something stupid, Buff.

You don't need to hurt your own image."

"I don't intend to."

There was a pause, and Samantha wasn't sure if they had moved or had just grown silent. She didn't dare poke her head around the corner to look; she didn't need to be seen.

"Where is your new girl, anyway?" Jennifer asked.

He scoffed. "Really? She was a dumb actress. She had the beauty, but not the brains."

"Hey Buff," someone shouted across the club.

The conversation ended abruptly. Just to be sure neither Bellano of Jennifer would find her, she waited a few extra minutes before leaving the bathroom.

She debated whether or not to tell Luke about the conversation that she just overheard. Because she didn't have any true proof that Jennifer was working with Bellano, she decided to keep the conversation to herself. Besides, Luke had enough worries, and she didn't want to add to them.

Chapter 21

What is Love, Anyway?

Publicity. It has the power to create, and the power to destroy. It can completely exaggerate or merely skip over the important details of a story. The Steel City Boys experienced a great deal of fame within those few months. The cigarette fiasco and the vandalism of the tour bus caught the attention of the cameras, but the news of the Grammy win turned everything upside down like an hourglass. The scandals were thrown aside, and all that mattered was the music. Record sales were climbing again, and no one complained. Luke, Ryan, Tyler, Adam, and Joe were still beloved heartthrobs.

Once the chaos was over, the band began working on their third album, *Heartfelt*. All five musicians wanted in on the songwriting, so they spent more time than usual at the studio.

One night, they stayed late to work. Luke's Corvette was in the shop, thanks to a fender bender, so Samantha decided to order takeout for the band on her way to pick him up in her white Camaro. She parked the car and stepped out carrying paper bags. Just as she was heading in, Ryan was walking out. "Hey, Ryan!"

"Hi, Samantha! How are you?"

"Great, thanks. Wait, shouldn't you be in there?"

"I have a date with Natalie," he said flatly.

"How's that going?"

Ryan shrugged. "Well, it's going. Where, I don't know."

"How's the new album coming along?"

"Fine. I'm pretty happy with it." Then he added, "But we're done with the album for tonight. The other guys left already. Jennifer wanted to go over financial and management stuff before she goes out of town for the week."

"Oh." She didn't know what to say.

Ryan smiled. "You know me, that crap goes in one ear and comes out the other."

Samantha laughed. "I know. Good luck with Natalie."

"Thanks!" Ryan moved further down the sidewalk.

She entered the building, a bit worried because Luke was in there alone with *her*. She hoped that nothing was happening—at least, not the movie that was playing in her mind. The third floor was dark and empty, except for the corner room at the end of the hall. She crept along quietly, even though it really wasn't necessary. Or was it?

As she grew closer, their voices echoed into the hall, indicating that the door was open. Before barging in, she waited outside the door, just to hear what was going on, to make sure that her fears weren't reality.

"If we're going to go ahead and make an appearance at Live Aid in Philadelphia, then we should make sure we have a new single ready to perform."

"What if the audience doesn't respond well to a new song at a huge concert like this?"

"Luke, why would you even think that? It's gonna be good, like always."

Silence.

The paper bags crumpled under Samantha's fingers, and its sound was echoed in the bare hallway.

"Did you hear that?" Luke said.

Her heart was racing. He would think that she was crazy for eavesdropping.

"What are you so worried about? You've been jittery ever since Ryan left."

"I should probably get home."

"We're not done here."

Silence.

"I should probably call her."

"Come on, your wife doesn't have to keep track of your every move."

"Jennifer, I love my wife, I'm not going to—"

Silence.

A giggle.

"I need to leave—"

"Hey," Samantha greeted sweetly as she popped into the doorway.

"Oh, hi!" Luke looked like he was in the midst of a heart attack.

"Hi—What's your name again?" Jennifer tilted her head to the side.

"Samantha," she answered with no emotion. "I brought food." She set the bags on the table. "But, I see everyone else already left."

"Thanks, Babe, I'm starved. Look, we still have a bunch of things to get through before I can head home." He sounded disappointed.

"I can wait."

"You don't have to. In fact, I can catch a bus, or Jennifer can drop me off."

"I don't mind," Jennifer jumped in.

"Neither do I. I can stay." Samantha crossed her arms.

Luke could tell instantly that she was exhausted, but still frantic about Jennifer being there. He didn't need her worrying on his account, and they did have a few loose ends to tie up. "You look really tired. Why don't you head home?"

She stared at him.

"Hon, it's okay." He looked into her eyes. "I'll be home

soon, I promise. You don't have to worry about me."

Finally giving in, Samantha kissed him goodbye.

She was only about halfway down the hall when she heard them.

"Relax, she's gone. We don't have to worry about her."

"Jennifer, no! Let's just get this done so we can go home."

Samantha had to fight the urge to run back and strangle the woman. No. She remembered the honest look that he just gave her. *If he really loves me, then he'll stand by his word. I have to trust him.*

She drove home in silence. Her head was pounding from the jumble of thoughts running through it. She tried to fight the tears and the rain as she turned on her windshield wipers and slowed down for a stoplight. Glancing across the street, she noticed a music store with a flashing open sign in the window. She had an idea.

Stepping into the old store, she weaved her way through the rows of shelves until she found her way to "V." She didn't even bother looking for The Steel City Boys or The Leather Heartbreaks. Thumbing her way through the records, she began to doubt that she'd find what she was looking for. Finally the second to last record caught her attention. There she was: Velvet.

Jennifer Mignonne's face and figure hadn't changed at all over the past few years. Her bangs were curled just as tight, and the heavy layer of eye shadow made her stare sharper and even more tempting.

Samantha hated it. She wished that she had a marker so that she could cover Jennifer's voluptuous smirk in black smudges. Jennifer's sensual pose on top of a bed with velvet sheets didn't help.

Pushing down her anger, Samantha made her way to the register, realizing that she was the only customer in the store.

The elderly store owner glanced down at the album cover as Samantha handed it to him.

"Now that's a name I haven't heard in a few good years. I wonder what happened to her. That girl was a dream alright. And when she sang—pure velvet, just like her name."

Samantha fought the urge to roll her eyes. Instead, she dug in her wallet for cash. She wasn't truly satisfied until the owner slipped Jennifer's arrogant smile into a plastic bag.

Before she pulled into the mansion's driveway, she hoped that a light would be on in the house, but the house was pitch black. She trudged into the house with the record bag tightly clenched in her hand. Making a beeline for Luke's studio, which had a turntable, Samantha tried to keep herself calm. She didn't bother turning on the lamp in the studio, but she closed the door before unsheathing the record.

As the first guitar chords rang out, Samantha plopped into Luke's black leather swivel chair. She shut her eyes, breathing in Luke's cologne. When she heard the lyrics of the song, she dug her fingernails into the arms of the chair.

I got you on my mind
All the time.
You never leave my brain,
Think I've gone insane,
Ooo, baby that's okay,

What do you say?

Already, Samantha couldn't handle it. What was going on in that room with just the two of them? How dare Jennifer try to steal her man. Samantha just couldn't fathom how she could be more attractive than Jennifer Mignonne. After all, Jennifer had to have been fully confident that her seductive powers could charm Luke. Otherwise, she wouldn't have cared about Samantha's coming to the studio or have made those comments after she left. But would the two of them do anything? Samantha didn't know what to believe. On one hand, Luke would never betray her like this; on the other hand, Jennifer seemed deadly. How could Jennifer simply walk away from a married man she desired?

Samantha couldn't take the mind games any longer. She hadn't trusted Jennifer from the start, and her worst fears may have been coming true. Even worse, there was nothing that she could do about it.

The anger raged in her. She jumped up from the chair and pulled the record from the turntable. With one swift motion, she hurled the record toward the back wall and let it smash into pieces. She didn't care anymore. She just wanted her husband back, if he was even gone. But with Jennifer around, how could any man resist her?

After dumping the record pieces in the garbage, Samantha tried to calm herself by working on the details for a huge photography gala that was soon approaching. She played around with pictures and business papers just to keep her mind off of Luke, until she couldn't think anymore.

Sleep wasn't even a possibility. Tossing and turning didn't help her forget about her worries. Finally, she heard the door. She rolled over to look at the clock: 1:07 A.M.

She pretended to be asleep. He came in, making as little sound as possible. Any optimism she had tried so hard to hold onto vanished immediately. The strong perfume she got a whiff of wasn't hers, not by a long shot. Sure, he was in the same room with Jennifer all night, but unless she bathed in it…

Then, she heard the shower running, and a chill waved through her body. It had to be true. On the TV shows she watched, characters always took showers after affairs.

He didn't talk much the next morning. She figured it was guilt. What else could it have been?

Samantha couldn't say that she was completely heartbroken. She had been expecting something like this to happen. She continued telling herself that it was all in her head: a horrible fantasy. The urge to come out and ask him if it had happened tormented her, but she couldn't bring herself to do it. If he wouldn't even say good morning to her, then why on earth would he admit to sleeping with Jennifer? Envy began to slink its way in. What did Jennifer have that she didn't? What was wrong with her?

Nights passed, and they didn't really talk anymore. The conversation never went farther than meaningless chit-chat. Dinner was unusually quiet. After they ate, he would disappear into his studio and then head to bed a few hours later, leaving her alone.

"Luke, are you okay?" she grew the nerve to ask one night, peeking her head into the studio doorway.

Luke, who was usually at his desk or behind the keyboard, sat on the floor surrounded by toppling stacks of records. The air conditioning was on the fritz, so he only had on a dark blue pair of pajama bottoms.

"I'm fine, why?" He kept thumbing through his records.

"You haven't said much lately. You keep to yourself a lot."

He lifted his head, but his blue eyes weren't full of their normal energy. "We've been so busy. I'm just tired, that's all."

She dared to dive deeper. "Are you sure? It feels like you're holding something back."

"Samantha, honestly, I'm okay. I just need some time to decompress and clear my head."

"What are you doing?" She pointed at the piles of records.

"This? Oh, I'm reorganizing. I think I might give a few away."

"Alright. Well, I'm going to bed. Goodnight."

After tiptoeing over the litter of records, Samantha bent down and kissed him.

"I love you," she exclaimed.

In return, he smiled weakly. "I'll be upstairs in a couple of minutes."

That was proof that something was wrong. Luke hadn't said those three precious words in weeks. He hadn't said them since that night with Jennifer, and he never normally refrained from verbally expressing his affection for her.

Tired? No, it had to be more than that. She was sure of it. As time dragged on, she wanted so desperately to call him on it, but then it would genuinely hurt her because the confirmation would be coming straight from his lips. Then again, if she was making it up, then she would just look stupid in front of him, and she couldn't bear that humiliation either.

A few weeks later, Luke received news from back home that his uncle had unexpectedly passed away. Luke was determined to fly back to Pittsburgh to attend the funeral. This uncle had inspired Luke and introduced him to the world of music. Secretly, he was hoping that he could sing for the funeral Mass.

Samantha, unfortunately, could not accompany him because the weekend of the funeral was the same weekend as the gala.

She was finishing up last-minute work for the gala. It had only been a day since Luke had departed—he hadn't even kissed her goodbye. She sighed heavily when she heard the doorbell.

The housekeeper answered the door and hurried to Samantha. "It's Mr. Ryan Delhart, ma'am."

"Let him in. I'll be right out."

"If you don't mind, I think I'll head home then."

"Okay. Have a good night."

Samantha shoved the papers that she had been handling into a manila folder and exited the room. Out in the hall, she discovered Ryan standing there, looking lost and broken.

"Ryan?"

"Hi, Samantha. Is Luke around?"

"No, he left yesterday for his uncle's funeral."

"Oh, right. I won't bother you then."

"Ryan, is everything okay?"

He paused, and then shook his head. "She cheated on me and stole my money."

Samantha exhaled. "Come on, let's sit and talk."

She led him to the living room couch. Ryan was pale

and defeated. He sat there, silently at first, until he opened his mouth and waited for sound to come out. Nothing happened.

"Well?"

"I don't know, what's there to say?" He paused. "Natalie cheated on me. And, from the sounds of it, multiple times with multiple men. She's been using me for money and status. She played me like a fool."

"She's a heartbreaker, that's for sure."

"Let's hook her up with Bellano."

They laughed, allowing all of their troubles to dissolve for a minute.

"How're you holding up?"

He shrugged. "Horribly, I guess."

"Oh, Ryan, I'm so sorry. I hate to say I told you so."

"But you did tell me so, and I didn't listen."

"Is there anything I can do?"

He thought for a moment, focusing on the ground. "Can you tell me what's wrong with me?"

She was taken aback. "Nothing! Ryan, you're a charming guy. You're kind-hearted and compassionate. You've got a great sense of humor, too. The girls should be after you."

"They used to be. Maybe they still are. I don't know anymore. How'd you and Luke get so lucky?"

"I'm not exactly sure myself. Never in my wildest dreams did I think I'd find the love of my life so soon. But Ryan, we're so young. It's not over; you'll find her. You'll find the one."

"Yeah, but I feel like I've never been loved. No girl has ever wanted a serious, long-term relationship with me. Then again, I didn't want one either. Natalie was the first woman that I thought about being serious with, and now look, she broke my heart. At least a girl as good as you doesn't have this problem."

She scoffed. "I wouldn't be so sure of that."

Ryan gaped at her. "Why, what happened?"

"I think Luke cheated on me with Jennifer," she whispered, as though Luke were still in the house.

"No, he wouldn't! He loves you. Wait, with Jennifer? You're still on that?"

"He's been weird ever since that night at the studio with Jennifer. I walked away that night and it sounded like she was trying to come on to him. He didn't come home until one in the morning!" Samantha explained everything that had happened.

"Wow. And now he won't talk to you, let alone say he loves you? I find that difficult to believe. Luke actually—no way. Well, maybe she pressured him. She definitely is… attracting."

"I don't know, Ryan. It doesn't make any sense, but all the signs point directly to it." Talking about it made her depressed again. She was on the verge of breaking down.

"Want me to confront Jennifer? I'll do it."

"You're too eager. No, but thanks. I don't see how it'll help matters any."

"But what if it isn't true?"

"I—I don't know!" The tears were streaming. "Do you think I haven't thought of that? I'm not even sure if this is love. Maybe this was all too premature. I just feel lonely and confused, helpless and shattered. The worst part of it is that I have no one to talk to because nobody understands—"

"I understand," he said softly.

"I mean, if nothing happened," she continued, "Then why is he acting like he hates me? He can't be that tired—"

"No."

"Why are you agreeing with me? He's your best friend. You're supposed to defend him."

"I know Luke. This is literally what he's like when he's guilty or feels bad about himself. He stops talking and keeps to himself. This is exactly what he did when the record labels kept rejecting us. I can't believe I didn't see it sooner. Now that you mention it, things have been kind of awkward between him and Jennifer."

"I can't compete with a goddess."

"Samantha, you're beautiful, and you're the coolest girl I've ever met. It's not fair to compare you and Jennifer. I'd make you mine if you weren't already taken."

Then he quickly leaned in and kissed her. It was brief, but still eloquent. In an instant, she pulled away and stared at him wildly.

"No," she whispered. "What are you doing?"

"Sorry!" Ryan turned his head and rubbed his shoulder nervously. Then he repeated, "What if it isn't true?"

She sighed shakily, still trying to absorb what had just happened. "Either way, I'm a fool. I've wanted to ask him about it for so long, but I just can't bring myself to face the confirmation or the humiliation."

Out of nowhere, the phone wailed, and both Ryan and Samantha jumped, hearts racing.

He looked at her.

"Just let the machine get it," she said.

Several rings later, the answering machine played a velvety voice that echoed through the mansion.

"Hi, Luke, Jennifer here. I know you're out of town, but I just wanted to let you know that the band has been approved to play at Live Aid. Also, I can't wait to blow your mind again. Hope to be with you soon!"

Samantha couldn't help it. The bitter tears once more slid down her cheeks. "This is a nightmare," she choked.

"I can't believe she just did that," Ryan said. He thumbed her tears away and, for a blurry moment, she saw Luke's face instead of Ryan's.

"It'll be okay," Ryan said.

She blinked and Ryan's concerned expression was back. Without hesitation, Samantha allowed all the anger, betrayal, and pain to control her. She kissed Ryan and let the meaningless passion go from there. She figured that if Luke wasn't going to treat her right, then she may as well share the night with someone who understood how she felt, someone who cared. She just felt so numb inside. They journeyed upstairs, two lonely people searching for bliss.

Chapter 22

Snatched Away in a Second

Luke was shocked to find the Firebird parked in his driveway. He had to cut his visit to Pittsburgh short because he wanted to beat an incoming storm. He had less time to be with his family, but at least he had attended the funeral. Exhausted, he parked his Corvette adjacent to Ryan's car. The dash said that it was 2:02 A.M. *What's he doing here so late?*

Taking his suitcase out of the trunk, he pondered this question until he got to the front door. He dug out his keys and leaned against the door as he jammed the key in the bottom lock. Before he could unlock the top deadbolt, he dropped his keys and only sluggishly made his way to the ground for them. He was so tired, he almost fell over as he stood back up, so he grabbed onto the doorknob. To his surprise, the door opened right up. *Huh. She must've forgotten to lock the deadbolt.* Still trying to figure out why Ryan's car was there, he meandered into the house. He switched on the hallway lamp and set his suitcase at the foot of the stairs.

Slowly, he ascended to the second floor. A sudden, eerie sort of warmth flooded through him. About halfway up, a wooden stair creaked as he stepped on it, and he stopped. He didn't want to wake her, but something was wrong. Very wrong. Nothing was adding up.

He stepped into the doorway of the bedroom, and a patch of moonlight from the window helped him discern a body-sized lump on the left side of the bed: his side.

They were asleep, but they were still in each other's arms.

"Oh, my God," he yelled, part in rage, part in trembling disbelief. He didn't even care about taking the Lord's name in vain.

Ryan and Samantha woke up instantly. At first, they

seemed confused, but reality soon crept in.

It felt like someone had kicked Luke hard in the stomach. He was suffocating. His wife and his best friend had both just stabbed him in the heart, but Samantha's knife was sharper.

Samantha screamed. The shrill terror in her voice made Luke think that it was a dream; it definitely wasn't.

Ryan sat up at once. "Luke, it's not what it—"

"Looks like?" Luke turned on the ceiling light.

They squinted, adjusting to the light, and then scrambled to get dressed.

Not being able to handle what had just happened, Luke left the room abruptly and tramped downstairs. Back in the hall, he picked up their wedding picture. He fixated on their bright and cheerful image for a second, before glancing down at the "Forever Mine" lyrics engraved into the frame. He slammed it to the ground and listened to the glass break. It knew how he felt.

Samantha almost fell down the stairs on her way to him. She covered her mouth at the sight of the picture. "Luke, it's not like that." Her voice was barely loud enough to be heard.

He shook his head. "You knew I loved you."

"*Loved?*" Her eyes popped.

"Let's hold on a minute." Ryan finally made it out into the hall, dressed rather slovenly. "We never meant to hurt you."

Luke took time to breathe. His emotions were beginning to roll as he turned to face her. "Why?"

"Because you cheated on me," she said softly.

"I—I cheated?" Luke couldn't string words together. His head felt fuzzy. "No, I didn't. I'd never—"

"But you did!" Samantha got feisty now. "You slept with Jennifer that night, after I left."

Luke scoffed in disbelief, trying to comprehend this. He couldn't stand it, any of it. The tears were starting to build up. "I didn't sleep with her."

Samantha was getting worked up too. "But that night I showed up—"

"It didn't happen," he shouted. "She came on to me. She tried and tried to make me, but I refused. She kissed me, but I pushed her away immediately! Samantha, the only woman I've ever cared about is you. I stayed true to you."

"Then why did you come home late that night? Why did you act like you didn't care anymore?"

Luke sighed. "After the meeting, I stayed out by myself, and I caught a bus home. I knew nothing had happened, but I still felt so disloyal to you. I just needed to clear my head and breathe. I never stopped loving you or caring about you. I told you I was tired from everything that's been going on lately. After everything, don't you get it? I thought we knew each other, Samantha. I thought we were on the same page. But one suspicion and you go jump into someone else's bed? Into our bed? With him? I leave for two days and you betray me with my best friend?"

Then, Samantha remembered the phone call. "Jennifer called tonight," she said suddenly, excited. "She left a message saying that she missed you and wanted to sleep with you again. Luke, she admitted to sleeping with you already!" She hurried over to the phone and hit the button for the answering machine, but Jennifer's message ceased to exist.

"Well?" Luke's impatience was settling in. "Where is it? Are you trying to cover yourself? You can't prove something that was never there."

"It was there!" Samantha said.

"I was here," Ryan jumped in. "I heard it; it's true."

"Of course you were here." Luke was filled with an uncontrollable anger. He could feel his face grow hot, and he was beginning to shake.

He glared at Ryan. "What's your excuse anyhow? Did you think I wouldn't find out?"

"No, Luke, I never wanted to hurt you!" Ryan defended himself. "I—I just felt so lonely and helpless after Natalie cheated on me. I needed someone who cared, and you weren't here. I just needed the pain to go away."

"Did it, Ryan? Did it go away? I was the greatest friend I could be to you and this is how you repay me? That's it, we're done. I don't care if I ever see your pathetic face again. Get out of my house!" Luke grabbed Ryan by the arm. He dragged him outside and slammed the door in Ryan's face.

Luke leaned his back against the door and closed his eyes. Upon reopening them, he glanced over at the photo of the blue boardwalk on the wall. Everything had made sense back then. Where was the familiarity that he saw when he first laid eyes on it? After exhaling, he focused his attention on the woman who, an hour ago, he was proud to call his wife.

"You don't love me, do you?"

"That's not why I did it."

"It's a simple question. Is that ring on your finger a lie?"

"NO!"

"Then why did you sleep with him? Him, of all people!"

"I told you, I thought you cheated on me."

"So, what, sleeping with Ryan was compensation?"

"I needed to feel loved."

"No, no, no. I know Ryan was having issues. He needs to feel loved. I've given all my love to you, and you just threw me away. Maybe all you use me for is money and status! Maybe Nick Anson was right after all."

"Nick Anson?! Don't throw him in my face! What did he tell you, that all I do is spend other people's money? I explained that to you a year ago. Luke, I love you. Why can't you see that?"

"Yeah, that's what they all say."

"But I do! I'm sorry!" She paused. "And how am I supposed to believe *you?* Prove to me that *you* didn't sleep with *her.*"

He scoffed again. "You are *so* stupid! If you really understood me, then you'd know that I'd never betray someone I love. I don't have to prove anything to you. You know what kind of man I am. I don't cheat, and I don't lie. What, you were afraid to know the truth, so you didn't talk to me about it? How was cheating the answer?"

She opened her mouth a few times, but no sound came out at first. "So, I'm just supposed to take your word for it? Why would you think that I'd lie to you? Have I ever? That message was on the phone. I didn't make it up. What other reason would she have to call if you two weren't having an affair?"

"I never thought you'd be one to make up stories."

"You can't even answer the question! Do you realize that you've been distant from me for the past month and a half? You won't talk to me, let alone say you love me, and you haven't kissed me since that night at the studio. Every time I kissed you first, you acted uninterested. You were in your own little world.”

He shook his head. “I told you why I was depressed.”

“For that long after the fact? If anything, you should’ve given me all your attention instead.”

“That’s it, I’m done.” He threw his hands up in the air.

“We’re not finished here,” she protested.

“Yes, we are. I am.” He turned to walk away, then stopped. He spun around to look in her frazzled eyes. “Was he better than me?”

“WHAT?!”

“On second thought, I don’t want to know.” He realized that he was exhausted, but he was oddly wide awake at the same time. He knew that if he went upstairs, he wouldn’t fall asleep.

“Luke,” she said through the tears, reaching out to him.

“Don’t touch me!” He backed away like she was a snake on the hunt. “We have nothing left to say.”

She shook her head. “No.”

“I don’t care where you sleep from now on, but it’s not going to be in my bed. Pack what you need and get out.”

She only stared at him.

“Go!”

Slowly, she took the stairs one leaden foot at a time.

While she gathered her things, he plopped himself on the bottom stair, defeated. He held his head in his hands and waited for her to come down.

Just before she opened the front door, he stopped her. “Wait.”

They locked eyes. He noticed that hers were full of sadness and dread, but he didn’t care. His own eyes were empty, yet brimming with agony.

"Keys." He stuck out his hand.

She seemed confused.

"I can't have you waltzing back in here whenever you want."

Reluctantly, she dug out her keys and gently laid them in the palm of his hand. She exited the mansion, struggling to carry three suitcases along with her.

The house was dead quiet. He lugged himself upstairs where he glared at the huge bed. The first thing that he resolved to do was strip off the sheets and put on a clean set. But, that didn't suffice. He couldn't bring himself to sleep on that mattress of misery, so he hauled his aching body to the living room couch. Still, sleep declined the invitation to arrive, and he found his usual pure mind wondering: did they do it on this couch, too?

The next few weeks were the hardest for Luke. He tried to blame himself for what had happened, but he decided that it was a ridiculous notion. He hadn't done anything immoral, and he sure didn't deserve to be cheated on. Maybe it would've been different if she had slept with a complete stranger instead of his best friend, his brother. It just didn't make any sense. He really thought that there had been a connection between him and Samantha, but he wasn't so sure. His thoughts were in a jumbled mess, and he couldn't make heads or tails of any of it. He was the best husband that he could be. The fans screaming "I love you" meant absolutely nothing. The physical attractiveness and seductive powers of Jennifer Mignonne could never tear him away from the one he treasured most.

Soon enough, the other big issue had to be addressed.

The Steel City Boys couldn't go on, at least not with Ryan. The rift between Luke and Ryan stalled the band's progress.

"Are you sure you want to do this?" Tyler asked Luke.

"I don't have a choice," he said. "I can't even look at him, let alone play onstage with him."

Just then, Ryan came into the studio.

"Ryan—"

"I know!" he exploded, flailing his arms. "I'm leaving. I'm finally going out on my own. I'm just here to pick up paperwork." He stormed back out the door and slammed it shut behind him.

"I'll go with him." Joe jumped up and started to follow.

"No, I will." Adam jumped too.

"What are you doing?" Tyler threw out an arm, forcing them to stop. "Neither of you are going with him."

"He needs someone. You know he'll be a complete wreck if he goes alone," Adam said.

"You think Luke isn't a complete wreck?" Tyler pointed at Luke.

"Adam, I'll go," Joe offered. "He'll need a drummer if he's serious about playing on his own. They'll need you because you can play any instrument they need."

"You condone what Ryan did?" Tyler still wasn't backing down.

"I—"

Luke shook his head. "Joe, go ahead."

"Dude!" Tyler shouted.

"No, Joe's right. Ryan needs him, and we can find another drummer. You know what'll happen to him if we leave him alone. The guilt will kill him."

"He screwed your wife!" Tyler insisted.

"Tyler! I'm not happy about it, and I'm nowhere near over it, but this is the way it's got to be."

With much persuasion from Mr. Langderate, though, Luke and Ryan agreed to perform a final concert in Pittsburgh, which would be televised live. After all, the devoted fans deserved to see them one last time. It was tremendously difficult for them to act happy while performing. They put on masks of amusement and attempted to have fun.

But, Luke's heart just wasn't in it. His voice soared like it was supposed to, but not like he wanted it to. A couple of times, he could've sworn that he was out of tune. His stage presence surely was. He barely moved around, and he hardly edged closer to Ryan. However, he did do his best to engage the audience, asking them to sing along on upbeat songs like "Music Man."

The ending felt awkward to Luke because he and Ryan couldn't bring themselves to hug each other. Instead, they took a prideful bow and proclaimed their gratitude.

"We want to thank you guys so much—" Ryan said.

"We truly couldn't have done it without you." Luke cringed as he realized that he was still finishing Ryan's sentences. "We regret to say that The Steel City Boys are going to have to undergo some… changes." He really had no clue how to let the fans down easy.

Ryan continued, "You guys have been absolutely amazing, and I've had a lot of fun sharing our music with you. Know that you'll always be in my heart. You'll always be 'Forever Mine'! But, I'm going to go out on my own for a while. Joe and I are going to form our own band."

Ironically, the fans had to go without hearing "Forever Mine" one last time. Luke immediately suggested removing it from the set list, and Ryan swiftly seconded the motion.

So, the last lyric was sung, and the last chords were strummed. The hollow beats from the drums echoed and faded away dolefully. The stage emptied, the crowd cleared, and the true, original Steel City Boys were merely a memory.

The press exploded. It couldn't wait to expose a failed friendship and plaster headlines everywhere, even if the stories were untruthful. The rumors made Luke's head spin, so he stopped reading them after a while. Some stories insisted that Samantha had been bored with Luke; others claimed that the friendship between Luke and Ryan was never as smooth as presented. Every major interviewer wanted to talk to Luke, but he politely declined. From what Luke could tell, some fans believed what had happened, but most cried and mourned in denial. That wasn't the Luke Cavarelli and Ryan Delhart that they knew and adored.

Tension was high when the band came together for the American Music Awards. They didn't say much in their acceptance speech when they won an award for the *Steel City Pride* album.

The last thing that Luke wanted to do was think of his ex-best friend, but from time to time, he found himself wondering if Ryan's reputation was truly shot at this point. Luke watched and listened as Ryan went his own way and tried his best with Joe. The new duo called themselves The Enharmonics, but Luke didn't even chuckle when the thought crossed his mind that Ryan likely didn't know the music term he named himself after. However, Luke did know how talented Ryan and Joe were individually; maybe they could make it after all, but Luke had never wanted this. Growing up, he had always stayed up to date on band member changes. There were lead singer swaps, falling outs, side projects, and more. He wasn't ready to accept that the same phenomenon had just happened to his own band.

The Steel City dream faded away in an instant. A trusted and admired friendship evaporated with no indication of a reconciliation.

***

"What do you mean, you want to fire me?" Jennifer's face appeared, though she sounded so far away.

"I just think going forward the band needs—"

"Are you letting your feelings for your slut of a wife mess up your head? I've helped you get to where you are."

Then Samantha's voice echoed, "Luke, I still love you."

"Are you going to listen to *her?* She broke your heart, and you're going to fire *me?*"

"I—I—"

Suddenly Jennifer disappeared into the mist.

The alarm buzzed incessantly, reminding him that sleeping in wasn't an option. He sighed and rolled over. Nothing. He turned over and only met the tangled-up mess of bedsheets. Stretching out his arm, he only felt the cool touch of the mattress. He sighed again, this time letting his shoulders sag as reality set in.

He had that dream again, the one that was half memory and half fiction. The first half was exactly how Jennifer reacted to Luke firing her. Samantha intervening was his imagination. It was the third time that memory haunted him, but he hadn't done any wrong in firing her. He just couldn't bear seeing her anymore.

After dragging himself out of bed, he slowly put on his clothes and trudged down the stairs. He poured himself the usual bowl of cereal and flopped onto the living room couch. Flipping on the television, he found *The Today Show,* like he did every morning, and tried to immerse himself in the joyful happenings of the world. He was doing fine until a familiar, rough voice almost made him dump the milk into his lap.

"We're happy to announce that our new album, *Leather Stride,* is going to be released next month." Tony Bellano was slouched in the studio chair, the same smug grin on his menacing face.

The interviewer asked, "So, what's new about this album? What are you guys doing differently this time around?"

"I'm so glad you asked. Well," Bellano paused as if in thought, "this album features songs that I've actually composed myself. Leather Heartbreaks fans know that I don't usually get sentimental enough to write my own songs."

"What song off this album speaks to you the most?"

"Uh, that would have to be 'Secrets in the Dark' because it's a message to an old acquaintance of mine."

Luke couldn't believe his ears. Tony Bellano wrote a song? An album? Why would he start composing this late in his career?

"I'm pretty sure this song can finally trump Luke Cavarelli on the charts."

The interviewer saw the opportunity. "How did the changes to The Steel City Boys affect The Leather Heartbreaks?"

Suddenly, Luke grabbed the remote and turned up the volume.

Bellano shook his head. "It's made it even harder for us

to reach the top. That Cavarelli kid's got a voice, and it's gotten even better. That's the only thing he's got going for him."

"How does it feel to be competing with a fan?"

"It's incredibly frustrating," Bellano was frowning. "I've been doing this a lot longer than he has, and it's not fair to us. Anyone who knows me knows that I always demand control. There's no way I'm backing down now."

Neither am I, Luke thought.

"Honestly," Bellano continued, "I don't think The Steel City Boys knew who they wanted to be when they were all together. One song was amateur with all that cliché romantic stuff, and then the next made them seem mature. They were too wishy-washy. With The Leather Heartbreaks, you always know what you're getting. They just got lucky."

"What about their success today?"

"Look, the fans only sympathize with Luke because his wife slept with his best friend. He's a sob story."

He chucked the remote, the indignation roaring inside of him. What gave Bellano the right? He had no idea what it was like to have an emotional storm constantly brewing in his heart and in his mind.

Luke marched into the studio that day and confronted Mr. Langderate, who was doing his best to find a replacement for Jennifer, while helping the band for the time-being. "I want *Heartfelt* to be released next month."

"Next month?" Mr. Langderate was taken aback. "Well, we can have a single out by then, but that's still a very tight deadline, Luke. There's still so much work to do on the album since you're replacing the songs Ryan helped write."

"A single is fine; I don't care. I'll work day and night to get it done."

Mr. Langderate must've seen the desperate look in Luke's eyes. He smiled. "Then your next song will be out soon. What do you have in mind?"

Luke grinned wide in response. "It's called 'Inspiration (I Believed in You).'"

Against his better judgment, Luke envisioned Tony Bellano rocking the stage with "Secrets in the Dark." He could see The Buff stalking fluidly from side to side, allowing all the screaming girls to reach out and touch him. Luke, however, performed in his own way, closing his eyes and allowing himself to be swallowed by the accompaniment:

(I believed in you...)
(I believed in you...)
You were my comfort,
You were my strength.
You turned wrongs into rights,
You made my confidence shine bright.

If i were a bad boy
Then we wouldn't have a problem!
But now I got the power,
You can't stand the heat.

Luke's aggression toward Bellano couldn't have been stronger in this song. Onstage, he always allowed his vocals to carry his feelings away. It was almost like he didn't have control of his emotions. The mix of emotions that was welled up inside of him flowed through the sieve, swirling into the ears of the hungry listeners; he couldn't contain the rage, hurt, and sadness any longer, going into the chorus:

Inspiration,
You used to bring out the best in me
Now darkness is the only thing i see.
Inspiration,
You made me believe
I could let myself be free.
Inspiration,
Where have you gone?

Some tabloids claimed that the song was about Samantha, but Luke had forgotten about her for a moment. Bellano was the focus of every lyric.

You were my idol
You were my joy.
You were always there for me,
But that was yesterday's fantasy.

His passion for music was at its all-time high. Whether a song was about Samantha, Ryan, or Bellano, every little lyric and every single note came straight from the heart, no exceptions. Depression made the songwriting process challenging, but nothing could stop him. In barely any time at all, his songs rose to the top slots on the charts.

The problem? Luke Cavarelli had once again managed to beat Tony Bellano out of the top spots. Luke had heard that the crowds weren't responding much to Ryan after the scandal, so they clung to Luke even more. But, that wasn't all. Luke's voice had grown more fortified and mature. The fans couldn't get enough of his sound, especially his octave jumps. If Bellano wanted competition, bring it on. Luke was ready to do whatever it took to be his best self, musically. If Bellano needed the competition gone, then he was out of luck.

Chapter 23

Shattered Lens

Samantha would have never classified herself as a slut, yet the word Nick Anson had shouted at her echoed in her mind as she drove away from her home that night. With tears still streaming, she checked into a hotel. Flashbacks of her Pittsburgh poverty haunted her. Deja vù.

She didn't have even half of her belongings packed into those three suitcases. At some odd time in the morning, she thrust the clothes that she had into a dresser and flopped onto the rigid bed. Her eyes were heavy, but every time she closed them, she remembered everything that had happened that night. She stared at the ceiling, not even knowing who she was anymore. Just a few hours ago, she felt so betrayed by the man who she had given her whole heart to. But, then she gave herself to his best friend. No, tonight wasn't love, and she knew that. But, in the moment, she had thought that Ryan understood her better than Luke ever had.

She couldn't believe her own actions. She was no longer jealous, only guilty and ashamed. She could tell by the look in Luke's eyes that she had really wounded him. A couple of days ago, she doubted their love, but it was clear to her that they did still love each other. She loved him so much that the thought of losing him was unbearable. Why had she torn his heart in two? Was she that selfish? There were so many things that she still wanted to say to him, but she couldn't utter a single word.

Just as she nodded off, she woke herself with a start: it was time to set up for the gala.

The gala was an all-day affair, and she had to arrive early to set up. Since she was in charge, the weight rested on her already weary shoulders. She had been excitedly planning this event on her own for so long, but she didn't feel in the mood for a grand photography party. What success did she have to celebrate?

Her supervisor, Mr. Rostraver, greeted her right away. "Good morning, Samantha! I know you've worked very hard planning for today. I want to tell you how proud I am of your growth over this past year."

This comment didn't make Samantha feel much better about herself, but she nodded and smiled as she headed into the main event room.

"Hi, Samantha!" A bubbly co-worker ran up to her. "The artists are starting to arrive. They're ready to know where to put their work."

Samantha felt like an anvil had been dropped on her. She left all of the papers that she needed at home. Among those papers was the order of the photos, and that was a huge deal.

"What's wrong? Are you okay?" Her co-worker saw the panicked look on her face.

"I—I forgot the papers."

"Just go home and get them."

"I can't."

"Sure, you can. You have plenty of time."

"No, I—I can't."

She walked away in a daze, heart pounding, brain racing. She couldn't go back there.

"I—I don't have my key," she said, which was the truth. She couldn't go back to the mansion, even if she wanted to.

So, she directed the photographers according to her rattled memory. However, she couldn't remember everyone. She should have known better than to put Monessen and Youngwood next to each other. The photographers had a blood-boiling feud, but their skyline photographs fit well next to one another. The bright stars in one highlighted the glittering moon in the other.

Throughout their careers, Monessen claimed that Youngwood was guilty of plagiarizing him, and Youngwood claimed that Monessen spread rumors that caused him to lose profits and hurt his reputation.

When the men looked at each other's pieces, which were side-by-side, a violent brawl broke out between them, and it just couldn't be stopped. The guests, who were beginning to file in, landed in the crossfire.

"So, I see your background is the same hue as my 'Darling Starlight'?" said Monessen, a short and slightly-hunched-over man with a receding hairline.

"Getting blind in our old age, are we? My photo was taken in Hollywood, and yours was clearly taken in your dingy backyard!" Youngwood's towering figure and bushy white hair made him look more important and imposing than Monessen.

In a rage, Monessen flipped Youngwood's photo off of its display and slammed it onto the ground. In return, Youngwood flung food from the refreshment table. Then, the fists went flying. The place quickly became out of control. Samantha rushed in to break it up, and got rewarded with a punch in the eye. Meanwhile, the guests stood back, and some couldn't refrain from laughing.

Eventually, Samantha's boss intervened and broke up the fight. "Men!" Mr. Rostraver yelled. "You fight like action figures!"

The people in the room laughed lightly.

"Now let's please get on with this gala and put away our

differences. Cocktails will be free," he added as an incentive. Then, he pulled Samantha aside and gave her ice for her eye. "What are you doing?"

"What?" She hoped she could act innocent.

"Why do you have nothing organized? You let this place turn into a zoo! Monessen and Youngwood—really?"

"I'm sorry, I—"

"I don't want excuses! I want the job done right. We seek perfection in everything we do here. You know that." Mr. Rostraver's tone softened. "You just haven't been yourself lately. Clearly, you can't keep up with us anymore. I'm afraid I have to let you go, Samantha. You're done. I need you to leave."

She didn't know how to respond. Slowly, she nodded and trudged her way out of the building. She felt so dead inside. The interior of her Camaro was blazing hot, but she sat in there anyway, crying her eyes out. Her life was over. In the past 48-hours, she had managed to blow up her marriage and her career. How could she ever move on? What was she supposed to do?

Over the next few weeks, she wracked her brain for a solution. She couldn't let her dreams be washed away. At last, she put her finger on it: she had to open her own photography studio. She had always wanted to open her own studio, and here was the perfect opportunity. Easier said than done. A few years before she met Luke, she had saved a chunk of money in the bank. It almost killed her to not spend it, but she knew that she had to keep it in case of an emergency. She withdrew the money and bought a space that used to be a small insurance office. After remodeling, advertising, and buying materials and equipment, there wasn't much left over, so she had to dip into her checking account just to stay in a hotel. She was only able to spend about a week and a half in the hotel. She tried sleeping in her car, but the backseat was so uncomfortable, and she may as well have been using a rock as a pillow. At last, she bought a cheap pillow and blanket set and resorted to sleeping on the studio floor.

And if not having sufficient funds to live on wasn't bad enough, business was even worse. She knew that she deserved the blame, though. The entire media hated her, thanks to the affair. In their eyes, she was a complete monster. Her reputation, like Ryan's, had been nearly murdered. Some people dared to never set foot in a photography studio run and owned by the woman who ripped out the heart of the beloved Luke Cavarelli. Those same critics said that anyone who entered either had no morals whatsoever or distanced themselves completely from the world of music. One morning, she found notes under the door with hateful messages: *You never deserved Luke Cavarelli* and *How many Steel City Boys does it take to satisfy you?*

Her days became lonelier, and she found herself thinking about Luke constantly. She was determined to win him back, if that was possible. During the evenings, she would park outside Sforzando Records and watch him walk over to his Corvette and drive away, back to their—no, *his*—home. Every night, she drove away in tears.

One day, while she was trying to busy herself in her vacant studio, the door opened, and the UPS guy asked her to sign for a package. Her mind swirled about all of the things that could be contained in a brown box. After breaking the tape with a pair of scissors, she lifted out something that almost made her heart stop. She picked up a beautifully-crafted wooden frame that held four photos, which she instantly recognized as her own work. Two of them had been taken on the night of the Hexton wedding. One featured Luke at the mic, the other of the whole band. The last two were of Luke and Samantha on their honeymoon. She had forgotten that she had shipped them off to a friend of hers who did extraordinary framework. It was supposed to be her anniversary present to him.

She didn't want it. She couldn't even tolerate looking at it. At first, she grew angry and wondered how it had even shown up at the studio. After a moment, she remembered that she had all of her mail sent to the studio instead of the mansion. Right when she was going to get rid of it, an idea popped into her head. What if this changed the game? What if four tiny photos could spark the making-up process? Wasn't it worth a try?

Quickly, she worked to get the frame repackaged and mailed to Luke at Sforzando. This way, she could sit outside and wait for him. If he carried it with him and took it home, then there was hope.

She parked outside the next day and tried to hold in her anxiety. She watched him exit the building, and her heart jumped for joy: he had the package in his hands! Her eyes followed excitingly and then widened as the frame tumbled into the garbage. "No," she screamed, but she wasn't heard. She slammed her forehead on the steering wheel and wept. It was truly over. She had officially ruined everything. She smashed Luke's heart into glass fragments, and she just couldn't glue it back together. He'd never trust her again.

Minutes later, she lifted her head. Wiping away the tears, she took a shaky breath. As much as she didn't want it, she knew that she couldn't just leave the photos in the garbage. So, with as much pep as she could muster, she hurried across the street, in hopes of not being seen. Peering down into the red barrel, she saw it right away. The sight of it shattered her heart even more. She closed her eyes. *I can't pick it up.*

"Are you okay?" A deep, familiar voice from behind her.

"That's none of your concern." She sniffed, realizing that she was still a crying mess.

"How've you been?"

She stopped and turned around. "Look, it's bad enough I cheated on my husband with his best friend; I don't need to be seen talking to the enemy."

"Hey, don't be cruel," Bellano said. He came up alongside her. "I know how you feel. I can relate to you."

She scoffed. "You're Tony Bellano. You don't relate to anyone but yourself."

"You're upset."

"Of course I'm upset!" She started into the street, forgetting that she had left the frame behind. "Just go away!"

"Can I ask you something?" His voice flowed into her ears as he followed her.

She headed for the sidewalk so that she wouldn't be in the middle of a traffic zone. "Fine."

"Why did you cheat?"

Did he seriously just ask this? "Why do you care? You hate Luke."

"Yeah, but even I can't ignore a woman in distress." He shot her a sideways glance and a genuine-looking smile.

She sighed. "It's because of Jennifer. Do you know her?"

Bellano nodded. "Sure I do, the band's manager. I've worked with her a few times."

"She kept coming onto him, and I thought—"

"That he cheated on you."

The more she talked about it, the more irritated she became; Bellano, however, kept pushing.

"What're you gonna do now?"

She shrugged. "My reputation's not too hot. I need to keep getting business to make money."

"You and Luke have a joint bank account, right?"

"Yeah," Samantha said, seeing where he was going, "But I'm not taking that money. I still have respect for him. I'm the one who did him wrong."

"But it's yours too," he protested.

"No," she said.

Bellano leaned forward. "It sounds to me that you just need to get rid of Luke."

Samantha smiled weakly and tried to laugh. "I'm not sure I know what you mean."

The heartbreaker cocked his head. "You know, bop him off." He slid his finger across his throat, mimicking a knife.

"What, for the life insurance? Absolutely not! I'd never try to hurt Luke. I love him." Samantha couldn't believe how quickly Bellano's tone kept changing. *He is joking, right?*

All of a sudden, Bellano became dead serious. The look in his eyes was wild and strange. His lips formed a straight line when he said, "You kill him, and I'll double what money you get from his life insurance."

She didn't know how to react. He wasn't joking; he meant it. "Um, I have to go." She rushed for the driver's seat and sped away, not daring to look back.

With her mind buzzing, she drove for a while. What had just happened? Why on earth did Bellano approach her with this proposition? Was he crazy? She'd never kill Luke in cold blood for money.

Luke. Once again, she was reminded of him and the pain she had caused for both of them. She doubted that her life could ever be the same. She hated herself to the point where she refused to even look in the mirror every morning. She never cut herself a break, and she never thought of herself as worthy of anything, especially of Luke. As she drove, she felt all of the rage building up inside of her. She felt like she needed to break free from the prison she had created for herself, but to what avail? Luke wouldn't take her back, and the world despised her with a burning passion. How could she reach out and touch her independence?

Then, another idea formed. She redirected her route and took off for an expensive little house on the other side of town. She had only been there once. She and Luke had been there for The Steel City Boys' Christmas party.

When Jennifer Mignonne responded to the violent rapping on her door, she won a rough slap in the face. Bringing a hand to her pink cheek, she glared at her assailant. "What the h—"

"Don't even!" Samantha shouted. "You are the one who sent me into this nightmare."

"Me?" Jennifer pointed at herself. "You're the one who had sex with your husband's best friend."

Samantha slugged her again. "Because you acted like you slept with my husband!"

"Well don't have a cow about it," Jennifer said. She cocked an eyebrow. "He was absolutely amazing, by the way."

"Liar!" Samantha dove for the next punch, but Jennifer

caught her arm mid-swing and pulled her into the house.

"Stop attracting attention." Jennifer shut the door and spun around to face Samantha. "What do you want from me?"

"I want you to tell Luke the truth. You made me think you slept with him."

The manager scoffed. "And why would I do that?"

"Because—I—"

Jennifer folded her arms. "You can't even finish a threat."

"Don't you have a heart?" Samantha was beginning to feel like a fool. She cursed herself for taking so long to realize that Jennifer called that night on purpose just to upset her. She only had to prove it.

Just then, there was a knock on the door. "Come on in, Buff," Jennifer called.

Bellano looked twice before grinning devilishly at the sight of Samantha. "Well, hello again, Mrs. Cavarelli."

Samantha couldn't believe it. "What're you doing here?"

Jennifer stalked over and hugged Bellano. "What's it look like?"

Bellano eyed Samantha with a sly grin. "Velvet, do you have something to tie her up with?"

"What?!" Samantha's nerves instantly worked themselves into a huge knot.

"Yeah," Bellano nodded. "We're gonna go have a little chat with your hubby."

"I'm not going anywhere with you." She headed for the door.

Before she could make her escape, Bellano captured her

throat with his large hand. "Don't make this harder than it already is. I have a reputation to keep, you know. This is for the best."

Her throat was on fire, but she kept gasping for air. She tried to pull his hand away, but he was too strong. She managed to kick him, forcing him to release her. Right when she got free, Jennifer came back into the room and grabbed her.

"What's the plan?" Jennifer asked as she tied Samantha's arms together.

"We'll take her car, so Luke won't be suspicious."

Bellano pushed Samantha from behind. "Get moving."

"He won't take the bait," Samantha interjected.

"That's all up to you, sweetheart." Bellano shoved her out the door.

"Now I know what a leather heartbreak is," she snarled.

"Gag her, would you? And make sure you get her car keys." Then he muttered, "Luke Cavarelli had better say his prayers tonight."

Chapter 24

Music Man

Light shone through the stained-glass windows and cast colorful rays on his weary face. The wooden pew creaked beneath him as he shifted his weight. Luke sat in solitude in Blessed Virgin Mary Cathedral; his eyes followed the burning sunlight up the aisle and to the altar. There was a chalice positioned in the center of the altar, and just beyond it rested the golden tabernacle with a bunch of grapes and a grain of wheat engraved on the otherwise-smooth door. He examined the huge crucifix mounted on the wall above the altar. It shamed him to know that he was only feeling a small fraction of the pain and despair that the Son of God had felt, but at least he knew what it was like to have a Judas and a Peter. Or was it a double dose of Judas?

His mind swarmed with thoughts. The picture frame had shocked him. It was like Samantha stabbed him in the heart yet again. He hated to admit that he felt so lonely. He missed her so much, despite the fact that she had betrayed him.

The thought of an annulment was impossible to him because—deep down—he still loved her. He didn't want another woman; he wanted her and only her. He said that he would know when he met the one, and he did know. Her sweet smile danced before him and he felt like he could throw up. How could he forgive her and trust her again? It was just a never-ending circle that he couldn't resolve himself. He hadn't even brought himself to recreate the circle with Ryan.

He glanced down at the cassette case that he was rotating between his fingertips. *Leather Stride* was by far the best album that The Leather Heartbreaks had ever produced. As a fan, Luke loved the sound, but, as a competitor, it made him wonder if some days he was just throwing bricks at a wall. He'd never win Bellano's respect or admiration.

But, that wasn't all. Flashbacks of Bellano's *Today Show* appearance raided his brain. Something just wasn't adding up. The songs were too well-written for an amateur composer, yet the songs were Leather Heartbreak style. And who was the "old acquaintance" Bellano referred to? He chased the meaning behind "Secrets in the Dark" as it played over and over again in his mind.

You're still here,
I thought I told you to go.
I guess by now
You gotta reap what you sow.
I've never loved you,
You knew that right from the start,
But that doesn't seem to stop
Your golden heart.

Well, I'm gonna teach you a lesson,
One that you soon won't forget.
Oh, how I love to get inside your head,
You'll never know about that night full
of dread

358

Secrets in the dark,
You'll never shed light on the secrets of
the heart.
Secrets in the dark,
I always demand control.
You've hurt me once,
You'll never hurt me again,
So I hold on tight to those secrets of
the heart.

Was he the boy with the golden heart? That would've made sense, but then what was with the night full of dread? What did that even mean?

Luke cracked open the cassette case and let his eyes roam on the back of the front cover. When he made the tiny printed discovery; he thought that he was imagining it: *all songs cowritten and arranged by Velvet.*

He read it again. And again. Then, he just stared at it. Wasn't that Jennifer's stage name? They were working together? The timeline for the album meant that the songs were definitely written before he fired Jennifer, which wasn't that long ago. Were they both trying to end his music career? It all made a perfect sort of sense. Or did it? They paid off Mark Arrowitcz, sure, but the night full of dread… That still didn't make sense.

The more that Luke thought about Bellano, the more worked up he got. He started to believe that he had been a fool to fall for Bellano's bad boy charms. Luke was no better than an innocent girl who experienced a "leather heartbreak." Slowly, he felt the anger rise through his body and settle in his chest. As the rage grew, he gripped the cassette case in his hand even tighter. When he couldn't stand it any longer, he threw the cassette case, and it hit the edge of a pew. Even from Luke's pew, he could tell that Bellano's arrogant grin didn't have a crack in it.

"I haven't seen you here in a long time."

Luke glanced back to find Mr. Langderate in the pew behind him. "What're you doing here?"

"I could ask you the same question."

Luke sighed. "I feel bad that I haven't been here in months. I've just been so depressed."

"I know." Mr. Langderate handed him a wooden frame. "Does it have something to do with this?"

His eyes enlarged. "Where'd you get that?"

"I saw you throw it away before. I think you should keep it."

"What for?" Luke got gloomy again.

"She's still your wife."

"So?"

"Don't be like that," Mr. Langderate snapped. "It's obvious that you still love her. I can see it in your eyes."

Luke hung his head. "But, how do I forgive and forget?"

Mr. Langderate moved up into Luke's pew and made him slide over. "Luke, marriage is a covenant, you know that. You two are supposed to help each other get into Heaven, fix each other's faults. How're you going to do that if you can't forgive her? God's already forgiven her. It's up to you now."

He let this sink in. "You're right."

"I know I'm right," the old man joked, "I've been a Catholic for 60-some years and married for 40! Believe me, I know what it's like to forgive and move on."

Luke smiled faintly. "Mr. Langderate, is any of this my fault?"

"Your fault? Well, maybe you could've told her about what happened with Jennifer."

"It was just a kiss!" Luke exploded. "I pushed her away. She came onto me when I wasn't expecting it!"

Mr. Langderate laid a hand on Luke's shoulder. "Calm down. I'm not condemning you. I'm just saying that maybe you should've been a bit more open with her about it. You were awfully depressed."

"I couldn't talk to her. I felt guilty about letting the kiss happen. Besides, Samantha was already paranoid that Jennifer was going to steal me."

"Isn't it all a misunderstanding, then? I'm sure she didn't mean to hurt you. Yes, she was afraid to confront you about what she thought was happening, so she allowed her emotions to control her sense of reasoning. You kept your distance from her because you felt guilty for something you may have been able to control, but the relationship between you two isn't a failure. The love is not dead, but merely lost. It needs to be rekindled. If you really love her, and I know you do, then you know that you won't be at peace until you have her back in your arms. You two couldn't talk to each other, so you were pretty much in the same boat."

Luke thought for a moment. "Y—yeah. I—I guess so."

"Her sin hurt more than yours, sure, but it's still forgivable. Luke, you love her. Don't let this good thing slip away. You love her." Mr. Langderate paused for a moment. Then, he said, slowly, "'Love is patient and kind; Love is not jealous or conceited; Love is not proud or selfish; Love is not ill-mannered; Love is not irritable...'"

Luke hesitated before continuing: "'Love does not hold a grudge; Love is not happy with evil; Love is happy with the truth; Love never gives up; Its faith, hope, and patience never fail.' 1 Corinthians. 13, 4-7." Silence prevailed for a few minutes longer. "I do love her. I'll get her back."

"Wonderful!" Mr. Langderate started to stand up.

"But, how can I just take Ryan back after everything?"

Mr. Langderate slowly sat back down. "He's your best friend, and you two need each other. You just caught him at a low moment in his life. I think we both know that he didn't mean to hurt you."

"Do you think we can get the band back together?"

"I don't see why not. Do you want Jennifer back?"

Luke shook his head. "Apparently not." He showed Mr. Langderate the album.

"No indeed," Mr. Langderate said. "Don't worry. "

Luke groaned as another thought popped into his head. "Bellano will come at me even harder if we make a comeback. I'll have to deal with him again, plus Jennifer because she's on his side."

Mr. Langderate looked Luke straight in the eyes. "Don't let his jealousy get to you. Stand up for yourself."

"I can't; I'm too weak." Luke turned away.

"Don't say that! You're one of the best musicians I've ever worked with. Your heart and soul go into all of your music. It makes you who you are. The man doesn't just make the music, Luke, the music makes the man. And you are a man by my standards, not by Bellano's tough guy philosophy.

You should be extremely proud of yourself. You're a music man."

* * *

The first person Luke decided to make amends with was Ryan. He said goodbye and thanked Mr. Langderate before leaving.

Despite being filthy rich, Ryan had never moved out of their old apartment. A rumor floated around that he had plans to buy a grand beach house, but Luke knew that, in his current state, Ryan was all talk and no game.

Luke pounded on the door.

No answer.

Again, even harder.

Then he heard the gentle strumming of a guitar, and the wail of a mournful voice from behind the door:

I know sinners have a lot more fun,

But I'm so tired of hurting everyone.

I tried changing my heart around,

But found myself flat on the ground.

My heart's a time bomb ready to blow,

With a pain that's more ebb and flow.

Tears of a sinner ain't too cool,

I'm just here, one among the fools

He listened carefully to these lyrics. Wow. Ryan really did want to redeem himself. He needed Luke more than ever. So, Luke pounded harder on the door.

This time, the door opened a crack, and Luke could see that the chain was on.

"Go away," Ryan sneered.

"I need to talk to you."

"I'm busy."

"No, you're not."

"You don't know that. Didn't you hear me practicing?"

Luke sighed. "If you were that busy, you wouldn't have answered the door at all. Face it, Ryan, I know you. Now, will you please let me in?"

Ryan grumbled and thrust open the door. He stood back and let Luke in.

Luke barely had one foot in the room when he was attacked by the unbearable reek of smoke. Turning to look at his old counterpart, he said, "You haven't stopped, have you?"

"Does it look like I've stopped?" Ryan picked up a pack of cigarettes from the coffee table and worked on getting one lit.

"Dude, those things are going to kill you."

"Chill. It's not like you really care anyway. Besides, I deserve the worst for what I did to you. Why are you being nice to me all of a sudden?"

"I wanna talk to you about that, actually."

"Then talk." Smoke poured out of his mouth.

"Can we sit?"

Ryan shrugged and plopped himself on the farthest end of the couch.

Luke's feet shuffled on the floor before he chose to sit on the other end. Taking a deep breath, he said those precious three words: "I forgive you."

"I'm sorry, what?" Ryan pitched the cigarette, which was still sending up smoke signals, in a nearby ashtray.

"I forgive you, Ryan. I'll admit, I miss singing with you. You're my best—"

"Not anymore."

"Just hear me out! Look, I've finally realized that I can't hold this grudge. What you did was a mistake, and I know that you were weak at the time. The truth is, I miss being on-stage with you. Maybe you don't want to get the band back together—"

"No, I don't. Joe and I are doing fine on our own."

"Are you serious?"

"Dead." Ryan stared off into the distance, puffing on the cigarette again. His face was pale, and he looked like he was hypnotized by faraway thoughts.

"So, this is it, then." Luke couldn't believe his ears. He knew that he shouldn't have expected Ryan to jump on board so quickly, but he did try to have hope.

"We don't deserve each other as friends, so you may as well leave."

Luke sighed and headed for the door. He looked over his shoulder at Ryan, and his friend was almost a stranger before his eyes. He closed the door behind him, but he couldn't leave. He sank to the floor and sat against the wall in the hallway, thinking. For a while, Luke heard the strumming of a gentle guitar, but eventually that faded. The apartment was completely quiet, and Luke didn't like it. Something felt wrong, just like it had on the night of the affair. He got up as fast as he could and burst through the door.

Ryan was in a deep sleep on the couch and the cigarette wasn't in his hand; it was on the shag carpet beneath his feet.

Swooping in, Luke slapped Ryan awake. Ryan, dazed, took a few seconds to register Luke's face. "What do you want now?"

Silently, Luke pointed to the cigarette on the floor and bent down to pick it up before it could cause any damage. "So you're doing fine?"

Again, Ryan stared off into the distance. "Did you really say that you forgave me?"

Luke smiled. "Yeah, man. I forgive you. I want you and Joe to come back. We're not The Steel City Boys without you. Let's get the band back together."

"Can we?" Ryan lit up a little, becoming a bit of his old self.

"It's not impossible. I've seen other bands break up and then miraculously reform."

Ryan focused on the ground. "You know that I never wanted to hurt you. Natalie cheated on me, and it crushed me. Honestly, I should've known better. I'm such a fool."

"No, you're not. You were broken and needed fixed. You just went about fixing it the wrong way. I understand now. I had to have time to sort things out."

Ryan tried to smile. "I had forgotten that you left for the funeral, and Samantha was the only one around to console me." He scoffed. "I guess she did that all right. I don't even know what was going through my head. Apparently, noth-ing."

"I really believe we can move on, Ryan," Luke said.

But, Ryan had gone silent again. "Luke, I have a confession to make, and I hate the thought of what I'm about to say." He took a deep breath. "Ever since you met Samantha, I've been a little jealous. She's right for you. She's a wonderful girl. On the day we left for LA, I wished I were you. I hated the fact that you always played things straight and I could never settle down. I promise, I never wanted to do this to you or Samantha. I'm sorry."

They looked at each other for a moment; neither one knew what to say.

Luke was still absorbing what Ryan had just said. He only wished that Ryan would have confessed these emotions earlier. But, he wanted to forgive him. He needed to, or he would never have peace of mind.

"I still forgive you," Luke said softly.

Ryan nodded slowly. "Just give me some time, okay? I'll give you my decision about the band."

"You still want to be out on your own?" Luke asked.

"Look, man, I don't know. Give me time to think on it."

Luke agreed. Before he left, he showed Ryan the cassette case.

"Jennifer's working with Bellano? She was on his side the whole time?" Ryan gaped at him.

Luke nodded. "I don't want to say anything yet. This is between us and Mr. Langderate."

"Fine."

This reaction wasn't what Luke was expecting. He was waiting for Ryan to say something to the effect of, "I'd rather tell Jennifer off and take a few swings at Bellano."

But, Ryan remained somber and quiet as Luke slipped out the door.

Chapter 25

Monetary Visions

Luke's tires crunched in the driveway, and the front door opened and shut. "Samantha?"

For a brief second, relief flushed through her body, and it felt like nothing had changed. "I'm up here."

It didn't take him long to make his way into the bedroom.

When she laid eyes upon him, it seemed like the nightmare was over. He would save her.

In mere seconds, he sprinted across the bedroom and met her on the balcony. He kissed her without thinking. "How'd you get in here?"

"Housekeeper let me in before she left. Wait, why aren't you mad at me?"

"I forgive you," he whispered lovingly and kissed her again.

The passion that hadn't been there in ages came rushing in.

She felt so alive inside, and the moment couldn't have been more perfect. She pushed him against the rail of the balcony. She longed for him so much, but everything changed instantly when Tony Bellano's voice crept into her mind and began to taunt her.

"Samantha?" Luke held onto the railing with his head cocked to the side. "Are you okay? You're shaking."

Suddenly, her mind was frantic with thoughts. *Why would he forgive you now? He must want something. He doesn't love you anymore. If he did, he would've forgiven you months ago. Come on, just do it already. You know you want the money. You want this house all to yourself...*

Her jaw was set, and her hands were clammy. Her heart beat rapidly, and the fire in her eyes burned intensely. She seized his shirt violently, almost unaware of her own actions.

"Whoa, babe, what're you doing?"

He'll be going on tour soon, Bellano continued, *Love? Lust? No! He'll find a hotter replacement once he gets out of the city. You're entitled to this place. It's there for the taking. What are you waiting for?*

"I'm not going to let you use me. All you use me for is status—arm candy. I'm not going to let you throw me back out in the streets when you're done with me."

"What? Wait a minute! Honey, what are you talking about?"

She was pushing him more and more over the balcony rail.

Bellano's voice still resonated loud and clear. It reminded her of Nick Anson's snake-like taunting. *You've worked so hard for all of this. You're entitled to the money, the house. Just do it. If you don't, he'll tie you down, making you feel guilty for the rest of your life for sleeping with Ryan. He may say he forgives you, but you'll be his captive forever. You'll spend the rest of your life trying to please him, but you won't make him any happier. If you want to be free, push him off the balcony. He can't make you happy anymore. You can't live your life as a slave to his will. He'll use you for sure now. It's a dream to live in this house and have all this money. Don't let that slip away. Do you want to go back to the poorhouse again? He's the only thing standing in the way of your true happiness. Can't you see that? What are you waiting for?*

All she craved was money. She just wanted to live in this lap of luxury forever. Why should it end? If she could get her hands on the money, why not? The only thing she could think about was getting the mansion. It didn't register that the man she had in her clutches loved her unconditionally. It didn't cross her mind that he would give his life for hers. She couldn't go back to watching her pennies and dimes like she had in Pittsburgh. She wasn't a college student anymore. She wasn't still suffering with the Hextons. It was her life to live, and she wanted to be free.

Just as she went to finish the job, another voice intervened: her own. Samantha Cavarelli. Luke wouldn't do that to her; Nick Anson would. Tony Bellano would. Luke loved her, and she loved him. There wasn't room for anyone else. Bellano was just playing with her mind. She liked having money, but Luke had given her much more than access to colored paper. He had given her his heart and his life. He understood her. He set her free.

Samantha released her husband. Panting, she stared down at her hands like they weren't hers.

"I knew you wouldn't do it. You don't have it in you."

She whipped around to find Tony Bellano standing in the archway. She had been so absorbed that she had forgotten he was there. She forgot his threat of what would happen if she didn't kill Luke. After all, she was the bait.

* * *

"Bellano!" Luke exclaimed, coming away from the railing. "What're you doing here? How'd you get in?" Luke's mind whirled in a frenzy.

"Oh, I have my ways," Bellano cunningly dropped his catchphrase. He stood against the sliding door of the balcony with his arms folded and one leg crossed over the other. His eyes turned to Samantha. "So, you didn't want the money?"

"What are you talking about? You leave her alone." Luke pointed at him.

Bellano shrugged. "Your loss, Samantha. Go on, why

don't you tell him."

"Tell him what, that you're insane?" She became angry.

He grinned. "That you and me had a little visit today."

"Samantha?" Luke's heart dropped, and his eyes pleaded with her.

She looked at Luke. "He kidnapped me and brought me here. He said he'd double the inheritance I'd get when you die if I killed you. If I didn't do it, he said that he'd kill me too.

Luke began to pounce, but a second voice stopped him. Jennifer appeared, strutting along in her black sundress and narrow heels. She went over to Bellano and draped an arm over his shoulder.

Luke blinked. "So, you are working with him. But why?"

"Come on, Cavarelli, don't be so dense," Bellano said. "Jennifer here is my girl."

Luke shook his head. "So that is why Mark Arrowitcz left so quickly. You paid him off and became our manager."

"Well, the brain *does* work." Bellano lit a cigarette. "Hope you don't mind."

"If you have a purpose for being here, get to it." Luke felt himself grow hot.

"I have plenty of purposes in life," he mumbled with the cigarette still in his mouth. "You know, I thoroughly enjoyed the artwork you guys did on my tour bus. I suppose you could say I earned it."

Luke took a minute to think. "You did set that fire."

"No, actually," Jennifer jumped in. "I did. And it wasn't really a fire, you know. Just smoldered and made smoke."

"You?"

"Don't act so surprised," Bellano said. "You know I

hate you. You threatened my spot at the top of the charts. I'd do anything to break up your little boyband."

"But see," Luke said, "That's what I don't understand about you, Bellano. You want to be on top, sure, but you have to realize you're not the only one in the industry. What, you'll go after any new band that hits the charts?"

Bellano rolled his eyes. "Of course, not. I'll only knock down bowling pins like you. You got me all wrong, Cavarelli. I'll always adore the screaming fangirls, and I don't have an issue with other dudes, whether they're fans or new bands. Hey, I'm all for spreading the leather. But you? You're just a wannabe. You can't be me. You're not the Buff, and you never will be."

Luke scoffed, still in disbelief. "You actually think I want to be you? I'm nothing like you! I may make music like yours, but I am not you. I actually care about what I'm doing."

"So that's the way you're going to play it, huh? Looks like you grew some balls, Cavarelli, but you'll never be as tough as me, kid. You may kiss my leather, but you're not cutthroat enough to claim your own place in this industry. You have to claw your way up, no matter the costs, whether it's fire or love."

Samantha glared at Jennifer. "She purposely flirted with you, Luke, just to make me jealous. She wanted us to be distant."

Jennifer rolled her eyes. "I couldn't care less about your love life."

Luke's eyes widened. He couldn't believe that it took him this long to discern what was actually happening. "You made Samantha and Ryan sleep together." He'd been so blind with the pain that it hadn't crossed his mind.

"Indirectly," Jennifer said.

"You paid Natalie to break Ryan's heart so he'd be sensitive towards me."

"He'll get over it."

"How'd you erase the message you left on the answering machine?" Samantha demanded.

"Picked the locks on the door while you were upstairs—"

Luke raised his hand. "That's enough." He shifted his attention back to Bellano. "You dared to stoop that low? I don't care if you're tough. I used to look up to you."

Bellano shrugged. "You're a fool, then. He tossed the cigarette into a nearby flower pot. "Like I said," he reached into his leather pocket, "I'd try anything." His hand emerged, aiming a .38 Special.

Both Luke and Samantha froze. Luke took a deep breath before trying to talk Bellano down rationally.

"You don't want to do that."

The heartbreaker cocked the gun.

"If you kill me, then you'll hurt your own image."

"I'll take my chances. I can always frame someone." He stole a glance at Samantha.

Luke couldn't see how they were going to get out of this. Out of the corner of his eye, he saw his wife trembling. He had to think fast. He glanced back into the bedroom. "Ryan!" he shouted.

As expected, Bellano turned his head to find out for himself, giving Luke just enough time to topple him to the ground. The gun flew from Bellano's hand, but that couldn't deter him when he owned a pair of fists that would work just as well.

The first punch threw Luke off guard, so he retaliated, prepared for the second. The sensation of fighting was completely new to him. He didn't feel like himself at all, but it was oddly satisfying to strike Bellano's smug face.

Luke was able to duck Bellano's swings, which allowed him just enough time to swing back and push Bellano away. Luke jumped at Bellano and used his body to tackle Bellano to the ground. Taking advantage of this strike, Luke dragged Bellano by the legs over toward the balcony door. But, as he went to pick up the gun and dispose of it, Bellano grabbed his leg viciously and pulled him to the ground. Once Bellano managed to get to his feet, he smacked Luke in the eye as revenge and scurried to retrieve the gun. His cheek was bleeding, and even that had no effect on him.

Samantha went straight to Luke's aid, but Bellano would have no such thing. He tugged her up from the floor by her shirt collar and pressed the .38 to her temple. "Told you I'd kill you."

Luke scraped himself up and stood wobbly in front of them. "You don't know what you're doing." He watched his wife struggle in agony.

Breathing heavily, Bellano struggled to talk. "What're you gonna do now, tough guy?"

"What do you think you're going to accomplish by killing her, huh? You think I'm going to get so depressed that I'll quit the music business?" Luke shook his head. "No. I'll come back even stronger. See, you don't understand what it's like to put real emotion in a song. You kill my wife, and I'll write a song that's so deep and sensitive I'll be at the top of the charts for a year. You can't stop me." Luke was immersed in confidence.

"I'm killing you anyway," was the calm and apathetic response. "I just want you to suffer first by watching me shoot her brains out."

"Tony, stop it!" Jennifer shouted. "This has gone far enough."

"You turning on me now?" He strained his neck to look at her.

"If you really love me, you'll let her go."

Bellano tightened his grip on Samantha, and she cried even harder. The sweat poured off of him, and his eyes darted back and forth. Within a few minutes, he released his vise grip on her.

She ran to Luke, but he sent her away. "Go back there where it's safe," he whispered.

Before Bellano could point the gun back at him, Luke made an attempt to knock it out of his hand. They tugged and yanked until the barrel was tilted towards the darkening sky.

Bang! Bellano accidentally sent a bullet flying through the air. Luke snatched the gun away when Bellano loosened his hold. Luke turned back and started to throw the gun over the balcony. His effort was in vain because Bellano drew him once more into a deadlock.

Between the punching, kicking, and defending, Luke couldn't tell who was winning. He found it impossible to wrench the gun out of the conflict. There was no Ryan to save the day.

Luke got the upper hand and had Bellano pinned up against the railing. Due to his determination to escape, Bellano kept inching up over the railing.

Luke didn't know how much longer he could persist.

Bellano couldn't keep this up forever, could he?

"You can't beat me," Bellano said through clenched teeth.

"I already have," Luke answered smugly. "Remember 'Forever Mine?' Or how about 'Music Man?' Our songs beat yours on the charts a long time ago."

The gun clattered onto the floor, and Luke kicked it away. Bellano, however, was still going strong. He pushed Luke down and flipped open a pocket knife. With his arm lifted high, he started the plunge.

The next bang compelled three out of the four people on the scene to jump.

Luke couldn't breathe at first. He was in shock. He held on tightly so that Bellano wouldn't fall over the balcony. "Call 9-1-1!" Bellano's glistening face was already turning pale.

Samantha made a beeline for the bedside telephone, and Jennifer dropped the gun, hurrying to her boyfriend.

"I'm so sorry," she said. "I couldn't let you kill him."

Luke still had Bellano in his arms. He could feel the body start to give up and fall backward, but Bellano was still alive.

"Y—you win."

"This was never a game to me." The tears welled up in Luke's eyes. His idol was dripping a steady flow of blood droplets from his chest. Luke's rage toward Bellano suddenly dissipated, and the man in front of him was the same one who had inspired him only a few years ago.

For the third time that day, he wearily said, "I forgive you."

Bellano smiled with what strength he had remaining. He mumbled something, and Luke thought he heard, "If only I could be more like you…"

The final thing Bellano did was turn his head towards Jennifer and say smoothly, "I love you." Then, his eyes fell to the side, and he sighed, emitting a trickle of blood.

Luke was really losing him. His body was over the rail too far, and Luke's grasp started to loosen. Jennifer tried to help hold him up, but she was too hysterical, and her manicured fingertips slid right off of the leather jacket. They watched the corpse of Tony Bellano tumble over the balcony and plummet into the pool below.

"Tony!" Jennifer shrieked. She stayed engrossed, weeping.

"Are you alright?" Samantha hugged Luke for the first time in months. "I don't know where the ambulance is."

He sniffed. "Don't need it now."

He was absolutely crushed. Memories of his teenage years came rushing in: all the times he came home and sought out the glory of Tony Bellano. He may have had animosity towards him, but he still listened to the man's music. Deep in his heart, he secretly craved new music from the man who had given him all the confidence in the world. He never truly gave up on The Buff. It felt like he had just watched a family member die.

"LUKE!" A voice bounced through the hall. Ryan paused in the doorway, panicked. "I heard gunshots."

"Ryan, what are you doing here?" Luke asked in a trance.

"I—I came to say I accept your apology, but what happened?"

Luke looked down at his shirt, finally noticing the splattered blood. "Jennifer killed Bellano," he said shakily, still in disbelief.

Meanwhile, Jennifer's sobs grew louder, so Samantha ushered her inside to calm her.

Ryan quickly approached his friend. "What? Why?"

"To save me." He quickly recounted the events of the night.

Cautiously, Ryan walked over and examined the pool with a big, shadowy object in it. "He was rotten."

"No," Luke disagreed. "He was just a very flawed man who couldn't help himself."

Chapter 26

Love is an Undying Flame

The weeks following the incident were the most difficult for the Cavarellis. Their house was off limits for a couple of weeks due to the investigation of Bellano's death. Luke crashed with Ryan, as their friendship gradually improved. Meanwhile, Samantha insisted on staying at her studio, though she was already behind on rent. Luke had suggested that they stay in a hotel, but Samantha argued that it would be best for both of them to process the night's events alone.

The media went insane. The music world was heartbroken by the death of the beloved lead singer of The Leather Heartbreaks. The lead singer of The Steel City Boys was— oddly enough— no exception. He kept playing that nightmarish scene over and over in his mind. Where did it all go wrong? What could he have done differently? Nothing. He got the gun away from Bellano. How was he to know that Jennifer would pick it up?

Sometimes, when he thought about what had happened, he remembered the day Ace Holloway died from a drug overdose. For a few weeks after, Luke had felt sick to his stomach every time he heard one of Ace's insane guitar riffs. Luke didn't feel normal again for months. He felt like he lost a friend that he had never met. The Leather Heartbreaks were one of a kind, and Luke had always seen the good in them, even if their personal lives seemed to ruin their reputation.

He held this belief about Bellano until the feud began, when he couldn't see any light at the end of the tunnel. Bellano's memory haunted him for a while, but, after reflecting and blasting The Leather Heartbreaks albums, he realized that he forgave Bellano; it was okay if he moved on.

Luke refused to comment to the press, since he was

fighting his own emotions about Bellano's death. Instead, he headed to the studio, and The Steel City Boys were back in business.

Except that every headline read something different, often trying to make Luke out to be the bad guy. Fans of both bands were unsure. Bellano did die at the Cavarelli mansion, so was Luke to blame? Then again, Bellano was no saint either. It also didn't help that Luke welcomed Ryan back into his life as though nothing had ever happened. No one was able to shape the narrative into something coherent.

But, one thing bothered Luke more than headlines: Samantha. Before he had the chance to seek her out on his own, he came home to find her there. This time, he didn't need to ask how she got in.

"What're you doing?"

"What does it look like I'm doing? I'm trying to get my stuff out of here." She was stuffing clothes into a suitcase.

Luke's face twisted in both pain and confusion. "Why?"

"You know why." Samantha pushed down on the suitcase. It was too full, and the zipper kept jamming.

He took notice of her growing frustration and reached over, grabbed a stack of the clothes, lifted them out, and gently placed them on the bed. "Please don't leave," he said softly.

She met his gaze and frowned. "What, you can't make up your mind?"

Luke looked defeated and sighed. "I forgive you."

"Yes, you said that before. I don't know why you want to."

"I overreacted the night it happened."

"No, you didn't! You had every right to throw me out."

"I just wish you would've talked to me before you went off and slept with Ryan," Luke continued as if he didn't hear her. "Seeing those pictures you sent reminded me that I don't want us to be separated. Samantha, I still love you, and I always will, no matter what you do."

Samantha began to tear up. "How can you forgive me out of nowhere?"

"Because I know that you didn't mean to hurt me."

"Just because you forgive me doesn't mean that I forgive myself. And I *did* want to hurt you that night."

"Because you thought I cheated. After you learned the truth, you started to beat yourself up. I saw it in your eyes that night, but I was too mad to care or to let it go."

She shook her head. "What're you trying to say?"

"I'm saying that we were both afraid to talk to each other. I didn't want to admit what happened with Jennifer, and you didn't want to ask me about it. We both made mistakes. Let's take the high road and move on."

Luke sat on the bed with her and put his arm around her. The warm breeze from the open window blew back her light hair. She let him hold her tight, and she laid her head on his shoulder.

"You have to let it go," he whispered. "If I could do it, then so can you. You know you want to."

"But I was so stupid to think that you'd—"

"Shh," he pacified her and caressed her arm. "That doesn't matter now. Neither of us are perfect."

"But you gave all your love to me, and I just threw you away!"

"Samantha, you can't obsess over this. Look, I know the affair meant nothing. I was livid and hurt when I found Ryan on my side of the bed, but I never forgot the pain I saw on your face that night. I pushed it out of my mind for a while, but then it nagged me, leaving me confused about what to do. You didn't want to betray me. If it weren't for Bellano and Jennifer—"

"Don't make excuses!" She shot up now, clearly upset again. "I should've known better. Just because Jennifer made me think you were cheating on me doesn't mean that what I did is justified. I shouldn't have just slept with Ryan. It wasn't right, and you know it!

"Do you know how much I wanted to come back and beg on my knees in front of you? There was nothing else for me to say. There was no excuse. I didn't know how to make you see that Jennifer did call that night. But that didn't matter. Even if you had believed me, it didn't let me off the hook for breaking your heart.

"When I saw you throw that picture away, I knew my life was over. I needed something else to make the pain go away. I kept reliving everything over and over again; I eventually put two and two together that Jennifer and Bellano were working together. I overheard them at the Grammy after party, but I wasn't sure if they really knew each other. That's why I drove over to Jennifer's and confronted her. She was the only other one who would know about the phone call. Then, Bellano showed up and they kidnapped me, bringing me back here. He told me that if I didn't kill you, he'd kill me. If I did the job, then I could have the mansion and all the inheritance, plus the extra money he offered me. Luke, he knew about my vice: my greed. He knew I needed—craved—the money, and he pressured me to try and get it. I—I—" She broke down again. The sobs kept pouring out of her.

Luke absorbed all of this, finally hearing the full story for the first time. Witnessing her pain made him want to cry too. He couldn't stand to see her hurt herself for his own benefit.

When she could utter words again, she said, "I don't care if it's because I'm human! What I did to you was unspeakable, and I don't deserve to be with you. I refuse to hurt you again, and I can make sure of that by leaving for good."

"But I know you won't hurt me again," he answered calmly.

Then they were silent, with Samantha turned away from him.

What could he do to convince her? He closed his eyes and began humming. Gently, he sang:

You look, for something that don't exist
Her lips, I vowed to resist
Why do you keep holding on to
A cheap love in the air?

'Cause it's you and me
It's us forever.
Humans make mistakes
But we're not to blame

Do you remember that night on the
boardwalk?
How a photograph could set you free?
How a song can strum the heart
And join two souls in one.
Won't you let me hold you?
On the boardwalk

We've been, distanced for months on end
As she, tries to lure me to her bed
Don't go believing the lies, girl,
I'm the one you should trust

'Cause it's you and me
It's us forever
Humans make mistakes
I tried to pull away

Easily tempted,
Far from immune
I've loved you forever,
Not a moment too soon.

Remember those lights,
Oh, how they glowed.
Snapshot, shutter click
Will it never be the same?
If only we could go back...
If only we could go back...

Samantha looked up at him. "Did you just write that?"

He nodded slowly, still surprised that he actually sang what was on his mind so beautifully.

"I have a confession to make," he said. "I understand now why you thought I cheated on you with Jennifer. That night after she kissed me, I did go down to the beach to just reflect on what had happened. I did feel disloyal to you. I shouldn't have led you to that awful conclusion. This is just as much my fault as it is hers and yours."

Then he sighed. "Don't you get it? I don't want to let that hold us back anymore. It wasn't a great situation for either of us, so now we have to make the best of it."

She buried her face in her hands, muffling her voice. "Any other guy would've given me up."

He laughed lightly. "We all know I'm not like other guys. Yes, I may be sensitive, but I don't just abandon the ones I love." He pulled her closer. "I believe that we're supposed to forgive each other's faults, and we're supposed to help each other get to heaven.."

She lifted her head and smiled weakly.

He was relieved to see that smile return. He had really missed it. "Well?"

Samantha wiped the tears from her eyes. "I love you!" She tackled him down to the middle of the bed with a kiss.

* * *

The boys commenced their comeback with two new singles: "Boardwalk" and "Brothers." Because of the fans' hesitation, it seemed as though the road to success wouldn't return as easily. On the management front, Mr. Langderate had been generous and offered his services until he could find them someone else.

Staring at a tabloid that was tossed onto the conference table in the studio, the boys talked about what they should do.

"We could do another charity concert, this time just on our own," Adam suggested.

"That's dumb," Tyler said while taking off his denim jacket. "That won't get us anywhere."

"I don't get it," Ryan said. "The album explains everything. If the fans would just give it a listen, they wouldn't hate us."

"They hate me, not you," Luke said dully. "Bellano died at my house, and I let you back in the band."

"Now, boys," Mr. Langderate's voice was calming, "It's all just a matter of marketing. He leaned back and shot the boys a reassuring smile.

"We have some extra money," Joe pointed out, "We just have to figure out what to do with it."

The guys around the table became quiet. Meanwhile, Luke traced the large white letters on the magazine: The Steel City Boys use new album to cover up what happened to Tony Bellano.

"We're not covering anything up!" Ryan insisted. "The songs say it all. How else can we get the fans and media to understand?"

Mr. Langderate's confidence was waning. He muttered, "Always hated this part of the job. That's why I left managing full-time and went to A & R."

Luke shook his head. "It's me they're after. I know what I have to do." He stood up.

"Where're you going?" Tyler asked.

"There's someone I have to see."

"Then I'll come with you," Ryan jumped to his feet.

"No!" Luke put a hand up. "Ryan, I'm sorry, but I have to do this alone."

Before Luke got to the door, Ryan stopped him. "Hey," he whispered. "I'm proud of you for doing this, whatever it is."

Chapter 27

Buff and Velvet

As the guard led him down the dull hallway, Luke felt his shoulders tense up. He could barely believe that he was doing this.

The guard stopped and motioned to the chair in front of him. "You have fifteen minutes," he said.

Luke nodded and scooted the chair closer to the glass. As he sat down and glanced up, a pair of glacial eyes met his own.

Jennifer smiled weakly and pushed up her long denim sleeves before reaching for the phone receiver.

Luke took a deep breath and grabbed his phone. "I got your message," he said, "But I didn't really come here because of that."

"Then why are you here?"

"Look," Luke leaned forward onto the counter. "I'm forever grateful to you for saving my life, but now I need you to defend my image. The Steel City Boys are being blamed for what happened to Bellano, and you and I both know it's not true."

Jennifer cradled her head in the hand not holding the phone. "I can't tell you how sorry I am for everything. By the end, I pleaded with Bellano to ditch the plan and leave you alone. I—I got too close and learned who you truly are. You're nothing like he is—like he was." A tear slid down her cheek.

Luke shook his head. "I just want to know why, Jennifer. Why did you do this to me?"

She stared at the counter and sniffed. "Buff and I went way back. We helped each other through tough times. I felt like I was indebted to him, an old friend, an old flame. Besides, given his messed-up childhood, I wanted to help him keep his confidence and status alive. I felt bad for him, Luke. But I also felt bad for you. You didn't deserve this, any of it."

"And yet you did it," Luke said. "How could one man hate me so much? I had nothing but love and admiration for him!"

"He didn't always hate you," Jennifer mumbled.

"What?" Luke asked, his voice sounding angry instead of shocked. He was still annoyed that Jennifer brought up Bellano's childhood. Luke knew Bellano's biography backwards and forwards, and he had never heard anything about her.

"When he heard '(I Want You) Next to Me,' he was in awe. He adored you for a bit, albeit secretly. He even considered paying you to quit The Steel City Boys and become his songwriter, but that would prove you were better than him."

Luke couldn't believe his own ears. "You mean to tell me that Tony "The Buff" Bellano had one inkling of respect for me?"

Jennifer nodded. "I know he seemed like a hateful man, but he did care about others, even if his self-love still overshadowed him."

"So that night at the Grammys?"

Shaking her head, Jennifer said, "He was livid when you won the award, but he really enjoyed singing the song with you."

"I know." Now Bellano's odd smile made sense. Pausing, Luke realized that maybe he had known Bellano after all. Bellano was a man who always knew what he wanted. If Bellano wanted Luke as his songwriter or seemed to be having fun at the bigtime music awards, then he meant it. Luke felt like a fool for a moment. How could he not have seen that sooner? No, he told himself. He couldn't have known without Jennifer telling him.

He looked up at the goddess in front of him. Even when she was in prison for involuntary manslaughter, attempted arson, and kidnapping, Jennifer Mignonne could turn heads, but Luke wasn't tempted. Behind her ageless beauty, he could tell that she was mournful and exhausted.

"Does this mean you'll help me clear my name… Velvet?" He smiled at her.

Hesitantly, she returned the smile. "It's the least I can do for you. Just say the word, Music Man."

If Luke had any shot of getting the truth out to his fans, then he needed to score an interview with Carrie O'Brien. Famous for her grilling nature, the woman could be an absolute demon in the media world. She asked so many questions, to the point that it was almost impossible to hide the truth. If a celebrity wanted to lie about his life, then Carrie O'Brien was the last person that he wanted to be interviewed by.

"Thank you for booking this interview on such short notice. I know you're busy and this is live and all," Luke said, trailing Carrie into her spacious studio.

She waved her hand. "No problem. If you want to get the truth out there, then I'm your girl. Don't worry, people crave this stuff."

Just then, two guards led Jennifer into the room and plopped her into a metal chair, her hands still cuffed.

"Whew!" Carrie said. "This is going to be an interview like I've never hosted before."

Luke took the chair next to Jennifer, and Carrie sat

across from them both.

"We're going live," the cameraman said.

Carrie stared straight into the camera, her poufy blond hair and large, serious hazel eyes making her unmistakable. "Tonight, we bring you a special broadcast. Luke Cavarelli of The Steel City Boys and Jennifer Mignonne, former manager of the band, are reaching out to talk about what really happened the night Tony Bellano died." She turned to Luke and let the questions fly.

He answered as calmly and thoroughly as he could. He didn't want to seem uncomfortable, but he wanted to say everything that he needed to say. He just hoped that Jennifer would do the same.

"I don't want fans to think that Tony Bellano was a terrible guy," Luke said. "As a musician, he had all the confidence in the world, and his songs were amazing, but I think it's important to explain what happened between us."

"But you yourself were a fan of Tony Bellano, right?"

Luke nodded. "I had been a fan for years. He was always my outlet."

"Then what happened?" Carrie asked.

"When we began recording at Sforzando Records, we ran into Bellano, and he didn't exactly give us a warm welcome… to put it mildly. He didn't like the competition. We were too much of a threat, especially when 'Music Man' went to number one."

"So, you were rivals."

"Yeah, but it was more than that. Bellano would stop at nothing to break us up. Even after Ryan and Joe left, Bellano and I were still battling each other. It turns out that his 'Secrets in the Dark' was directed at me, while my 'Inspiration (I

Believed in You)' was directed at him."

"How exactly does his song relate to you?" Carrie asked, thoughtfully.

"Well," Luke repositioned himself in the chair as things were getting serious. "It has to do with the fact that he made my wife think that I was cheating on her with our manager. See, nobody knows that that's why Samantha cheated on me with Ryan."

Carrie took a deep breath and then shifted her gaze to Jennifer. "And you, Ms. Mignonne, are The Steel City Boys' manager?"

Jennifer nodded. "I was."

"How well did you know Tony Bellano?"

"Very well. I knew him for a long time. We both helped each other out years ago, and our paths just kept crossing. I used to be a singer, and then I went to full-time managing. Bellano helped push me to that point in my career. He was always in my corner, and I tried to always be in his."

Luke cringed as Carrie then asked:

"So to 'be in Bellano's corner' means to destroy a marriage and start fires?"

Luke took a deep breath as he glanced over at Jennifer. She looked like she would strangle Carrie if only the guards would give her the chance.

"Look," Jennifer as she leaned forward, "I admit that I was on board with Tony's plan in the beginning, but that was because I thought The Steel City Boys really were a threat to The Leather Heartbreaks. Once I became the new manager, I saw Luke and Ryan for who they really are, and they are nothing like Bellano."

Carrie responded to the heat. "Yet, you still made Luke's

wife think you were sleeping with him?"

"What choice did I have?" Jennifer spat back. "I loved Bellano, but he was a man who could be blind to reason when it came to something he craved. He wanted Luke out of the picture, and I had no choice but to go along with it."

"No choice? Dearie, do you not see that this whole escapade put you in chains, behind iron bars? Sweetie, listen, you didn't do Bellano any favors. All you did was ruin Luke's—"

"That's enough!" Luke stood up suddenly. Then he sighed. "Carrie, I realize this is the way that you interview your guests, but I have to say something."

Carrie bit her lip and slumped back in her chair, speechless. For once, she didn't have to dig for the truth. It was all right in front of her and the viewers.

Luke told as much as he could about the affair and the night Bellano died. It hurt to say it all out loud, but he knew that he had to do it if he wanted to keep his dream alive. "Jennifer shot Bellano to save me. I can't blame the media and the fans for not believing me. If I was them, I wouldn't believe me either. Look, Tony Bellano was a determined man. He made his own way; everyone knows that. But, even though he caused this trouble to begin with, I still love him. Part of the reason why I wanted to come into the music business was because of him. Sure, my heart ached every time he blasted me with a new insult, but he was Bellano. I wanted to be like him, and, even though I still made my own way, I followed my dream and found success. Bellano made me, and the music made me.

"You know, people today look for any bit of dirt they can use against one another, especially in the entertainment world. I'm not like the rest of them, and I never have been.

I know that some can't understand why I took Ryan back as a friend and bandmate and Samantha back as my wife, but isn't that what you do if you truly love someone? Don't you eventually forgive them, no matter how many shreds they've ripped your heart into? I'm just trying to inspire others through my music. I'm trying to connect with others through what I think and feel. Losing Bellano was a tragedy. Part of me died when he died. His death showed us all the meaning of a 'leather heartbreak,' but, on the night he died—" Luke had to pause so that his voice wouldn't break—"I forgave him for everything he'd done to me. And I know many of you won't believe it, but I forgive Jennifer, too."

Luke only hoped that he had opened hearts with his speech. He couldn't expect everyone to believe him, but he had to make his stand. Through his honesty, he hoped that his fans would understand, forgive, and maybe even admire.

Chapter 28

To the Rhythm of Love

"Listening to your own song on Christmas? Never knew that Luke Cavarelli was such a narcissist!"

"And I never knew that Ryan Delhart, a ladies' man who was almost a drop-out, knew big words." Luke shut off the radio. "I was trying to find a decent Christmas station. Come on in. Merry Christmas."

Ryan stepped into the mansion's living room with a girl trailing after him. "Thanks, same to you. So, anything new?"

Luke laughed. "Yeah, actually. Say, do you remember that song, 'Young Guns (Go For It)'?"

His friend nodded. "Yeah. Look how far Wham! has gotten. I remember when we first saw them on TV. What about it?"

"Let's just say I'm really not a 'young gun' anymore. I'll have to get used to 'sleepless nights.'"

The guitar player stood for a moment in thought. "No." He shook his head.

"Oh yeah."

"Daddy Cavarelli!" Ryan shouted. "Man, that's awesome! Congratulations."

Luke grinned. "Thanks."

"And where's the beautiful mother?"

"Right here." Samantha came into the room, glowing like a New York City night.

Emily appeared from behind Ryan. "Congrats!" She hugged Samantha.

"So, how are the wedding plans coming along?" Samantha asked.

Emily beamed. "Perfectly."

The girls strolled into the kitchen, leaving the guys alone. The Steel City Boys' new songs and Luke's interview helped promote Samantha's photography business. Emily opened her own bakery next to Samantha's shop.

"I just bought the beach house," Ryan whispered.

"You finally did it? Good for you."

"Yep," Ryan flopped on the couch. "Gonna be the honeymoon present."

"Oh, how original. I think I know someone else who did that," Luke said flatly, but then laughed again. "You know, you're not exactly young and free yourself."

Ryan shrugged it off. "I've moved on I guess."

"Told you. Sometimes it's good to be tied down. No more wandering around lost." Luke switched on the television and started channel-surfing.

"I still disagree with you on that, but I am glad Samantha hooked me up with Emily," Ryan continued. "She's what I was looking for."

"I knew that when you met her back in Pittsburgh at the café." Luke paused on MTV. They were once again playing the tribute concert he did for Bellano. He remembered how awkward it felt to be in Bellano's shoes, singing lead on The Leather Heartbreaks' songs. The crowd before him had clung to every lyric.

"Ladies and gentlemen," the Luke Cavarelli on the television announced, "Whether you're out here in the audience tonight or watching at home, we're all together to celebrate one singer whose confidence and stage presence captivated each and every one of us. Tony 'The Buff' Bellano was a bad boy who wanted everyone to forget their problems and live life to the fullest. I myself took to Bellano's carefree, party-all-night anthems when I was down…" He turned it off. "Still can't believe it."

"I know." Ryan put a hand on Luke's shoulder and got up and stretched. "Do you ever miss those days playing at Silva's?"

Luke shrugged. "A little. But look where we are now. Why?"

"No reason. It just feels like it was so long ago."

"Dinner's ready!" Samantha called.

After the four friends ate, they laughed and reminisced the night away. Then, Luke remembered the last wrapped present under the tree. He handed it to Ryan, who didn't waste time in tearing it open.

"A Rolex?" Ryan was grinning widely. "You know I always wanted one!"

"There, it makes you a 'cool kid.'" Luke joked.

Ryan didn't want to take his eyes off it, but he went and grabbed Luke's present from his coat pocket. He handed it to Luke, who wasn't sure how to respond because, clearly, it was a wrapped cassette case.

"Please tell me you didn't wrap one of our own."

"Oh, shut up and open it!"

Luke ripped off the shiny paper. He was confused at first when he laid eyes on Tony Bellano's confident, gleaming smile. "It's their first album. I have this."

Ryan shook his head. "No, you don't. Look at it closer."

Luke did. No way. It was a special edition of *Heartbreakers Only Live Once.* It had all the extended versions of his favorite songs, and it was autographed in the lower corner by Tony "The Buff" Bellano. He couldn't speak. "H—how?"

"Oh, I have my ways," Ryan said as he smiled devilishly, impersonating Bellano.

"I loved this album."

"Come on, you still do."

"Dude, I only bought you a watch!"

"Well, now maybe I'll be on time for something," Ryan said with a wave of his hand. "Don't worry about it. This was the least I could do for you. I know how much you admired the guy. It broke your heart when he died."

"Aw, you made him cry!" Samantha got up from the armchair and went over to Luke on the couch.

"I'm not crying!" Luke sniffed.

"He's always been a softie," Ryan said, "But I wouldn't have it any other way. He's come a long way from where he was, though."

Finally, Ryan and Emily decided to leave. When Ryan opened the door, he found an envelope tucked inside it. "I guess this is for you." He handed it to Luke.

"It's probably just from one of the neighbors." He pitched it onto the dining room table, not giving it another thought. "Man, I still can't believe I'm going to be a father."

"Remember, I'm *Uncle* Ryan."

"Don't worry," Luke said. "You'll be the favorite uncle." He changed the subject. "So how long has it been now?"

"About a year. Can't stand the sight of a lighter or the smell of smoke."

They high-fived in celebration. Things couldn't have been better.

Luke and Samantha watched the Firebird drive away. He looked at her and smiled. "Race you to the balcony."

"Huh-uh."

"Come on, you're not even a month along."

"Nope."

Luke sighed. "Okay, I'll escort you, then." He held out his arm, and she took it.

Upstairs, he embraced her as the moon began to peek out from behind a cloud. It was tradition for them to host this vigil every night. Out on that balcony, no one could hijack their love. They could be themselves, and no one would point a finger and judge. Why should Christmas have been any different?

"Everything's so quiet," Samantha said.

"So why are you complaining?"

"I'm not complaining! With everything that's happened, it's nice to just be with you alone."

"We're on top of the world up here. Our world."

Crickets chirped in the background, and the wind rippled the pool water below.

Luke looked over at her and found her staring off into the distance, thinking about something in another dimension. "You ok?" He reached out and touched her arm.

She jumped, coming back to real life. "I'm fine. Just wondering."

"About?"

She sighed. "I was just wondering what life would be like if this was a year ago and this was Ryan's baby, not yours."

"Hey!" He turned her so their eyes would meet. "You promised me we wouldn't go down that road again. We're moving on."

"I know," she whispered. "I'll get there," she added with a weak smile.

He kissed her tenderly and then felt her warmth slip away.

"I'm going to turn off the Christmas lights," she said as she started to leave.

Now alone, Luke looked out over his property, imagining thousands of crazy fans anticipating him to take a microphone in his hand. He could feel the energy from the imaginary crowd. He loved connecting with fans. They were human, just like him.

Luke blinked, chasing away the shadows of the night. What he dreamed of was his actual life. He had made it, and he would continue his passion until the good Lord chose to ease him into sleep. Despite all of the trials and tribulations, he had his band, his best friend, his loving wife, and, soon, a child. Luke Cavarelli's life couldn't have been any sweeter.

He tip-toed closer to the edge. The warm breeze comforted him as he took in the world around him. He laughed lightly and smiled to himself, breathing in a sense of pride and exultation. "Thank you," he whispered in prayer. "You really are good."

"Luke?" Samantha laid a hand on his shoulder. "Who is this from? It's not from the neighbors." She handed him the envelope that Ryan had found in the door.

Perplexed, he opened it carefully and unfolded the letter that was inside. It read:

Dear Mr. Luke Cavarelli,

You don't know me, but you and I have a lot in common. We are both music men. Your personality is a lot similar to mine. Honestly, you have inspired me to become a better musician by teaching me to craft as much emotion into my music as I can. Not only that, but I've learned to put myself into my songwriting.

Luke, I admire you so much that I finally decided to come out of my shell and try my hand at being a professional musician. And, somehow, my fortune has skyrocketed. I was just offered a contract with Sforzando Records. My band and I are planning on taking the deal, which means I'll be living my dream in the same building as you. I truly hope to meet you soon and that things won't be awkward.

Merry Christmas!
Gregory Edwards, Lead singer of upcoming Rad!

Looking up from the note, Luke couldn't believe it. A flurry of emotions swirled through him. This meant the world to him, but it had the ability to take him down in an instant. He pushed the negative out of his mind. He wasn't Tony Bellano, so there couldn't possibly be a feud between The Steel City Boys and Rad! like there had been between The Steel City Boys and The Leather Heartbreaks. No way. They were just a new breakout band; that's all. So, a band looked up to the five boys from Pittsburgh? Now that *was* totally rad. He wasn't alone. Finally, someone else understood that, indeed, the music does make the man.

Acknowledgements

Tyler: I cannot express how grateful I am that we were able to bring Luke and Ryan into existence. Thank you so much for your expertise on the finishing touches! Besides, "once a bearcat, always a bearcat!"

Julia: WE DID IT!!!

Family and Friends: Thank you so much for supporting me on this journey. I can't wait to hear your reaction after reading this debut novel. I also can't wait to continue this journey with you in the future!

Randy: Your service to the Johnstown Fire Dept. does not go unnoticed. Do you remember when I asked you about what would happen if a lit cigarette fell onto a carpet? Surprise! That question was for a novel plot, not for a school project. (P.s. I'm now a Great White fan, but I'm still too nervous to look up the stage fire video you told me about!)

Ms. Gil-Montero and Mr. Reger: Thank you for all your support and expertise during my time at SVC. Mr. Reger: although I never took one of your classes, your being a beta reader for this manuscript gave me a real sense of hope that Luke's story had potential!

Mme. Gilmore: thank you for being much more than a cameo. You were there when I needed a shoulder to lean on, and you helped me to accept my old soul personality. Our '80s music bond began with Wham!, but it sure didn't end with Pete Burns and that music video!

Donna, Lily, Brenda, Sandy, and Anyone who has been a beta reader or has answered any of my bajillion questions in the past seven years: Your help has been, and never will be, in vain! This book you hold in your hands is proof.

To all '80s musicians: You helped me to fuel my journey. Without you, this "Steel City dream" would have never been possible.

About the Author

An English major alumna from Saint Vincent College (SVC), **Nicole Fratrich** has won various poetry contests, including ones sponsored by The Ligonier Valley Writers and The Catholic Daughters of America. Her short story "The Key" was selected as the winner of the 2018 Emerging Mystery Writer scholarship contest for undergraduates; the story was published in the November 2018 issue of *Mystery Weekly Magazine.* In 2019, her short story "The Branded Shadow" was published in an anthology titled *The Twofer Compendium* by Celestial Echo Press, an imprint of Gemini Wordsmiths. Nicole has also had several chapters of short stories published in the Johnstown *Tribune-Democrat* newspaper. When she is not writing, she jams to '80s music and chills to classic horror movies! Check her out on www.nicolefratrichauthor.com, and also subscribe to her blog, *Confessions of a Classic Soul.*